OUTSIDE
the LINES

ANNA ZABO

Riptide Publishing
PO Box 1537
Burnsville, NC 28714
www.riptidepublishing.com

Outside the Lines

Cover art: L.C. Chase, lcchase.com/design.htm
Editor: Carole-ann Galloway
Layout: L.C. Chase, lcchase.com/design.htm

ISBN: 978-1-62649-653-8

First edition
December, 2017

Also available in ebook:
ISBN: 978-1-62649-652-1

OUTSIDE the LINES

ANNA ZABO

RIPTIDE
PUBLISHING

For R. This isn't your family, but it's a little closer to your truth.

TABLE OF CONTENTS

CHAPTER ONE

IAN

I t was amazing how fast two weeks' worth of work could be destroyed. I mean, I'm used to it—half the models I built were meant to be blown up or set on fire or otherwise obliterated in a sea of special effects. This one wasn't any different, a lovely detailed miniature of a sacred grove, complete with altars and idols—everything the larger set had—surrounded by trees in the heart of the forest. My miniature had been destined to be burnt to the ground in a spectacular magical explosion, since the EPA kind of frowned on pyrotechnics in the forest on the Olympic Peninsula. Apparently, fire and trees didn't mix.

At least, that had been the intended fate of my model *before* Anderson had fallen backward into the damn thing and crushed it into tiny little bits. Stunt actors, I swear—bones made of steel. Poor set was absolutely no match for two hundred pounds of falling man.

My heart stopped, or tried to.

Would have made a great shot had Anderson been in a giant rubber suit. But this was *Wolf's Landing*, not some science fiction show with mecha and monsters.

Ginsberg helped Anderson up and looked at the ruins of the model in the same way someone peered at roadkill. Pity mixed with revulsion. "Oh, shit."

"Sorry, dude." That from Anderson.

I couldn't speak. Didn't know what to say. We were supposed to film the scene this evening and now my model was . . . gone. Anna was going to have kittens. Large hungry kittens with claws and teeth and a taste for blood.

You think stuff is safe on set, that people would be careful. I croaked, still looking for the right words.

Anderson scratched the back of his head. "Can you fix it?"

I met Anderson's gaze. Behind him, Ginsberg's eyes were wide, and he backed away, his hands raised in surrender.

"Did you . . . really . . . just ask me that?" I barely recognized my own voice. It was too calm and cool. Nothing like the litany of *oh fuck, oh fuck, oh fuck* running through my soul.

Anderson flinched and glanced at the shards of wood, clay, and paint—he'd also managed to bend the metal leg of the table my model had been sitting on—then met my stare again and hunched his shoulders. "I mean— I'm sorry. It was an accident."

"Tell that to Anna." I jammed both hands into my hair, and the trembles started. Holy shit. Two weeks of work undone. I barely had any supplies left, and the production schedule was so damn tight, I didn't know if there was any time for me to rebuild the set.

"Tell me what?" Anna Maxwell's voice cut through the air like the thin blade of a utility knife. Her footfalls followed until she stood next to me and oh, the look she gave my ruined model . . .

Yup. Kittens. Mountain lion kittens. I pressed my lips together and tightened the grip on my hair.

"Um." Anderson shifted back and forth from one foot to another. "We were fooling around with a hacky sack and I, uh, fell."

"Hacky . . . sack," Anna said.

Claws and teeth and blood.

"Yeah, it's that game with that kind of ball—"

"Oh, for fuck's sake, I know what a hacky sack is." She waved Anderson quiet and turned to me. "Don't tell me that was tonight's shot."

"That was tonight's shot," I whispered.

Anna closed her eyes, and I could almost hear her counting down from ten. She let out an exhale. "You . . ." She pointed at Anderson. "Get your ass to Natalya for some *extra* training."

Anderson didn't have to be told twice. He didn't walk away—he fled at top speed. Anna turned back to the model and rubbed her chin. "Fuck."

I slipped my fingers from my hair. Yeah, that was about all I had too.

"How fast can you rebuild it?"

Not fast enough. "I don't—"

"Ian."

Oh, man. I hated when Anna looked at me like that. It wasn't anger, but there's this . . . stare . . . directors got. One that made you want to cower in fear.

"Like . . . a week? Maybe?" If I worked around the clock. If I had what I needed on site, which I *didn't*.

"Specifics, please."

Shit. Well, it was Wednesday, so I had the weekend. "A week. Seven days. This time next week."

She nodded. "I think we can live with that." Some tension eased in her shoulders, and her razor-sharp expression softened. "I know this wasn't your fault. I'll have a talk with the crew and remind them to be careful around the sets."

I really, *really* didn't want to be there for that. "Thanks."

We parted ways; her to scare the pants off someone else, and me, after gathering the sad wreckage of the grove into a box, back to my shop.

Didn't take long to pull out the reusable bits from the detritus— pretty much only the stuff I'd sculpted out of polymer clay. At least that was good—those had been a pain to get right.

What wasn't good was the level of supplies in my shop—I was more or less out of *everything*. I'd used so much shit making this model that I'd burned through the bulk of my stock. I had supplies on order, but who knew when that would show up in this little backwater town.

I huffed out a breath. Bluewater Bay wasn't *that* bad, but shipping shit here took *forever* for some reason.

And I'd told Anna I'd have the model built in a week. *Oh, God. Ian Meyers, you are well and truly screwed.*

Desperate times and all that. I parked my car along Main Street in lovely downtown Bluewater Bay and tapped my fingers against the steering wheel. Usually when I came to Main, I went two blocks down to Stomping Grounds for some caffeine. I tended to avoid this part because it was home to Howling Moon, the mother of all

Wolf's Landing merchandise shops. The tourists were plentiful around here. Down at Stomping Grounds, the townsfolk ran interference for us, especially when we were wearing our crew jackets or hats. Kept the gawkers from doing more than gawking—like that time when a guy tried to swipe a grip's badge.

Unfortunately, Howling Moon was next door to where I needed to go: End o' Earth Comics and Games. I'd already come up bust at the local craft stores. I'd managed to secure some items—mostly balsa wood—at the art-supply place, but I needed model paint. For that, you had to go where they sold models and miniatures.

Only one place in town had what I needed—End o' Earth, unless I wanted to buy official Wolf's Landing miniatures. Hell, maybe Howling Moon had a freaking Sacred Grove™ set. Plop *that* down for Anna to use.

I giggled. She'd *kill* me. Probably for real.

Right. I'd left everything that could possibly signal I worked on *Wolf's Landing* at home. Should be safe enough to head into End o' Earth. Up and out. Lock the car. Slink past the visiting tourists. Through the door and bang straight into my youth.

Oh my God. The colors. The glint of bags. The collectors' issues carefully hanging on the wall. All of it sent a tingle up my spine. There was the swooping thrill in my chest at the sight of the racks. I gravitated toward the new comics. I was so out of the loop, I didn't recognize many of the titles—and half of those I did sported unfamiliar faces.

But the shop as a whole? Like an old boyfriend standing there at the corner. *Hey, sweetheart, where ya been?*

I stared at the covers. *I'm seeing someone now. No time for old loves.* I'd get lost in too many other stories and aesthetics. I barely had enough time to keep up with my own sculpture, and it was hard keeping the Wolf's Landing aesthetic from seeping into my own creative work.

It *smelled* like a comics and games shop, though. All ink and paper and . . . paint. Specifically, miniature paint.

The guy behind the counter was youngish, maybe in his early twenties, and had several piercings in his ear. Given the pink *Yay for Gay* T-shirt and lacy scarf ensemble, he clearly wasn't afraid of his feminine side at all.

He let me browse for a bit, but eventually coughed to catch my attention. "Let me know if you need any help."

What I wanted, for an insane moment, was one of everything on the racks. But I didn't have that kind of cash, and I certainly didn't have that kind of time. I tore my attention away from the new issues. "Actually, what I need are miniature supplies."

The clerk nodded to the right. "They're in the back, behind the board games. Simon's there and he's the man for miniatures—he'll give you a hand." A nice professional smile. "Follow your nose."

"Thanks." When I walked past the graphic novels and games, I understood what the guy had meant. The familiar delightfully pungent smell of paint wafted from deeper in the store. At the back was a man painting a model at a table, and for the second time, I was struck by color and light. Not from the starship in his hand or the one next to it, but from the man himself.

If I'd known they grew them like *him* in Bluewater Bay, I'd have spent a hell of a lot more time on this end of Main Street. Mahogany hair, thin elegant fingers that held the brush *just so*, cheekbones that went on forever, and pale-blue eyes, like the sky sometimes got out here—when you could see it.

I must have made some sort of undignified noise, because his intense focus shifted and pinned me to the ground.

As did his wide smile. "Hey, hi! Give me a sec to finish this, and I'll be right with you."

Simon. The clerk had said his name was Simon.

"Yeah, okay." Stunning first line, that.

With trepidation, I moved closer and followed the flow of his fingers to his brush, to the model. It was better than staring *at* Simon, but not by much.

Because his painting? Superlative. Maybe better than mine. Yeah, he was using a magnifier, but I did that too. His hands were so very steady and the line he drew—utterly straight. Perfect. That starship could easily have been at home in a prop shop.

How had I missed a guy like this? I'd been in Bluewater Bay almost a year and had *never* seen him. Before I started making any additional strange noises, I stepped away as quietly as I could, and took stock of the area around me. Tons of supplies. My geeky little artist heart flipped over—what was left that wasn't already tumbling from watching Simon. Yeah, they had a lot of what I needed.

And something I wanted. I swallowed against desire. Down boy. *You know nothing, Ian Meyers.*

Simon exhaled. "There." He set the starship down, cleaned his brush, and stood. "Now, what can I help you with?"

My brain locked up. He wasn't particularly tall—we were about the same height—but the way his jeans hung on his hips cupped him perfectly. Legs and torso and, God, that bemused expression. "Uh."

I'm so fucking eloquent.

"Paints?" he said. "Models? You working on something particular?"

Apparently, a nice boner. Boy, I needed to get a grip. "Yes, paints." I swallowed. "And yes, something in particular. But it's not a commercial model." I waved at the kits.

He lit up. "Are you sculpting? I've wanted to do that, but I have no talent, whatsoever."

I did sculpt. Stuff that would work in a shop like this too. Dragons. Fantasy beasts. Weird organic spaceships. "Your painting is exquisite. That takes talent *and* a steady hand."

He snorted. "It's not horribly artistic."

I stepped closer to the table and him. "It can be." The detailing on the ship—it wasn't any particular film or television property's merchandise—was not what was on the cover of the nearby box. "You're doing your own thing."

"I usually do," he murmured.

When I glanced up, I got the distinct impression he was checking me out. Delight clashed with fear and zinged down my legs. "Me too."

He met my stare, and his smile could have been called cocky in some script or another. "You still haven't told me what you need."

A one-night stand? A quickie in the back room? Dinner and a movie? *Shit.* "I'm here for work. It's kind of a desperate situation."

"Work?" He pursed his lips.

Simon had a mouth that begged to be kissed. Plump, wet, and lovely. I quieted my voice. "I make miniature sets for *Wolf's Landing.*"

His breath hitched. Wasn't sure if it was me or what I'd said, but it didn't matter. There's something about flustering a guy that drives my pulse skyward. I'd take it.

"What happened?" he whispered.

I told him, and he tried hard not to snicker. Failed. By the end of my tale, I was laughing too. The absurdity of it all, Anna's reaction, and what the stunt guy would probably go through during training. "So," I said, "can you help me?"

I hoped he could, because if the answer was no, I was out of options. And I'd never get a chance to take him out for a beer, 'cause Anna would have me buried out in the forest somewhere.

CHAPTER TWO

SIMON

C *an you help me?* The words rang through my head and it took all of my restraint not to blurt out *Yes, yes, I can!* Help someone from Hollywood, someone from *Wolf's Landing* with anything? Oh God, I wanted to jump up and down and beg.

My wife, Lydia, called it my inner fanboi, and she was right. I squeed with the best of them, though not in public, especially not about *Wolf's Landing*. Not when they'd revitalized the town.

"Yeah." I tried to keep my voice steady and smooth. Didn't help that this guy was Hollywood gorgeous and everything I liked in men. My height, dark hair, rich brown eyes that I could spend eternity falling into, a waist I wanted to hold, and shoulders made for biting.

I was *hopeless* when it came to men.

"We certainly have paints and most of the other supplies. I might have some stuff at home, too."

He shoved his hands in his pockets. "I don't want to cause you problems. Get you in trouble with the boss."

My laugh bubbled out, high and giddy. "I *am* the boss."

The way his smile crinkled around his eyes set my blood alight. His gaze darted down and up my body, and every bit of me heated. No, I hadn't been imagining him checking me out.

Damn. *Damn.* "I'm Simon Derry." I offered him my hand and he took it in a warm, strong grip. Rough skin.

Electrifying. *Hell.*

"Ian Meyers."

His shy smile played with my nerves in wicked ways, and we both let go at the same time. I could almost hear Lydia whispering in my ear, *Go for it*. Except whenever I did, I got shot down hard. I'd given up on men long ago, at least in these kinds of situations.

Being poly *and* a bisexual guy was asking for trouble. We stuck to swinging with other couples and all the guys were straight, so I got to look, but not touch. Bi guys aren't exactly welcome as swingers.

Ian? I really wanted to touch Ian. Would never happen, though. "Do you need somewhere to build it, too? I mean, if the paint has to dry quickly, this is a great space. We keep the humidity down, or try to, for the books and comics." I nodded to the bread-and-butter section of the store. "Plus, if you need anything . . ."

Ian's grin wasn't so shy now. "I suspect you don't have stunt artists running around playing hacky sack in the aisles, either."

"No, not usually." I laughed. "Though some of the crew do come in for their comic fix. Not sure who's who."

Ian seemed startled by that tidbit of info. "You don't have any trouble with the fans?" He nodded in the direction of our next-door neighbor, Howling Moon.

"You'd think they'd come in here too, right?" That had been our hope when they'd opened next door.

Ian nodded.

"Some do, but far fewer than you'd expect. They can get Wolf's Landing comics at their local stores. Here, they're only interested in the stuff you can't find anywhere else. Other than the comics and the books, we can't sell anything Wolf's Landing, so they glance around at the comics and leave."

Ian wore a shocked expression again. "You . . . can't sell Wolf's Landing stuff?"

"Not anymore. They licensed all the merchandise to certain vendors once the TV series hit big." Which had been about the same time Howling Moon had opened. "Makes sense, in a way. Don't want one shop poaching from another."

"But you can still sell the comics?" Ian focused on the new issues racks with such a longing that I wanted to slide up to him and give him a hug. Desire, loss, and need played across Ian's face. Part sexy, part heartbreaking.

I'd seen that before. In parents who wandered in with their kids and in those who came in off the street "just to look around," as they said. Had usually collected comics as kids, but stopped, or had their issues thrown out, or something like that.

I wondered what Ian's story was. "Well, there's really only one distributer for comics. Not even Hollywood can break that monopoly. We get the Wolf's Landing issues in with all the other comics."

Ian nodded absently, that yearning still etched in his face. He clenched and unclenched his hands.

So far gone. "You collect?"

He shoved his fingers through his hair. "Used to. No time now, and Anna will have my balls if I don't get this set finished."

I croaked, and he got the most wicked smile.

Yeah, I kind of wanted his balls. In my mouth. But explaining everything about my life? That shit took time, and I wasn't fooling around with anyone until I told them about my situation. Of course, that inevitably led to never seeing the guy again. Ah well. "So, when do you want to get started?"

Now his grin was straight from the devil. "On the set?"

Fuck, yeah, he knew I was into him. "I— Yeah. The set." Heat on my face. "I'm in the shop every day, so I'm available whenever."

"For the set." That smoldering gaze burned straight down to my dick and balls.

I wasn't going to get out of this gracefully. Might as well head toward what we both wanted . . . and then get shot down in flames. I swallowed my fear. "Let's start with the set."

Ian had eyes I could drown in. A smile too. "Okay," he said. "Then you're on for tomorrow."

I struggled to find a sexy or witty reply, but was saved by Ian's phone whistling.

"Fuck," he muttered, and whipped the cell phone out. "Shit. I'm gonna be late for a meeting." He met my gaze. "I'm sorry. I gotta run."

"No problem. I'm sure we'll be seeing a lot of each other."

His grin was perfection and he did that up-down number again, practically undressing me with his eyes. "I hope so." He turned and headed out the door.

Well, here we go. I watched the trail Ian blazed and returned to my model. It seemed such a dull, amateur job now. Much like my flirting.

But if there was one thing I'd learned over the years—you had to keep trying.

I spent the rest of the day attempting to work, but thinking about Ian. After he left, I'd sat down at my table and picked up a paintbrush, but my hands had been too unsteady to go back to painting the model.

Instead, I wandered up to the front of the store to help Jesse shelve and board issues until I'd stopped vibrating. If he noticed my distraction or bounciness, he gave no sign. Sometimes, I wondered if he'd put some pieces about me and Lydia together—we tried to keep our polyamory on the down-low in town, but you couldn't hide everything. And Jesse wasn't an idiot.

If he knew, he obviously didn't care. He was our best employee. Lydia and I often talked about making him assistant manager, should her career take off.

Once I calmed my ass—and dick—down, and my hands were back to their steady state, I returned to my models.

A little before four, Lydia emerged from her studio in the back of the shop and found me with a brush in hand. Sometimes, we worked the same hours, sometimes not, depending on the schedules of our other employees and what freelance lettering and coloring jobs Lydia had going on. She'd been on several tight deadlines for clients the past week or two, but given her bright smile and the crinkles around her eyes, she was done with at least one of them.

Which meant Chinese take-out for dinner. God bless her clients and deadlines. Pretty much the only time I got my egg foo yung fix was when she turned impossible tasks around on time.

I put down the ship I was painting—same one I'd been working on when Ian had come into the store. Lydia leaned over and gave me a peck. Her lips tasted faintly of tea.

"You seem happy." I cleaned the brush I'd been using in a cup of water, shaped the tip, and laid it down to dry.

"Finally finished one of my lettering jobs. Wasn't easy with all those different speech types they wanted, but God, the comic's great."

She peered down at me. "Si, you're beaming. What's up? They let you order those Wolf's Landing miniatures in?"

Heat rose to my face and Lydia's lips parted a fraction. "Kind of, but not really?"

She gave me her patented *do go on* look.

"One of the prop guys came by from *Wolf's Landing*, looking for supplies. Some stunt dude fell on his miniature set." I filled her in on the rest of the story and how Ian would be rebuilding the set *here*. I left out the part about him seemingly mentally stripping the clothing from my body with every glance.

"The sacred grove. Oh my god, Si, that's fantastic!" She gripped my shoulder. "And you get to help?" She knew it was a dream come true.

"Maybe? We'll see." I paused for a second and gulped down a breath of air. Time for the rest. "I think he was checking me out." *Think?* Knew.

Lydia's smile widened. "Please tell me you flirted back this time?"

Yeah, my wife knew me well. To be honest, I was hopeless with any gender and turned klutzy and dorky the minute I was the least bit attracted. I didn't flirt well—but I did flirt. She'd seen that firsthand.

"Maybe we should talk about the rest of that over dinner?" Some close friends knew about our open marriage and our polyamory, but it was not exactly something we went around blurting out, especially not in the middle of our store. Washington state may lean liberal, but not every place here did.

She glanced at her watch. "Let me ask Jesse if he wants anything, and I'll go grab some Chinese." A moment later, she vanished past the graphic novel display.

Score. Egg foo yung heaven awaited.

I eyed my half-painted spaceship. I wouldn't be finishing it tonight, not between talking to my wife and chowing down, so I closed up the paints and packed everything away.

If only most things in my life were that easy to handle.

CHAPTER THREE

IAN

Standing in Anna's office, I watched as she perfected her expression—a cross between *you're out of your mind* and *explain that to me again*. "You want to build your set in town, in a comic-book store?"

I tried not to shrink into myself, because my plan was a good one. Anna was intimidating, but fair when she understood why you wanted to do something unorthodox. "It's been raining all day. It's going to rain for the next couple of days."

She rubbed her forehead. "Don't remind me." The shooting schedule had been upended completely due to the weather, which happened pretty much every month unless we were filming scenes in the rain. On the other hand, everyone marveled at how authentic the downpours appeared on the show.

It had also been warmer than normal for this time of year, leading to very sticky and damp conditions. "I know the shop trailers are supposed to be cool and dry and—"

"They're swamp-like right now."

"The set will dry faster at the store. There's supplies on hand, and the owner offered me a space to work free of falling stuntmen."

Anna flinched. Not much, but enough. "Build a set in public, though?"

I shrugged. "Everyone knows the grove's going up in a fireball. The book's been out for years. And the graphic novel. And the comic. And . . ."

Anna held up her hand. "You'll have it done when you said?"

"Cross my heart." I did too. Still had enough Catholic in me for that.

"Fine. Go. Do." She gestured at the door.

She didn't have to say it twice. A moment later, I was out of her hot and humid trailer, and heading across the lot to my car. All the salvaged bits from the miniature set were packed, along with the base, the plans, and the few supplies I had. I'd loaded my Mini as soon as the drizzle started. Waiting for rain to let up was pointless out here—it only ever got worse before better. That could take days. Ah, the Pacific Northwest. So very . . . moist.

I booked it to the parking lot though I didn't know if it was the rain or the prospect of seeing Simon again that had me walking so fast. Oh hell, who was I kidding? It was Simon. His eyes, his hands, the way his shirt clung to his chest. Yeah, lust had gotten a grip on me, but there were things I liked about Simon other than enough perfection to get my dick hard.

Simon was kind. Friendly. A geek, like me. And he could *paint*. Understood miniatures, even if they weren't the movie-set kind. Not the type of guy I normally found around here. Mostly, I ended up meeting men who were only interested in *Wolf's Landing* or worse— they were *employed* by *Wolf's Landing*.

Lots of people on set fished off the same pier. It worked for some, like Carter Samuels and Levi Pritchard, our star-crossed big-name actors. And Anna and Natalya.

Heck, I'd gone spelunking into the pool of available guys a couple of times, but it was damn awkward when a one-night stand fizzled into regret . . . and you had to say "*Yo*" to that dude the next day. And the next . . . and the next. After the third "*Oops maybe not, man*," I'd stopped. Better to take things into my own hand, so to speak, than spend weeks cringing when we bumped into each other on the job.

But Simon? Simon was gorgeous, engaging, and *worked in town*. Couldn't ask for a better chance. I was dying to see if I'd imagined that spark of interest. Still, I took my sweet time driving over to the shop. The cops liked to sit on this stretch of road, and the rain had gone from annoying to insulting. Fastest setting on the wipers wasn't cutting it. I'd bought this car for sunny and dry California, not rain-soaked Washington state.

By the time I pulled up in front of End o' Earth, my heart was thudding against my ribs. This was the start. One set. One comics guy with a wicked smile, and me. Had it been my imagination yesterday? Na. Dude was a flirt. I was a flirt.

We could be flirts together.

Before I unpacked the monstrosity of the base and all the items stuffed into my car, I ducked into the shop to see if Simon was ready. It was after lunch and I didn't know if he was in. We hadn't discussed the time—only that I would be here today.

I dashed through the door, and this time, there was a woman behind the counter: neon red hair, a nose piercing, and some wicked tats up her arm. Her smile was bright. "Hey, how's it going?"

"Good! Well, other than the rain."

She gave me an eyeroll that I recognized as *Oh, this one's a California boy.* "Yeah, puts a damper on the day, huh?"

I snorted. "Or at least makes everything damp."

Apparently, my charm washed out, given her unimpressed raised eyebrow.

I cleared my throat. "Is Simon in? He was expecting me."

That had her straightening up. "Yeah, hang on." She opened a door behind the counter and called inside. "Si? There's a guy here for you."

Yeah, I was here for him. I had to bite my tongue to keep from smirking. I had no poker-face whatsoever, and I wasn't certain I wanted the fiery comics gal to know I was macking on her boss.

Simon appeared at the door and met my gaze . . . and I'm not sure what expression I had, because comics gal took one look at me and punched him in the arm. Simon only widened his grin, which formed dimples on his cheeks.

Glad I hadn't tucked my shirt in, because dimples were kryptonite to my self-control. "Uh . . ." And to the ability to put words together. "I have . . . stuff." I pointed behind me. "In the car."

Sometime during my brilliant use of the English language, Simon had rounded the counter and had come to a stop next to me. He was slightly taller. Right. I'd forgotten that part.

"Shall we get your *stuff*?" Simon held my gaze a bit longer, as if he knew he'd shorted out my mind with his smile, his hair, and those lips. Then he peered out the door and crinkled his brow. "I think there's a lull in the rain."

That's when my brain engaged. "I didn't think rain ever lulled here." We moved toward the door, side by side, but he paused to let me go first.

"Been known to happen. Count your lucky stars."

"Astronomical or Hollywood?"

Simon let out a bark of laughter as I unlocked the car. He sobered pretty quickly. "I can't believe you got that much into a Mini Cooper."

I shrugged. "I'm good at squeezing things into tight places."

Simon made a sound that might have been a swallowed giggle and wouldn't meet my eyes at all. His skin held a blush nicely, though. "I suppose that's a good talent to have."

"Never got any complaints from my ex-boyfriends."

Simon met my gaze, and his smile was wicked. "Really?"

Gotcha. "Really." I opened the Dutch doors to my Clubman. "Ten more inches than the regular Mini, and I know how to use every extra inch."

"Wow." Simon's eyes never left mine. "Your exes must have been fools."

Some of them, yeah. But I was far from perfect. I bumped Simon with my shoulder. "Let's get this *stuff* unloaded before it starts raining again."

His smile was a nice combo of turned on and shy. We pulled out bags of supplies and boxes and ferried them all into his shop. Didn't take long to unbury the base of the set.

"It's bigger than I thought." Simon rubbed his chin.

"Too big?" I didn't want to overtake his store with my problem. The guy still had a business to run.

"No." His grin was toothy and melted my bones. "I can take it."

Holy shit. My turn to have screaming hot cheeks. I totally deserved that line, and the smirk Simon gave me.

"Mostly, I'm worried about getting this through the door."

We managed, though, with a bit of maneuvering and help from comics gal, whose name turned out to be Dexy.

"That short for anything?"

She sighed. "Yeah. Dexys Midnight Runners, the eighties band. Dad *really* liked them."

When I glanced at Simon, he held up both hands. "Honest to God, it's true."

Dexy showed me her license. Given that her middle name was Eileen, Dad must have been a huge fan. "I'll be damned."

She gave a little rueful smile. "I like it now. It's unique."

Sure was. With her help, we got everything back to the tables Simon had been painting on the day before. "You boys have fun," she said, before sauntering off to the counter.

"Um. Is she actually old enough to call us boys?"

Simon shook his head. "Not *nearly*." His delightful smile was back and it warmed my blood.

I focused on the table, rather than on Simon, and that kept me from being too obvious. I hoped. "Well, this is it." I waved at the base of the model and all the bits. "Looks great, huh?"

Silence. I chanced a glance over, and Simon was rubbing his chin. "You're gonna build a grove in a week out of *this*?"

"Yup."

His gaze met mine. "You've gotta be kidding me."

"Hey! I'm a professional!" I clapped him on the shoulder. "Trust me." Beneath my hand, he was warm and tense, and I loathed to let go. But that seemed the best move.

Such an adorable smile. "Tell me what you want me to do."

Oh, so *much*. But the clock was ticking, and Anna's exacting filming schedule needed a set more than I needed a blowjob. The latter could wait. "Start unpacking the bags, and I'll show you the plans and the photos of what this looked like before a stunt dude fell on it."

We got to work emptying the bags and setting out the supplies I'd brought, plus my tackle box of tools. Yeah, I could have used one of those expensive art boxes, but I liked going old school—with an expensive fishing box, instead. At one point, Dexy called Simon to the front of the store, and I took a moment to admire his back and ass as he headed to the counter.

I took another second to catch my breath. When this day was through, I was going to need a beer. Company too. Preferably the tall and lanky kind. Maybe nothing would happen other than flirting, but I wanted to know what was going through his mind. Or body. Whichever.

I dug out the set plans, my notes, and found an open space on the table. Simon returned while I was rooting through my supplies for paint. I had to have a bottle of the color I'd used under everything. Except I didn't. "Damn."

Simon's warm hand on my back nearly made me jump out of my skin. "What are you looking for?"

"Paint." It came out higher than it should have. "I, uh, used this particular sepia brown under everything, and I could have sworn . . ."

His fingers drifted down my back and fell away. "You wouldn't happen to remember the name?"

No. But I had lists for that. A few flips of the pages in my notebook, and I'd found it. "Here."

He took in more than the paint color above the tip of my finger. "This is high-end stuff."

"Dude. This is *Wolf's Landing*."

A little red in his cheeks. "Right. Hollywood. Sometimes I forget."

"Is that good or bad?"

He peered back at me, eyes the same shade as a morning sky. "Both, I think. It's weird. A lot of you guys have become local-ish. Settled in. That's good."

"And the bad?"

"I don't carry this brand of paint."

Yeah, that could be a problem. "We'll make do."

He stepped up to the model and peered closer. "I bet I can match the color."

Wouldn't you know, he did. Nearly perfectly. There was a touch of red in the brand he carried, but in some ways, that was better. We rebuilt the upright columns that acted as tree trunks and fixed up the altar base until it was as good as new, then started painting the whole contraption. Simon's color contrasted better when I added gray on top. While I touched up the paint, I set Simon to piecing together the shattered remains of the trunk texture. I'd spent so damn long to get those trees to appear real, especially in the flickering light that should play off them . . . right before the whole set blew up. I wasn't going to waste that work.

He hummed to himself. Nothing I recognized—might not have been anything but random notes—but it was pleasant and sweet, and I wondered if he puttered around his house like that, making up little tunes under his breath.

That led to visions of Simon, bare-chested, wearing nothing but a low-slung pair of gray sweatpants in his kitchen. Man, did I want to see *that*. There was nothing like slim hips in sweats that begged to be slipped off.

Oh yeah. I had it bad.

"I do love puzzles," Simon murmured, as he poked at pieces of tree bits on the table. He straightened and stretched his back. "I think I'm done."

"Nearly there, myself." I put a few final touches on the base, then stepped away. It looked decent too. Still a lot to accomplish, but my stomach told me we were close to dinnertime, and my watch confirmed. Nearly five thirty.

Not bad for a half-day's work.

On the other table, Simon had arranged the bits and pieces of cracked tree trunk material, and it did kind of seem like a pieced-together puzzle, had the maker been a sadistic bastard. Which I guess I was, since I'd asked him to figure out how they all went back together.

"There's parts missing." He pointed out some spots where there were noticeable gaps.

I chewed on the inside of my mouth, arms tingling, and nodded. "There's going to be, anyway." I waved at the model. "The bases for those trees aren't exactly the same as they were."

"I'm surprised you don't use real bark."

He wasn't the first to suggest it. "It looks wrong. Ridges are too big, since it's actual tree-sized and not miniature."

Simon snickered.

"What?"

"You drive a Mini."

I stared at him.

"A miniature guy . . . who drives a Mini."

Oh my God. "I . . . uh." Never crossed my mind.

"No . . . Don't fuck with me. You didn't buy it because of that?"

"I didn't! I got it because it's cute and yellow and gets good gas mileage!"

We couldn't stop laughing, and God, Simon was amazing. Dimples, laughlines, and a bright smile. His hair was disheveled and all I wanted to do was brush it out of his face.

Of course, we were still in his store, and *of course* that's the moment when we weren't alone anymore.

"Someone's happy." The woman who spoke was slightly shorter than me but elegant, unlike either of us, even in her jeans and plaid button-down. Long black hair that wasn't at all like my short mess. She had a bohemian look to her.

We, on the other hand, looked like guys who'd spent the day painting a model.

"Hey!" Simon lit the fuck up when he saw her, more than he should for an employee. Or friend. "I thought you were working tonight?"

I swallowed my breath and my heart. Oh shit, no. I couldn't have been wrong. No way.

"Oh, I am," she said. "Still have about two hours left on the lettering job. But a girl's gotta eat." She peered at me, her smile warm and inviting. "And I wanted to meet your friend."

I didn't want to meet her, because she was acting like a girlfriend and I wanted to take Simon out for a beer. I didn't want to know who she was, because I had to spend the next week working next to a man who moved like sin.

I must have hidden it well enough, because Simon's toothy grin was aimed at me. "This is Ian Meyers, the miniaturist I was telling you about."

At least he was talking about me? None of this felt right, though. My lungs were tight.

She reached out her hand and I took it. Warm fingers, but my blood was going cold.

"Ian, this is Lydia, my wife."

Fuck. Fucking *hell*. "Great to meet you," I said, and it sounded pretty good, despite the tumble in my head.

"Likewise." She was as charming as her husband. All good cheer and happiness.

We let go of each other's hands.

Great. Just . . . great. I really picked winners, didn't I?

After Simon and I cleaned ourselves up in the End o' Earth's tiny staff bathroom, the three of us headed down to Cougar Den, the nearest bar. Well, I shouldn't say three. It was Mr. and Mrs. Derry and me, the gullible and foolish third wheel. But the tavern had a good beer selection and decent food, both of which I needed. Especially the beer.

Seems like everyone did. We ordered a round of local brew for one and all. I doubted either of them had the same thing running through *their* minds.

Married. Fucking dude didn't wear a ring! Lydia did, though. A silver band with some etching on the side. It wasn't until the waitress brought us water that I recognized it. "Is that a Stargate?"

Lydia smiled as if she had no idea I'd spent part of the afternoon imagining her husband naked and under me. "Good eye." She glanced at the ring. "Do you want to see it?"

I kinda did, and maybe she could tell, because she pulled the ring off and handed it to me. Yup. Little miniature Stargate wedding band. Nice detail and the symbol band even rotated. There was a date inscribed inside. Quick math told me they'd been married ten years, which made me wonder about Simon. Gay? Bi? Trapped? Happy? He'd sure gotten a boner a few times, flirted like he wanted my cock, and yet here we were at a bar with his *wife*. I played with the spinning part of the ring. "Is this official merchandise?"

She coughed. "No. It was before the whole geek-ring trend became . . . well, a trend." A little color came to her cheeks. "The guy who made them doesn't anymore."

"There are official ones now, if you ever need one." Simon closed his menu. "Before Lydia was into—" He stopped and got this adorably sheepish expression. "Well, back when we met, Lydia was into *Stargate*."

I handed the ring back to Lydia. "Before?"

Now they *both* looked sheepish. Huh. I wanted to prod, but the server came to drop off our beers and take our order. To top off the weirdness of the night, they both ordered bacon cheeseburgers, which I desperately wanted . . . so fuck it, I ordered one as well. They both ordered fries. At least I got mine with onion rings . . . wouldn't be kissing anyone tonight.

I also wasn't letting them off the hook for earlier. "Before?" I repeated.

Lydia's face gained color, and she glanced around the bar. "Before I was into *Wolf's Landing.*" Low voice. "*Stargate* was my passion before that."

Which meant *Wolf's Landing* was her passion now. "Oh."

Embarrassment tightened her features. "I'm sorry. I try not to mention it, especially with people—" She waved her hand.

With people like me, who worked for the show. My stomach lurched. "It's okay, you know? To be a fan. Bunch of people on set are, too." Absolutely true. Couple folks had jumped at the chance to work on the show because they loved the books to pieces. Including me.

"I know." She tucked a strand of hair behind her ear. "But there's the whole thing about not shitting where you live." She met my gaze. "I live here. So does Levi Pritchard and Carter Samuels and Hunter Easton and a bunch of other people. I can't imagine what it's like with all the fans coming through. They don't need that from me."

Right there and then, I decided I liked Lydia. She was real and earnest and cared. Sure, she was also married to my walking wet dream, but I couldn't blame her for getting there first. "Hey, they need people to adore what they do, too. That's part of why they do it." I reached over the table, took her hand, and gave it a squeeze. "Just because you live here doesn't mean you have to stop loving *Wolf's Landing.*"

Man, the light in her eyes, and that little smile. If she'd been a guy, I'd have been all over her. As it was, it warmed my heart. No wonder Simon was with her. I let go and took a swig of beer.

Lucky bastards. Both of them.

She wet her whistle with a swig from her own bottle. "So, how'd you guys make out today?" Her focus shifted between the two of us.

Simon scratched the back of his head, as if he, like me, had zoomed right in on the words *make out.* "Well, I puzzled together some broken tree bits and Ian painted. But I don't know . . ."

He still had lovely blue eyes, and my body still responded to them, even if my brain slapped *married* all over that. "It was a good start. It's gonna be a long-ass week, but I got more done with your help than I could have alone."

They both smiled and parts of me zinged in ways I didn't understand. Good people. A hot guy. A *married* guy. His cool wife. None of it made sense.

I was so damn grateful when the burgers came, because they gave us all a chance to stop talking. But food only covers the lulls in conversation for so long. This time, I wanted the control. "When does the shop open tomorrow?"

Simon had a mouth full of fries, so Lydia answered. "Ten. But I'll be there, probably before eight."

"Takes that long to open up?"

"Only on Wednesdays—comic day." Which tomorrow wasn't. She continued. "But my studio's in the back of the shop, and I *need* to finish this coloring job, so I'll be in early."

"Wait, you work in comics?" Talented, too? Kill me now and put me out of my misery.

She picked up a fry. "Freelance. A little lettering here. Some coloring there." She smirked. "And like everyone, I'm working on my own graphic novel."

No way she was getting off that easy. "About what?"

Simon giggled, but said nothing. A moment later, he jumped. "Ow! Hey!"

"Don't you start, Si." There was laughter in Lydia's words.

"He'll love the idea, I'm sure." Simon poked his fry at me. "It's tons of fun."

His grin still pushed all my buttons. "What?"

"It's . . . pirates. Space pirates." She looked mortified.

"But with tall ships and lasers!" Simon had the glee of a kid with a thousand SweeTarts. He flinched when Lydia kicked him under the table again.

I could buy that, actually. I mean, why not? "And? What's the story?"

Lydia got quiet. "An older woman searching for her little sister she had to leave behind when their planet was taken over by the Tsar of the neighboring system. She was conscripted into the Navy, rose through the ranks, then broke away. Became a buccaneer and started her search."

Simon had been right. This was something I'd love. "Got queer characters?"

That made her laugh. "Oh yeah. Queer. Poly. People of color. Basically, I rage wrote this idea from all the stuff I loved but never saw. And now—"

"She's making it." Simon finished. The way he watched her . . . damn. He wasn't trapped. That was a man who loved his wife.

Why did such wonderful, beautiful people have to find each other? How did they? Because I needed to take some notes on that shit. I wanted Simon badly, but that wasn't going to happen, given his marriage. I might have been gay, but I totally got why he was into Lydia. Hell, I wanted *her* as a friend.

The conversation shifted and for a little while, Simon and Lydia talked shop—literally—and I got a small glimpse into running a comics store. Same pain points as any other business. Overhead. Margins. Scheduling. In some respect, I was glad for my paycheck. There were plusses to not being your own boss too.

When the tab for dinner finally came, I grabbed it, over both their protests. "Hey, you guys are doing me a huge favor. Least I can do."

After I got my card back, we left and fell into an awkward silence on the street.

"Um," Lydia said. "I need to head back to the shop."

"I'm parked there," I replied. "So I'm heading that way."

Simon gave one of his little shrug-and-smile deals. "I'll follow."

But which one of us was he following?

As it turned out, we walked in a row, with me in the middle. Nothing at all symbolic about that. My confusion raced back.

Married. Hot. *Shit.*

When we got to the shop, Lydia paused by the door. "Do you mind hugs?"

"Love 'em." Nice of her to ask, though.

She folded her arms around me. "Great meeting you, Ian."

I patted her on the back and enjoyed the warmth before we broke apart. I didn't get a lot of physical contact from anyone, to be honest. Hugs from friends? I liked those.

Of course, this meant I *had* slotted Lydia into friend already. I laughed at myself. Only I would end up liking the wife of the guy whose bones I wanted to jump. Speaking of which . . . Simon looked at me and raised a brow, the question pretty obvious. So, I hugged him too.

Hugging the guy you want to fuck while he was off limits? That's damn good as well. And maybe I lingered a little longer than I should have. Been a little harder than appropriate. Or maybe he did and was too. *Shit.*

Simon gave out a small sigh and let go. "See you tomorrow."

"I'll probably be here about eight thirty, if that's okay?"

Lydia nodded. "Come around to the back of the building and ring the bell. I'll let you in."

"I'll be in around nine thirty," Simon said. "I'm working the morning shift, but I can help when there's a lull."

"Or I can take over, and you can have him for the day." Lydia smoothed a hand down Simon's arm. "Let's see how much of this job I get finished."

I nodded because it seemed the best idea. "Tomorrow, then."

We said our goodbyes, and I climbed into my Mini. Simon's joke came back to me, and I chuckled, but sobered quickly.

He'd been so damn flirty. They were so damn married.

On the drive back to my apartment outside town, I ran the whole day through my head. I had no idea what to feel at all.

CHAPTER FOUR

SIMON

I followed Lydia into the store. I'd biked over from our house, so I had to grab my wheels to get home, and I wanted to make sure everything was fine with Ian's set. Most of our customers knew not to touch what was on the tables in the model area. But still.

Plus, I'd caught the look in Lydia's eyes. She wanted a conversation.

Jesse had taken over from Dexy, and he nodded. "Boss-people."

Lydia rounded the counter and gave him a playful bump with her hip. "We've got names, you know."

Jesse grunted, but his smile said everything. This was an old, *old* routine. He focused on me. "You heading out?"

"Yeah," I said. "Been here since opening. Gonna be here to open tomorrow." I tried not to work too many shifts in a row. That shit could burn you out.

"I'll hold down the fort, then."

"If you need anything, I'll be in back." Lydia met my gaze. "Got a minute, Si?"

"Always, for you." Yup. Conversation time. Probably about Ian. Everything about their interaction had told me she liked him, which was good. Still, I always got nervous about these talks. We headed into the employees/storage area and then a little deeper into the tiny room she'd claimed as her studio. It had a high window along one wall and her work covered pretty much every free surface.

I closed the door and leaned against it. "You like him."

"Of course I do. You have fantastic taste in men." She flopped into her chair. "He's charming and pretty and he's a certified geek."

Yup to all of those. "I didn't tell him I was married." Which I should have, but that would have shut down the flirting . . . and I liked that part.

"Figured that out pretty quickly when you introduced me."

I winced. Ian had held it together, but I'd been around the block long enough that I knew what shocked and confused looked like. "There hasn't been any time. We just met." I'd been trying to figure out how to say something—anything—about it to him.

"Sweetheart, I'm not chastising you." She twisted her hands in her lap. "I'm trying to apologize. I should've thought before bounding over and pulling you away for dinner."

Nope. Not Lydia's fault either. "Well, you *are* my wife." I pushed off the door, walked over, and took both her hands. "I can't ask you to avoid me because I'm shit with men and don't know how to flirt or talk or—"

She snorted. "Yeah, except he's into you, so you must have done something right." She gave my hands a squeeze. "And you're not shit with men. You're gorgeous, sexy, and funny."

"I'm really not." More nervous and geeky. "And you're biased."

"Maybe I am. But you didn't see Ian's face when you hugged him." She raised her gaze. "I did."

I hadn't, but I *had* felt the bulge in his pants. Even now, the memory got to me, and I gave a little sigh.

Lydia's smile widened. "I'll give you hopeless. Especially when a guy knocks you off your feet."

Couldn't help the laugh or the color to my cheeks. I slipped my hands free of hers. "He's . . . Oh God. I haven't felt like this in years." *Hopeless* was a good word for it. "I've only known him for a few hours!" Wanted to know *so much* about him.

I didn't know if I stood a chance, though. These kinds of situations were weird and . . . well, Bluewater Bay was an awfully small town to be poly in. Word got around. Breakups got awkward. We'd seen it happen with some other people, which was why we'd mostly gone swinging out of town. Besides, our one try in Bluewater Bay had fizzled out before it even began. Dude had been too into his ex and not into us enough.

Lydia wrinkled her brow. "What did you do the last time you felt like this?"

Her question stopped my breath, but I knew the answer. I'd flirted hard and stupidly. Made a fool of myself. Gone out on three dates, and then asked Lydia to be my wife.

That had been a rocky time, since we weren't each other's primary relationship. Given that I felt the same giddy, life-changing rush for Ian?

Oh shit, it worried me right down to the bones.

"Honey?" Her voice was soft.

"I married you."

So many emotions flickered over her features. This time, when I took her hands, I went to my knees on the hard floor. "I won't do anything." I wouldn't lose her. I loved her. Deeply. Astoundingly. Enough that I knew—without a doubt—that no matter who else she was with, she'd come home to the house we'd made.

I needed her to know that about me too.

"Si, don't." She freed one hand and cupped my face. "I'm not worried. I know who I married." She kissed the tip of my nose. "Go home. Get some rest." She chuckled. "If you start acting around Ian the way you acted around me, he'll have no choice but to fall hopelessly in love with you."

I wanted that. I feared that. Society told me I couldn't have that. I pulled Lydia into my arms. "You're the best thing that ever happened to me." The words fell into her hair.

She pulled back enough to kiss me—sweet and lingering, with enough tongue to curl my toes—before she backed off and sighed. "I need to work on this job. It's due in two days."

I stole a quick taste of her mouth. "I'll let you get to it." Rising made my knees creak like a set of stairs. Shit. I was only in my thirties. Unfair. "See you when you get home."

"Mm-hmm." She pulled me down for another kiss, one that left me a tad breathless. "Don't wait up."

I would. I always did.

On the way up to the front, I grabbed my bike from the employee area and conferred briefly with Jesse about Ian's set in the middle of the miniatures area.

"I'll make sure no one touches it, boss."

He would too. I had him hold my bike as I took one last look at what we'd accomplished today. Didn't seem like much: a painted base that could be a grove, and bits of shattered bark. Couldn't see how this all was going to go together in a week. But Ian had been pleased.

Ian.

I closed my eyes and remembered how his body had touched mine during that brief hug, and wondered what he'd felt. Wondered if I could build on any of it.

I'd never managed to get going on a relationship like this before. But Ian was different and he hadn't run away. I glanced around the area. Then again, I had his set, so it wasn't like he could.

Right. Enough rumination. I headed back to the counter, grabbed my bike, and rode home.

The sound of the front door closing startled me awake and the book I'd been reading slipped from my fingers and thudded to the floor. It took me a moment to figure out I was on the couch in the living room and not in bed. Mostly, it was the sweatpants that gave it away, and the fact that Lawrence Purrbody, our longhaired black and white troublemaker, was stretched out next to me, rather than on my legs. He preferred me under the covers. Apparently, without blankets, my legs were too bony for his royal fluffy butt.

From the entry into the living room, Lydia snorted. "It's past midnight."

I groaned. Getting up tomorrow would hurt. I had no idea how Lydia managed. She seemed to survive on a couple hours' sleep and coffee. "Guess it's time for bed?"

"Go on up, sleeping beauty. I'll take care of feeding Purrbutt."

Wasn't going to argue. I fished my book off the floor, found the last spot I remembered reading, and stuck in a bookmark.

I made it through my nighttime routine and was tucked under the covers when Lydia came up. "You look a little like someone dropped a brick on you, love."

"Gee, thanks, sweetheart." We both laughed, though I sobered first. "The brick is named Ian."

She nodded, but didn't say anything else before heading into the bathroom for her own pre-bed ablutions.

Ian. I ran bits and pieces of the day through my head. His smile. The sound of his voice. That hug that had lasted longer and been closer than a guy-hug . . . and that had just been day one. I groaned, grabbed Lydia's pillow, and covered my face.

"Simon?" A mixture of amusement and concern from the bathroom doorway.

Had to ditch the pillow to speak, so I tossed it back where it belonged. "I'm going to be spending an *entire week* with Ian." I mean, I'd known before. But it hit me now. A week of those bright eyes and those arms and that waist and . . .

I was hot for him. So much so. I blew out a breath.

My wife laughed at me. "You're adorable."

"But—what do I do now?" How do you tell a guy you dig him when he's met your wife and you haven't had the chance to explain? Hell, how do you tell a near stranger you're in an open marriage, and you'd like to get to know him better?

Lydia managed those talks, but my usual route was to get cold feet, a dry mouth, and not do anything. Because when I did, a lot of people pegged me as the "typical cheating bisexual." And I wasn't. I *wasn't.*

Once she'd undressed, Lydia slipped under the covers and curled up against me. "You talk to him, Si. You tell him what's up and see if he's interested."

"He's not going to be."

"Honey, I saw how tight the front of his jeans was."

Yeah, I'd felt that during the hug. "That's . . . lust."

"Lust's a good start."

It could be. I certainly had it in spades for Ian. There was also that same weird connection and longing I'd felt when I met Lydia all those years ago—right after I'd pretty much given up on women and gone exclusively to dating guys. Funny how life liked to play with me. Kind of like Lawrence McFluff liked to play with cotton balls—incessantly and without mercy. "Ethical non-monogamy is hard!" I mock whined the words.

Lydia kissed my shoulder. "It's not easy to say either."

Couldn't help laughing. She had me there. "God, I love you." Over and over. I couldn't have met a better partner.

"I know," she murmured against my skin. "That's why you married me."

Yeah, it was. "I can't imagine spending the rest of my ethically non-monogamous life without you."

"Ditto." Sleepy voice. "Never gonna—"

Before she could get the next word out, I pressed my fingers against her lips. "Don't you dare Rick Roll me in bed, Lydia Derry!"

Her eyes danced with an evil glint. She knew that song would be stuck in my head now. Probably would be playing there in the morning too.

I replaced my fingers with my lips and kissed her long and hard.

CHAPTER FIVE

IAN

I felt like some kind of weird thief or secret agent creeping around dumpsters and trash cans in the alley behind Main Street to find the back door to End o' Earth. Luckily for me, it was well-marked. They all were, actually. I guess that made sense for deliveries. Or weird miniature artists coming to work on models at eight thirty in the morning.

I had two cups of coffee from Stomping Grounds in my hand— coffee with cream for me and a latte with a touch of cinnamon for Lydia. It was her favorite. Or so the barista at the shop had said when I asked.

"You know, she's married," she'd said.

My chuckle had likely been as dark as black coffee. *"Yeah, I know. The Derrys are doing me a favor. I figured coffee wouldn't hurt."* And Lydia was totally not the Derry I was after. Had been after.

Shit.

Here I was at Lydia's door. I pressed the bell and waited. A few moments later, the door swung open, and she poked her head out. "Hi, Ian! You're here."

"Yup, as promised." I handed the coffee to her. "I'm told you'll enjoy this."

She pushed the door open wider and ushered me in. "You didn't have to get me coffee."

Her smile was bright and charming, and sent warmth into my soul. "Yeah, I did. You have no idea how much you're helping me, letting me borrow Simon." We walked down a small corridor past what was probably her studio, given all the art I spied inside.

"Don't worry about it. I don't mind." Lydia took a sip of her coffee. "And Simon likes to be borrowed."

I tried not to spew mine out through my nose. *Does he?* No, no. I was reading a little too much into that. We reached the main part of the shop and Lydia pointed the way to where Simon and I had been working before—though I'd guessed the direction. We'd come out behind the counter and I had excellent spatial memory. Had to. Kind of came with the territory.

"I suppose I'll get to work."

"Holler if you need anything." She swallowed another mouthful of coffee and practically purred in pleasure before heading into the back.

Same little flutter in my soul. Yeah, the coffee had been a hit. I'd have bought Simon one too, but by the time he came in, it would have been cold. Simon hated cold coffee. The barista told me that too. *"Even in the summer, he likes it blazing hot."* I had no idea what I'd do with that tidbit of information.

Nothing. I'd do nothing at all because I wouldn't be doing anything with Simon, other than working on my set in his shop.

I needed to get my head out of my ass. After another gulp of my coffee, I took stock of what needed to be done today, and started working. Some time passed and I was deep into gluing the bark Simon had pieced back together onto the tree supports when I heard the murmur of his voice at the front of the shop. Lydia's too. A zip of conflicting emotions went through me: Lust, jealousy, warmth, joy. I liked the Derrys. Both of them.

What a fucking hell *that* was.

I focused on the model and maneuvered another piece of bark into position while I listened to the soft fall of shoes on the carpet.

When I straightened, Simon spoke. "Hey." He was clearly a bundle of nerves, bright-faced and excited.

All my buttons got pressed again and I fought to shut that shit down. As adorable as he was—Simon was Lydia's. And she was his. They were so fucking lucky. That was enough of a rock lodged in my stomach to quell desire. "Hey. You free, or . . ."

"For the next fifteen or so, until it's time to open. After that, it'll be catch as catch can until Dexy comes in at two." He scratched the back of his head. "Is there anything I can work on that I can pick up and put down?"

There was. I had Simon find the bag that held the other sculpted pieces I'd made. The altar, rocks, all the details, and asked him to inspect them for chips or missing paint. "Any piece that doesn't look like that"—I pointed to the photos of both my undamaged set and the life-sized one—"needs to look like that."

"So, repair and repaint?" Simon peered at the photos.

"You up for the work?"

His grin took my breath away. "Dude, you have no idea." His smile became more serious. "I'm so glad you walked through that door."

His expression—I knew that twist of lips and frown. The longing, the need. Maybe it was sexual or artistic. Didn't matter. Sent blood to my cheeks . . . and lower. "Me too." It came out too deep, but it was true. Simon was like fresh air. I wanted to breathe in as much of him as I could, while I could. And like clean, crisp air, I hadn't known I'd needed him until I experienced his presence.

Except, of course, I couldn't have him. Not in all the ways I wanted. "If you want help . . ."

"I'll let you know." He spoke quietly, and for a moment, it looked as if he'd say something else, but he furrowed his brows, and bent to study the photos instead.

I went back to putting bark onto trees.

After a piece, Simon touched my shoulder. "Hey, Ian?"

I wanted more of that hand, more of that voice saying my name. Warmth spread through me like fire. "Yeah?"

"Can you see if I did this right?" Simon pointed to the table where he'd sorted through all of the remaining bits and pieces.

I wandered over. He'd created two piles. One obviously was for repairs and a much smaller one was for items that miraculously didn't seem to require touching up. I took a quick look through both, and damn, Simon had an eye for detail. He'd found little imperfections most people wouldn't, but that the camera would. "Man, this is great. You have no idea how much time you've saved me." Simon was so close and our hands brushed. I wondered if he felt the heat from my body too.

"Good." Relief was written into Simon's smile. "I have to go open, but when I get a break, I'll start on matching the colors and touching up the ones that only need paint."

"Sounds good."

Simon gripped me on the shoulder again, his expression so damned complicated, I didn't know what to make of it. Then he was gone, heading toward the front of the shop while every bit of my body tingled.

Talk about mixed signals. Or mistaken signals. I had no idea. Didn't matter in the long run. A few breaths steadied my nerves, and I got back to work.

Simon flitted in and out as he did his job in the shop. By the time he'd sorted out the paints and started touching up the bits that needed it, I was nearly finished placing as much of the bark as I could back onto the tree bases. Now all that was necessary was to fill in the gaps and sculpt it. I stretched out my back and my stomach rumbled.

"Hungry?" Simon set down a miniature rock he'd been painting.

"Yeah." I loathed to lose time, though. The clay would need to set before I painted it. If I didn't get the trees done today, I wouldn't be painting them until tomorrow. But damn did my back hurt. I'd been sitting for a good part of the work, but I'd spent too much time hunched over. "I probably should take a break for lunch. What time is it anyway?" I checked my naked wrist, then dug my phone out of my pocket.

Simon was quicker since he actually wore a watch. "Almost one thirty."

I didn't believe him, but my phone said the same damn time. "Fuck." I rubbed my forehead. "I need to get the trees done today." No lunch for me. I rolled my shoulders and tried to crack my neck. "I'll eat later."

Silence. When I met Simon's gaze, he tilted his head, inspecting me. Heat flowed to my cheeks, though the down-up he gave me wasn't sexual at all. "Did you eat breakfast?"

Coffee had been my breakfast. Always was. I rolled my eyes at him. "I'm fine."

"You're shaking."

I held out my hands. "Steady as a rock." They were. I ignored the muscle twinges in my legs and the pain in my shoulders.

"I don't want to clean your ass off my floor when you pass out."

Oh, the skepticism. "I'm not going to pass out." I sank down into the chair I'd been using, because falling over would prove Simon's point. "I don't want to lose my momentum." I probably should eat, but I could wait until dinner. I'd only ever passed out on the job once.

Well, twice, but the second time I'd had walking pneumonia, so that didn't count.

He chuckled, but didn't sound amused. "You know, I'm going to sic Lydia on you, right?"

"Dude, I'm gay. Your wife isn't going to charm me into lunch." Okay, that was a bit much, but after all the flirting—or not flirting—I was cranky with him. "Especially since you failed."

Same damn snort of laughter as before. "I'm not trying to charm you. If I were, I'd be whispering in your ear."

Oh fuck. Imagining that was such a turn-on—and from the uptick of Simon's smile, the bastard knew. "Wanna give it a try, straight boy?" I spoke through gritted teeth.

He closed in on me, and the intensity of his stare pinned me to my chair. He swung behind me, hands on my shoulders, fingers pressing down against my sore muscles. Warm breath caressed my left ear and he whispered, "I'm not straight."

"Married," I said, my own voice almost air. "Married, then."

Simon's chuckle was wicked and sexy and made my brain melt. He kneaded my shoulders and it was heaven and hell. "It's an open marriage."

Unfair. Completely unfair. "You've got to be kidding me." I glanced up, and there was Simon, close enough to kiss. All I had to do was reach up and drag his head closer.

"Not kidding. Come to lunch with us at two, Ian." Simon pressed his lips to my forehead, then stood back.

If I hadn't been dizzy before, I sure was now. Holy fuck. Took me a second, but I remembered how to breathe. Probably sounded like I'd run a marathon, though. Every bit of me tingled.

Not straight. Open marriage. I struggled to make sense of those two statements and of my own feelings. "I—uh. Okay." Not like I was going to get anything done after his little announcement.

Simon's smile was blinding. "I need to cash out the register before Dexy comes in. Come up when you're ready."

I nodded, since I didn't have any words left in my short-circuited head. I checked my phone again. Only a few minutes had passed, but the world had tilted sideways in that time.

At least my gaydar was working. Or bi-dar. Whatever. I stared at the *Wolf's Landing* model, and Lydia's earlier comment—that Simon liked to be borrowed—bounced through my head. *Holy shit.*

I'd spent *years* in Hollywood, so I'd seen the whole poly thing before. I'd dated a few guys who'd been dating other guys, but never anyone married. How'd that work? Did I want to get involved?

Did Simon?

I suppose his kiss on my forehead was answer enough.

Shit, yeah. I wanted involved. Tangled. Entwined. Guy like that? Sign me up.

I pushed back from the model and stood. First, find the modeling clay, then I could sculpt after lunch. I also cleaned up what we wouldn't need. I had no doubt Dexy would keep prying customers away, though a thought niggled. Eventually, the model would look less like a pile of crap and more like a *Wolf's Landing* set . . . and that might attract attention. I'd have to talk to Simon about a sheet or something to cover the grove when we weren't here.

I stopped short. Simon and sheets. Simon *on* a sheet, under me. Not the first time that thought had coursed through my body, but now there was actually a chance. Maybe. If this whole *open marriage* scenario were true.

Dexy's hello rang through the shop, and I swallowed hard against my desire and need. I'd worn my crappy loose jeans for painting, which in retrospect had been a good plan. By the time I made it to the front of the store, I was only semi-hard.

There stood the Derrys and Dexy. Simon had the expression of a cat who'd caught a bird. Lydia wore amusement.

Dexy plunked a cash drawer into the register. "Hey, Ian."

"Hey." I still sounded out of breath, but Dexy didn't seem to notice.

"If you guys go to Raven's Flight, the soup of the day is French Onion. And they've got that salmon burger of theirs on special."

The mere mention of a burger had my stomach growling. I pressed a hand over my belly. "Shush," I said to my gut.

"I thought you weren't hungry?" Simon's voice was like velvet.

I tried not to shiver, especially since Dexy and Lydia were both there. With my hand still pressed over my middle, I answered, "Never said I wasn't—just that I'd eat later."

Lydia looked for all the world like she was trying not to burst into laughter. She took a breath, but the smile didn't fade one bit. "Shall we head out?"

Simon rounded the counter and headed for the door. "Let's."

I followed, as did Lydia.

Once again, I was sandwiched between the Derrys as we walked down the street, only it wasn't quite as awkward as it had been the previous night. So much made sense now. "I guess we should have a conversation."

They both grinned, and my stomach flipped due to an entirely *different* hunger.

CHAPTER SIX

SIMON

I should have kissed Ian on the mouth. Cupped his neck, leaned down, and done it. I hadn't, because Lydia and I tried to keep our poly life on the down-low. Who knew what the hell he thought of polyamory, or my clumsy flirting, or Lydia's smile.

But he hadn't run. Hadn't turned down our offer of lunch. Then again, his set was sitting in our store, so this could be a captive-audience thing. Shit. I hadn't thought of that.

I stole a glance at Ian, but couldn't read him at all. "Anywhere in particular you'd like to go?"

He pursed his lips. "I'm fine with Raven's Flight. They've got great burgers."

"You like burgers, huh?" He'd had one last night, as well.

Ian glanced over. "I do. I'm also very fond of sausage." He said it in a totally deadpan manner, but there was an evil glint in his eyes.

Lydia snort-laughed while I reddened. But hey, he was flirting. That was a good sign. My insides tumbled.

At Raven's Flight, they sat us in a booth in the back, away from others and it was pretty private. Good. Lydia and I sat opposite Ian. After we got our waters and menus, Ian folded his hands and placed them on the table. "So," he said. "Open marriage?"

"Yup," Lydia said. "For all ten years."

Ian seemed to chew on that. "But still married."

"We love each other," I murmured. "Clicked exactly right. And since we were both poly before . . ." I shrugged. "We got married. Didn't change who we were."

Ian studied each of us in turn. "I've done poly, but usually it's been guys who like dating a lot of other guys, not—" He waved between the two of us. "A married couple. That's *usually* monogamy."

"You'd be surprised," I said.

"Maybe I would be." He read the menu for a moment before those deep brown eyes met mine again. "Why me?"

Lydia sat back and picked up the menu. I caught her little smile. Ian did too. Yeah, on the surface the reason why I was interested was obvious. Ian was *hot*. "Could ask you the same question."

He nodded and ran a finger down the lunch specials. "Well, aside from being sexier than sin, you're not *Wolf's Landing*, but you're a geek so you understand me." He looked up. "And you're really talented."

I hadn't considered that. I *was* a comics guy and a townie. But talented? "I—uh." I reached for my water. "I do paint by numbers, Ian. I'm not . . ."

His raised eyebrows stopped my breath. "Dude. I watched you working on my set. I'm *letting* you work on my set. Trust me. You've the skills of a pro."

Lydia flipped over the menu, then set it on the table. "He's got you there, Si."

"Is he always like this?" Ian sounded exasperated.

"Totally unaware of how awesome he is?" Lydia chuckled. "Yup. Always."

Well, now my face was burning. "I—um." I had nothing. Thankfully, the waitress came to take our orders. I quickly scanned the list and ended up ordering the salmon burger. Lydia got a steak salad, and damn him to hell, Ian ordered a sausage on a bun.

After the waitress left, Ian had the devil's grin when he picked up his water. "You didn't answer my question, you know."

Lydia snickered and leaned back. My lovely wife. Abandoning me.

Only one option: I told the truth. "You're stunning." I took a breath. "And you have a job I can only dream about. That you trust me to help—"

"Si, I told you—"

"It means something to me. You're witty, hard-working, and kind. You like comics and *Stargate* and . . ." I shrugged. "We clicked."

He took a sip of his water and set it down, but didn't say anything.

"Look," I said. "I know this is a different situation than maybe you're used to, but . . . I'd like to see where it goes."

"It is different." He studied me from across the table. "I've never had a guy ask me out with his wife sitting next to him."

Lydia shrugged. "At least you know he's on the up and up." Her smile faded to seriousness. "I have absolutely no issues with it."

Ian laughed and seemed to take stock of us both. "See, that's the thing. I've also dated married guys who pretended to be single. And pretended to be straight to their *wives*."

"Cheaters," I said. "Closeted."

He nodded. "You're not that. I *like* that you're not that."

"No. I'm bi. I'm married. I'm poly. I don't hide any of that from my partners." Never had, and I wasn't about to start now. I *hated* lying. And keeping secrets. "I get it, though. A lot of the guys I dated before I met Lydia were men who wanted a little meat on the side, but loved living the het lifestyle."

He sat forward. "You dated dudes?"

I rolled my eyes, and Ian had the wherewithal to look sheepish.

"Okay," he said. "So, how does this work?"

"Have *you* dated guys before?" I *loved* the taken-aback expression carved into Ian. "Dating me works the same way."

"But—" He eyed Lydia.

She shrugged. "Anything goes. Just don't break him."

He blinked a few times and a grin that boiled my blood appeared. "Could you define *break* . . . for me?"

"Oh," Lydia said in that lovely sultry voice of hers, "you two are going to have so much fun."

Ian's chuckle curled my toes, as did the sparkle in his eyes. Yeah. Lydia was probably right about that. She usually was.

After lunch, we all headed back to the shop, and Lydia checked in with Dexy to see if she needed anything.

"I've got about another hour's worth of work in the studio, but if you want help, give a call." Lydia nodded at me and Ian. "Don't bother the boys unless it's modeling-related."

Dexy nodded. "Figured that might be the case." Once Lydia had vanished into the back, she shuffled some papers and gave me a coy once-over. "You guys going to be working on that *Wolf's Landing* thing?"

"Probably going to be the schedule here until . . ." I met Ian's gaze.

". . . Tuesday," Ian said. "Anna wants to do the shoot Wednesday night."

A flicker of envy danced through me. Ian got to see *Wolf's Landing* shoots. "So, not too long, then all will be back to normal."

"Well, most nights when you've worked the morning shift, you paint anyway." Her smile was sly. "The only difference is you have a partner now."

Such innocuous words, but yeah, she knew something was up. She was a smart kid. Next to me, Ian shifted, his shoes scraping against the industrial carpeting. I clapped him on the shoulder. "Let's get back to work."

When we settled back in around the grove, he fiddled with the base for a second. "Does she know?"

"About us?" I shrugged. "She's good at deduction, and she's aware Lydia and I have an open arrangement."

"You, umm . . ." He glanced back at Dexy, then at me with a mixture of horror and curiosity.

Oh my God. "No! She's nineteen. I have T-shirts older than her!" I was thirty-five. Yes, it was legal, but I'd known Dexy since she was *twelve*. Did not compute. Nope. Nope.

The relief in Ian was palpable. He coughed. "Sorry, I . . . but she *knows*."

I suppose me having dated Dexy was one conclusion you could draw from that, even if it did freak me out. "Lydia had a relationship with Dexy's father a few years back. They were pretty serious, so we all talked about how that would work, and told Dexy what was going on."

Ian looked like I'd hit him in the head with a brick. "Oh." He chewed on his thumb, which was endearing, but man, I hoped he didn't do that while playing with paints.

"She knows to keep it quiet, and she can also read me like a book." I plopped into the chair by the pieces of the model I'd been repairing. There were a few rocks to touch up, and I wanted to tackle those before starting on the important parts, like the altar.

There was Ian's sexy laugh. "You haven't exactly been subtle about your interest in me." He spoke low and damn close to my ear. His fingers brushed the back of my neck, sending shivers down my spine, straight to my balls.

"I—I'm bad at flirting." The words tumbled from my mouth. I was screwing up horribly.

"Liar," he whispered. His lips replaced his fingers and I clung to the table, and tried not to moan. "The things I want to do to you."

I was rock-hard and he could've convinced me to bend over right there—if we hadn't been in the middle of my shop. "The things I want you to do." I swallowed. "In private."

He sighed and stepped back. "I know. And if I don't get this set done, Anna will eat me, and not in the pleasant way."

I'd heard about Anna Maxwell, the *Wolf's Landing* director. "So, these good?"

"They're fantastic. Keep going."

I did, all while trying to get my dick back down. Hell, I couldn't wait to tumble into bed with him.

Ian got out some kind of clay and started patching the tree bark together. At first, it looked like shit, and I bit my tongue. But as he worked and sculpted, the bark took on a life of its own. Even without the paint, the trees went from pathetic to realistic. I couldn't help staring at his hands as he pushed and prodded with a tiny sculpting tool.

"Where did you learn to do that?"

He paused and glanced over, all smile and light. "I took sculpture and pottery in college to get the basics, but most of this, you learn on the job. All the tricks and shortcuts and shit like that."

"Do you do any art outside of *Wolf's Landing*?"

Ian straightened slowly. "You're the first person to ask me that."

"Really?"

Something grim appeared in his face. "Guys I've dated from the show mostly wanna fuck and not talk about anything vaguely related. Guys outside the show only want to know *about* the show."

"Groupies."

Ian rolled his eyes. "I mean, I appreciate the fans. They're why I have a job—but I don't want someone sleeping with me to get on set, you know?"

A pang for my earlier thoughts. I wanted Ian. I also wanted on set . . . but no. I wouldn't ever use him for that. "So, art outside of the show?"

He nodded, his smile wistful. "Dragons," he said. "And gryphons. Used to do wolves, but I stopped when I got this gig." He set down his tool. "Wait, I have a few photos on my phone." After he pulled his phone out, he played with it for a second, and handed it over.

The photo was of a sculpture of a gold, red, and black dragon, launching itself into the air. Detailed and beautiful. I wanted to reach through the tiny screen and touch it. "That's amazing. That's . . . holy shit."

He reddened and put the phone back into his pocket. "The few friends I've shown keep telling me I should sell them."

"You should." Hell, we could move them in a heartbeat.

"Yeah, but . . ." Trepidation seeped into his voice. "This is going to sound strange, but I want to make sure they go to the right homes."

Beautiful works of art like that? Understandable. "Someone who'd appreciate them and not waste them?"

A croak of a laugh. "That desire is hubris, though. People are free to do what they want with 'em . . . but I put so much time into creating them."

"I get it." Without thinking, I took his hand. "You pour out your heart and soul." I gazed up into his eyes.

His lips parted and we stood like that for what felt like hours, but was likely a second. He squeezed my hand back, then disengaged. "I think you do that too." He nodded at the table, but I got the distinct impression he wasn't talking about my model painting.

"Sometimes. Maybe." Certainly with Lydia. I wanted that with Ian as well. I was an incurable romantic.

His smile was everything I needed to breathe. He shuffled his legs. "I should—" He pointed at the set.

"Yeah." When I turned back to my work, I spied the altar with the bit of the base missing. "Hey, Ian?"

"Yeah?"

"What should I do about this?" I held up the altar.

"I thought that was fine." He squinted at the faux stone block.

I rotated it to show where part of the base had been chipped. "Nearly fine, but . . ."

"Nearly won't do." He pulled his chair over and sat. "Want to learn how to fix that?"

Tips for repairing a model from Ian? I could mainline that shit. "Sure. If you're willing."

He scooted his chair closer. "So, paint isn't going to cut it, because there's never been a chunk missing from the altar on the large set," he said, and pointed at the plans and photos, "as you can see. Leave it like that and the prop director will have my head."

"So, fill it in like you did the trees?"

"Since we don't have the missing bit, yeah." He grabbed some of the clay he'd been using, and set it down next to me. Our arms brushed. "Use self-hardening clay to fill in the missing part, then make sure you feather over the edges of the repair, and you're good."

I eyed him. "That easy, huh?"

He laughed. "Well, in theory. Want to try it in practice?"

Hell yes! But . . . "What if I fuck it up?"

"This stuff takes forever to completely dry, so if you screw it up, I can fix it." He nudged me with his shoulder. "But you'll do fine. I know you will."

That Ian remained shoulder to shoulder with me made my bones hum. I swallowed and picked up the altar. "Okay. I'll give it a shot."

Ian laid out his sculpting tools and pointed out which ones I should use. First, I didn't take enough clay—then too much, but eventually I scraped off enough and the altar started to look whole again. A bit of simple sculpting later, and I was done. "Like this?"

Ian had returned to his trees, but put down his tool and came over. He clasped me on the shoulder and leaned in, his face far too near to mine. "Exactly like that."

Warm breath. Lovely eyes. His lips parted and he moved closer and the world narrowed down to me and Ian. Inches apart.

Voices from the front of the store jolted us both—especially when they came this way. Dexy spoke loudly, more so than normal, bless her. "If you want to know more about models and miniatures, you should talk to Simon. He's back here, working on a project with a friend."

By the time Dexy and the customer—an older gentleman with glasses and a thin face—cleared the rows of shelving, Ian had returned to his spot by the base of the set. I set down the altar.

Fear had done wonders on reducing my desire, though with Ian, that fire seemed to always be there, an undercurrent to our every interaction. Still, I was the consummate professional shop owner. "What can I help you with?"

Turned out, Mr. Sato had built models as a young man, but had stopped when family and work became his priorities. "Now that I'm retired, my wife wants me to get a hobby." There was a gleam in his eyes.

I showed him some of the less complicated model kits and he chose an old-fashioned street rod to build. I also suggested one of our magnification stands, helped him carry everything up front, then turned him over to Dexy for checkout. "If you need any help at all, stop back in."

The excitement I saw in his weathered features was like a jolt of joy-laden caffeine. This was the best part of my job—helping someone discover—or rediscover—a hobby they could love.

I wandered back to Ian, and my heart slid into my throat. We'd been about to kiss, in the middle of my shop, during business hours. Oh, I wanted that, but it wasn't the wisest of plans. A glance at my watch told me we still had two hours before the shop closed.

Ian had a contrite expression. When he spoke, his voice was so soft, it might have been a whisper. "I'm so sorry. I . . . got ahead of myself."

"So did I." The altar sat on the table—along with a bunch of other pieces I needed to repaint. "I guess getting interrupted like that is a good reminder that we're working."

He wore nervousness like a second skin. "All work and no play?"

"I didn't say that," I murmured. "Need to wait to play, that's all."

His smile returned, the glorious thing that it was, on those lips I so wanted to taste.

I glanced at my watch again. Playtime would come soon enough.

CHAPTER SEVEN

IAN

When it got close to eight o'clock, Simon set down the torch stanchion he'd been touching up. "I should go help Dexy close the shop."

"Or," said Lydia, as she rounded some shelves and paused to straighten the boxes on them, "you can keep working and let me do it?"

He sat back down and picked up another stanchion. "Who am I to argue with that logic?" There was sheer joy in his voice.

I realized that Simon's good mood was because he got to keep spending time with *me*, and Lydia had facilitated that. This whole open-marriage shtick was going to take some getting used to. I'd never dated guys in happily committed relationships before. There would be no sneaking around. No lies. No finding out the guy was on the down-low when the wife showed up screaming. We weren't cheating, at least not in Simon and Lydia's book.

I believed them, but it was hard to wrap my head around, despite Simon's need being almost a physical presence between us, like the mythical psychic link the show went on about sometimes.

This wasn't magic, but it was real and tangible and I couldn't wait to get my hands on Simon.

We kept painting until Lydia came back around. "We're all ready to lock up. You guys going to stay later?"

Simon gave me a sly look that Lydia couldn't have missed. "A little longer."

Her chuckle was low and she kissed Simon. Not a lingering taste, but not a peck either. "I'll see you later."

Something passed between them—a flicker of understanding that touched both their eyes and smiles—then Lydia pecked *me* on the cheek. "Have a good night, Ian." Her grin said everything—whatever happened between me and Simon was okay.

"You too." I breathed the words out.

After she left us, the lights near the front of the store were turned off and Dexy yelled "Bye, guys!" We yelled goodbye back, then there was a rattle of a lock. Then silence, but for the gentle hum of the HVAC system and the pounding of my heart.

Alone.

"Um . . ." Simon focused on the torch he'd been painting. "How much did you want to get done today?"

Good question. While I wanted to abandon my work and go to town on Simon, I needed to get the set repaired by Wednesday. We'd accomplished quite a bit, but more would be better. "We should finish all the items that need to be sculpted tonight, or the clay won't set in time to paint."

Simon sank onto his chair. "So, we're still working before playing?"

Goddamn did I want to play. I set aside my paintbrush and slid up close to Simon. "Don't drop that," I whispered, right before I tipped his head back and kissed him. His whole body trembled, and he opened his lips to my probing tongue.

He didn't drop the torch, but made these delicious helpless moans that I drank down when I took his mouth and lips. The pulse in his neck beat wildly against my fingertips. Kissing him had been worth the wait. He surrendered to me, but also tangled his mouth and tongue with mine. Simon was pliant, needy, and sexy.

I broke the kiss, and Simon stared up at me, his throat moving under my fingers. "I thought we were working?" Rough words, full of desperation. I bet if I slid my hand down to his lap, I'd find him hard and ready.

"We are." I kissed him again, with more force this time. He still didn't drop the piece he'd been painting. I worked my palm over his chest and then between his thighs, and yup. I'd been right about that. He spread his knees and rocked his dick against my palm, and I wanted him there and then, maybe bent over the table, or maybe with my cock down his throat.

I fucking loved how much he needed me. The kiss left him panting and I stroked him, enjoying the way his eyes glazed over. "How long have you wanted me?"

He gave me a chuckle that was half a moan. "Since I saw you that first day."

So, the same as me. "The sooner we finish, the sooner you can find out what else I can do to make you moan." I traced his length with my fingers.

"Incentive?"

"A promise." I relented on teasing him—we did need to finish. I had to get this set ready for shooting on Wednesday . . . but I also wanted to discover how loud I could make Simon yell before the night was through.

Simon gulped a breath and slowly examined the torch he'd been painting. "I like your promises."

So did I.

It took maybe another hour for us to finish fixing the parts and I had to resist touching, teasing, and kissing Simon.

Despite my previous distractions, Simon managed to finish the torch stanchion and repair a few other pieces as well. As it had been for the past two days, his work was excellent and his hands remained steady, though his neck was red and his glances smoldering. What fantasies were rolling through his mind?

I knew the ones going through mine, and as we cleaned up the area, I wondered how many of them he'd let me create. At last, we headed to the back of the store and Simon shut off the rest of the lights in the shop. When he turned toward me—and the door to the alley—I cupped a hand around his neck and pulled his lips to mine. Again, he opened to me, but now that his hands were free, those roamed down my back and he kneaded my ass while grinding against me.

I wanted that mouth elsewhere on my body. Between bites on his lips, I whispered, "I hope you like sucking cock."

He made the same little throaty noise as before. "I love it."

Grazing my teeth along his throat got me a deeper gasp. "Prove it." I needed him on his knees for me, his eyes looking up into mine, and those exquisite hands on my thighs.

"Not in the store," he murmured.

"That a rule?"

He opened space between us, though our hips stayed pressed together. "Yeah, actually." But his smile was warm. "Work is here. Play is"—he gestured toward the door—"for out there."

Out there was an alley with dumpsters and dimly lit pavement. Given that it was the main drag of town, it wasn't too seedy. I turned over Lydia's *don't break him* comment and a plan formed in my head. "Ever sucked a guy off in an alley?"

Simon's breath caught. "Not that one."

That wasn't at all a *no* to my question and I couldn't help my grin. "You should probably set the alarm."

"Mmm." He nuzzled my neck, his stubble scraping across my skin before he nipped me and sent my pulse sky-high. "Probably." He pulled away and did exactly that.

Half a minute later, we were outside and Simon was locking the back door. A moment after that, I had him up against it and moaning into my mouth. His keys clattered to the ground and his hands tangled into my hair. I rocked my dick into his thigh.

Did taking Simon apart count as *breaking*? I wanted him begging and screaming, dirty and willing to do anything I asked.

I wasn't sure which one of us swung the other around, but a second later my back hit the steel door. I pressed my thumb against Simon's throat and broke our kiss to catch my breath. Over his shoulder, wherever light hit the pavement, it shone from the earlier rain; bright dots of light in the inky night. "Get on your knees."

He met my gaze, and fucking kept it as he dropped down before me. "It's gonna have to be fast."

His hair was soft and long enough to grip tightly between my fingers. "Why's that?"

"'Cause Officer Phil Merrick always patrols the alley around ten." Nimble fingers had my fly open and Simon nuzzled my dick through the cotton of my briefs.

Fuck. That hot mouth. Those sinful lips. I needed inside both. I had no idea what time it was, but I bet Simon did. "I'm sure you can manage."

His dark chuckle sent heat into my skull. "Just you wait."

He had my cock out, and warm breath caressed me right before his lips slid over the head. I bit my lip and pressed back against the door to keep from moaning too loudly. If this area was patrolled . . . well. No need to call attention to ourselves, even if I was standing against End o' Earth's delivery door, in full view with Simon Derry sucking the tip of my cock. We weren't in the dark. Anyone walking by could see.

For all Simon's talk, he took his damn sweet time blowing me. He started by sucking and licking the length of my shaft and fondling my balls. But the heat of his mouth and the flick of his tongue kept me breathless despite his languid exploration.

I stroked his hair. "What would your wife think if she saw us?" Part of me still couldn't believe we were doing this.

Another laugh. "She'd pull up a chair."

That— Oh hell. I bit my lip and swallowed a groan. Voyeurism wasn't my thing, but that thought zipped from my brain straight to my balls anyway.

We were so going to get caught if we kept this up.

I gripped Simon's hair tight, and at long last, he took my shaft into his sweet hot mouth. His moan vibrated against my length. "Yeah." I tugged his head toward me. "Take my dick, Si. All of it."

Damned if he didn't do exactly what I'd asked. I'd had plenty of blowjobs before and from guys who could deep-throat, but none of them had ever done me like Simon Derry. Maybe it was the alley or his tight throat, or the way he inhaled me, but pure bliss rolled up my spine when he took my cock to the root.

Then he did it again. And again. And *again*—until my vision hazed and my balls were about ready to explode. His tongue was magic and he sucked me as if he wanted every piece of my dick—yeah. Simon wasn't a straight guy at *all*.

The light on the tarmac glittered and my sight blurred. This was fucking amazing. Better than porn, far better than my last quick hookup in the back of the prop shop. To top it off, I might get to take Simon home. Maybe fuck him until he screamed.

I whimpered into the night and tried to keep my mouth closed. I wanted to yell and curse and tell Simon he was one hell of a cockslut, but—alley. And perhaps a patrolling cop. I swallowed the words.

I was so damn close and that was unfair because I wanted so much more of the man kneeling before me. His eyes were closed, his mouth stretched wide, and he was fucking beautiful. A filthy angel on his knees, doing everything he could to suck the jizz out of me.

I didn't know how I heard the footsteps over the pounding of my heart or Simon's deep grunts, but I did. When I cranked my head to the left, over the dumpster that hopefully blocked Simon from view, I made out a figure striding down the pavement, a flashlight drawing curves on the ground. My pulse shot through the roof. "Si," I hissed. His eyes flicked open and, I swear to God, the look he gave me was pure lust and a little bit evil.

Bastard knew exactly what he was doing, I was certain. That was all it took. I locked my fingers into his hair, fucked his throat deep, and emptied my nuts into him. I tried to keep quiet—the cop was closer now—but I must have gasped or grunted or something—because the light flashed up into my eyes.

"Hey!" A cop voice—deep, gravelly, and intimidating.

Simon yanked my shirt down over my unzipped jeans, then wiped semen off his mouth with the back of his hand. "Help me find my keys." He was grinning like he'd won the jackpot. The bulge he sported in his jeans told me everything. *Someone* liked getting caught. Or maybe being watched.

I knelt down out of the flashlight glare and zipped myself up and struggled to catch my breath. "Think you dropped them over there." My voice sounded louder than normal, and way more broken than it should have.

Shit.

"Hey!" The cop yelled this time, and the light shone on both of us.

"It's okay, Phil. I dropped my keys." Simon lifted the bundle, and shook them in the beam of the flashlight. They jangled and clanked and glittered with water from a puddle.

I wondered if Phil noticed the ridge of Simon's dick, so prominent in his jeans, especially with the way he knelt. Or that Simon's lips were plump and bruised and glistened like the wet pavement, or that his jeans were far too damp to have been kneeling for only an instant.

"Simon Derry." The cop sounded exasperated. "I've told you not to slink around your own shop. Give me a heart attack."

Simon stood and rattled his keys again. The flashlight swung to me. I rose slowly on shaky legs, holding up my hand to shield against the light. I didn't like cops much—mostly because they always pegged me for a gay guy and gave me *that* frown—like the queer would get on them if I got too close. I knew they weren't all like that, but still. Trust wasn't exactly there.

"Who's this?" There was suspicion in Officer Merrick's voice. Bingo. He didn't like me either.

"This is Ian. I'm helping him with a project." I had no idea how Simon sounded so normal after swallowing me to the pubes repeatedly, but he did. He also had this incredible grin, like this was a picnic, and not the aftermath of a blowjob in an alley. "Doing a little work after hours."

A grunt from the cop. "Your wife know?"

Oh fuck. My cheeks went hot. I hoped that didn't show in the cop's flashlight, because I never could keep up the innocent act.

"Of course!" Now Simon sounded offended. "Who do you think locked us in?"

The light swung between us and then down to the ground. The cop sighed. "This place is way more trouble than Red Hot Bluewater." With that, he stomped away.

I exhaled, and Simon chuckled. "Come on, let's get out of here."

Didn't have to tell me twice. "Jesus, that was . . . something." My voice shook. "Fucking hell." Maybe Officer Merrick was an okay guy, but I was happy to see the back of him.

We walked around to Main to where I'd parked. I unlocked the Mini, then paused. "So, you wanna come over?"

Guess I spoke gruffly or sounded angry or upset, because he tilted his head, and for the first time since I'd met him, worry marred his features. His keys rattled. "If you don't want me to, I can . . ." He looked away, his voice dropping off. "I thought you'd like that, but . . ." A glance, and there was anguish there. He backed away from the car. "I'll get my bike."

Oh God. He thought I was rejecting him. "Si!" Maybe I said it too sharply because he jumped a little and his eyes went wide. If there hadn't been a car between us, I'd have taken his hand. "I want to spend the night with you." Peel those clothes off him and take him as high as he'd brought me. Maybe higher. I wanted to bury myself in him.

Feel him squirm under me. A litany of steamy fantasies we couldn't possibly accomplish in one night ran through my head.

"Oh." Sheepish and slightly mortified was cute on Simon. "Um. So, I should get in the car?"

"Yes, Simon. You should absolutely get in the car." I was getting hard again. Maybe voyeurism got Simon off. Taking charge? That was my kink. And Simon had the expression of a man who needed someone to tell him what to do right now. "Get in and buckle up. I'm taking you for a ride."

Simon did as told, belt and everything. In the dome light of the Mini, he appeared distinctly relieved. With the doors shut, no one could overhear us. "That was some goddamned magic you did back there. I hope you like being fucked, because I intend to return the favor . . . in spades."

"Yeah, I, whatever you want to do," he said.

Music to my ears. "As long as I don't break you."

"I'm very, *very* hard to break." That sly smile had returned.

When the dome light faded, I pressed the ignition button and slipped the car into reverse. "We'll see about that." I liked a challenge, after all.

CHAPTER EIGHT

SIMON

W e were heading out of town, vaguely toward where *Wolf's Landing* filmed. I tasted Ian with every swallow. Yeah, the blowjob in the alley had been risky, but damn, I'd wanted him. Wanted him to want me. After two days of sexual frustration, I needed him to use me for whatever he desired.

I still couldn't read Ian, though. Sometimes he seemed hot for me—then he didn't at all. The salt in my mouth and ache in my throat told me he had enjoyed the blowjob. But the budding relationship? Who knew.

Then again, I *was* in his car, winding through the woods outside of Bluewater Bay.

He hadn't spoken since town, since those words that had sent shivers through me. I remembered what Lydia had said at lunch.

I craved Ian breaking me. It had been so long since I'd been on my knees for a guy. Longer since I'd bottomed. Most men I did manage a hookup with figured I was a top.

I wasn't. Not with men. But people looked at me and Lydia and made assumptions that I was straight and dominant. That I went home and fucked my wife every night. It was tiring having two lives—the one people painted onto me and the one I actually lived.

I wanted Ian to shatter the crappy picture everyone else had of me and remind me who I really was.

"Hey, Si?"

I liked hearing my nickname on Ian's lips. Especially in the dark. "Yeah?"

"You think that cop knows what we were up to?"

I rolled that around in my head. Phil wasn't an idiot. Most of the townfolks were smart as whips. You had to be to live out here.

"I don't know. Maybe." That quip about being more trouble than the local sex shop poked at my brain. I had to wonder if I wasn't the *first* Derry to blow someone behind the store. "Maybe Lydia's lost her keys there, too."

Ian made this strange sound between a laugh and a choke. "How do you . . ."

So many endings to that question. So many questions he could be asking. "I know it's strange, but there's room for whatever you want." Sex. Love. A fling. Something longer. Hell, we'd talked for a long time with Vince, Dexy's dad, about him moving in back in the day. He was straight, but I'd been friends with Vince. We all still caught a beer together once in a while, and he'd been so pleased when we'd hired Dexy.

Ian was silent, though his fingers tapped on the steering wheel.

"Communication's important, though. I can't read minds." This wasn't some paranormal romance, but real life.

This time, the sound was a distinct laugh. "Says the man who up and assumed I wouldn't want him to come home with me after he swallowed my cock and load in a damp alley." Warm fingers stroked my thigh.

Okay, he had me there. I blew out a breath. "We were nearly caught."

Ian inched his fingers higher, and I pressed against the seat. His voice was soft and full of depth. "Why do I get the feeling you liked that part?"

He was so good at this, the teasing, the turning on. The sexy talk I failed at. "Maybe." I did like being watched, but there was more to it than that. I wanted to get caught. I wanted people to know I was queer and poly. Lydia and I had talked about being out, but always came back around to not rocking the boat. We were both worried about the shop. Her career. All of it.

Ian made me want to tip our lives over. But I was getting *way* ahead of myself. Two days and a blowjob weren't enough to build a relationship on, or rearrange my life with Lydia for.

Guess I'd been quiet too long, because the stroking went from sexy to comforting. "Talk to me, Simon." An edge of command there. I could get used to that.

"It's complicated."

"That's a Facebook status."

I barked out a laugh. "It's true, though. My thoughts." I took his hand in mine. "I don't always say or do the right things. I'm horrible when it comes to sexy. I always guess wrong about men." I shrugged, which he probably didn't see. "I *like* you, only I don't know how to tell you that. Don't know how to explain my life. Want to try, though."

He squeezed my hand. "I think I see why Lydia married you."

That made me warm all over. His words were so something she would have said, and I wouldn't have understood it from her, either.

He let me go. "We're nearly there, and I need both hands."

Stick shifts. Hot, but cockblocking at the same time. We pulled into a driveway and parked by a detached garage next to a large house set not too far off from the road. We were out by one of the fishing piers, and I knew the house wasn't Ian's.

"I rent the rooms above the garage." He parked next to, rather than inside, the garage, and shut off the car. "It's pretty quiet out here, and the Yazzies leave me be."

Ah. I knew the Yazzies. They ran a framing store in town. Good people. Usually helped with our small arts festival every year. Queer-friendly too. "Good choice. Nice place."

"Time to unbuckle," Ian said. "Ride's not over yet."

I wet my lips. Good. I wasn't nearly done being Ian's for the night.

A quick trip up a set of outside stairs, and then he opened the door into a lovely loft. I didn't get much of a view, partly because the room was softly lit, but mostly because Ian grabbed me by the shirt right away and pulled me to him. Our mouths met. He was hungry and demanding and each swipe of his tongue had me wanting to sink to my knees. Especially when he worked the buttons of my shirt open and slid his palms over my chest. I moaned into him.

"You're fucking dirty, aren't you?" Teeth grazed my chin and his fingers pulled at my nipple. "Bet I could bend you over and take you right here."

Yeah. He could. "Any way you want me."

"Oh, Si." He shoved my shirt over my shoulders and I shrugged it off and onto the floor. "Don't tempt me like that."

I met his gaze. "I mean it."

Ian got this ravenous look. "I'm sure you do. And I happen to have a laundry list of what I want to do to you." He unbuttoned my jeans and pulled the zipper apart, practically in one motion.

"You've known me two days, how long could it be?" Not that I hadn't been fantasizing about him. But still.

Jeans and underwear slid down my legs and pooled at my feet, then I was in Ian's arms and he was kissing me again like he could drink my soul down. His hands roamed my back and ass and he nipped my lip hard enough to sting. I couldn't help the gasp or the shudder that ran through me. I rode his thigh, my dick pressed so hard against his jeans that it hurt. *Heaven and hell.* He opened my crack and skimmed my hole and I nearly came right there and then. "Fuck."

Ian's lips brushed mine and he chuckled. "I have a vivid imagination."

And wicked intentions. He bit my shoulder, pulling a long moan out of me, then patted my cheek. "Lose the socks and shoes, then get your ass on my bed."

I could get used to this. Being stripped. Ordered. At Ian's beck and call.

He sauntered toward his bed, pulling off his shirt as he went. The muscles of his naked back rippled when he tossed the shirt away. He glanced back. "Move it, Simon, or it'll be a hell of a lot more fun for me . . . and less for you."

Someone liked games. Getting my shoes off nearly had me tumbling to the floor, but I was by Ian's bed as fast as I could manage. He was naked—wonderfully, gloriously naked—and stroking himself. On his stomach, a tattoo of thorns and roses swirled from his hip to his treasure trail. "Shit, that's beautiful."

He smirked. "The ink?"

"Everything." I breathed the word. "You— I." My brain couldn't gather enough thoughts to speak. Ian was stunning, and I was *here.* He wanted my scrawny, clumsy, married, poly, bisexual ass. I hadn't realized how much I'd missed that—a man's desire. That it was Ian's was exponentially miraculous. "Please?" I didn't know what I was asking for.

Maybe Ian did, because curiosity, then firmness flickered across his features. He stepped up and kissed me.

Unlike all the times before, this was tender and light. I closed my eyes against the dizziness of his taste. Fingers pressed against my hips and our cocks slid together. He hummed into my mouth and shifted me—us—until I felt the bed against the backs of my thighs.

"Sit," he whispered, and I did.

He had the biggest grin when I stared up at him. "Anything," I repeated. I'd swallow him again. Get on my hands and knees. Whatever he wanted.

"You trust me that much?"

I shouldn't after two days, but I always fell hard and fast, or I didn't at all. One of these days, that would get me into trouble. Not with Ian, though. I knew that like I knew my own name. "Yeah."

Tracing my jaw with his fingers, he spoke. "You're something else, Si." Warmth in his voice—he wasn't making fun of me. "Stretch yourself out on your back . . . Hands at the headboard."

He watched me as I moved, his dick pointing up at the ceiling and his focus on my face and arms. The headboard had slats, but they were too close together to grip, so I grazed my hands against the wood. Smooth and warm.

Ian drank me in, his gaze licking over my body as if it were a canvas and he was deciding where to place the first stroke of paint. His choice was the lightest of touches against my abs, above my cock. I bit my tongue to keep from groaning. Failed.

"None of that." Ian ran his nails up my chest and flicked a nipple. "We're at my place. You're in my bed. We're gonna play by *my* rules. I want to hear *everything*, Simon. Every moan, every curse, every scream. No hiding. Understood?"

"Yeah." I sounded shaky. Hell, I was. Trembling. Turned on and buzzing. Ian had barely touched me and I was high as a kite already.

"Good." He flicked my nipple again and I winced and groaned, my body on fire. "Much better." Ian patted my cheek once more, his eyes bright and cheeks flush. "I'll be back. I need to fetch a few items."

I exhaled and relaxed against the pillows. "Oh fuck, this is . . ." Good. Hot. Sexy.

A drawer closed and Ian clicked his tongue—a sound of disappointment that I'd held back my words.

"It's perfect," I whispered.

A huff, and he returned. Lube, condoms, and a black sash. "I haven't even started yet."

"I know." I focused on the sash and my heart ratcheted up a notch. Lydia liked tying me up, since it drove me crazy. Ian was bigger and stronger than Lydia by far. No doubt he could keep the rest of me immobile with his strength. Open to him. At his mercy.

That smirk told me he'd read my expression. He put the lube and the condoms on the nightstand, and straddled me with one acrobatic motion that had the bed bouncing. His legs pressed against the sides of my chest, warm and tight, his cock so close but too far to suck. I tried anyway, but he pushed my head back against the mattress.

He gave me a wicked smile. "You're too much."

Couldn't help the laugh. "I could say the same."

"Mmm. Don't move." He crawled up, took my wrists and wrapped them with the sash. Cool fabric chilled my skin. Soft enough, but not slick. Wouldn't chafe, but wouldn't slip either. I tried to concentrate on my wrists because Ian's dick was inches from my face, the slit glistening with pre-come. I wanted to suck and taste him again. Hear his groans . . . but I knew better. His bed. His rules. So, Ian's scent engulfed me, my balls and cock throbbed, and the sash tightened around my wrists. I let out a whimper, then another because the first helpless sound had felt so good. Slyly tortured by a cock, inches from my lips, that I'd been forbidden to touch.

Ian sat back and slid his ass over my shaft. The heat, the sudden weight of him, and the way he moved over me sent sparks up my spine. Breath left my lungs and I pulled against the sash. "I'm gonna come. If you do that . . ." I didn't want this to end, not yet, but I was so on edge.

"Be a shame if you did." Ian rocked on me. "Especially before I fucked you."

He didn't want me to hold back, so I gave in to the gasps and moans when he skimmed his hands up my chest and kneaded my pecs.

"Thing is, I want to see you come like this." He leaned forward and ground his cock into mine. "Undone by a sash and a little frotting."

Yeah, and also the way he stared at me, that openmouthed smile, like I was the only guy in the world he wanted. The sweat at his brow, how his hair fell over his forehead . . . It was all too much. "Oh god, I can't last much longer."

His lips grazed mine. "Then don't."

When he kissed me, the world vanished but for his body, the heat and friction between us, and my utter helplessness. He sipped my groans and whimpers and curses, all while I twisted beneath him. His rhythm was insistent as were his bites and nips and the wicked whispers that ghosted over my skin. "Yeah, that's it, Si. Come on. I know you want to."

I couldn't string words together, only grunts and moans. The tension was so close to cracking into bliss and light. I only needed . . .

"I want your come all over me."

. . . that. Ian's dirty voice in my ears. Desperate sounds poured out of me into Ian's kisses, and I came and came until we were slick and I couldn't see or think.

As I floated back down, Ian grazed his teeth over my chin. "So fucking hot."

His cock was hard against my stomach and every inch of me tingled. I pulled at the sash. Still snug and tight. Comforting in a way. "Yeah." I sounded as breathless as I felt. "God, I can't believe you want me."

He coughed a laugh. "Si, you're gorgeous. Who wouldn't want you?"

Most men. And a whole bunch of women, but I wasn't going to argue with him. He was like Lydia—biased as all hell. "I'm grateful you do."

He landed a kiss on my nose. "Still want you. Still plan to have you. Figure I can get you up again before the night is done." He worked down my body and took my flagging dick into his mouth.

Totally unfair, especially given how sensitive I was. I arched against the rasp of his tongue and lips as he licked and sucked me clean and damn if I didn't start rising to the occasion. I guessed there was still a bit of teen left in my bones, or at least in my dick.

"Goddamn, I love how you taste." Such warm breath, and there was that zing again, but this settled somewhere in my chest, heating me in a way that had nothing to do with how much I wanted him inside me.

Words sawed through my brain and spilled out my lips. "You . . . are amazing." Not the most clever response, but I was never good at talking romantically. Usually left my partners giggling.

Ian wasn't laughing, though. He grinned, and licked up the rest of my spunk. No one had ever done that before and his mouth left me hissing and shaking against the bed. He traced his hands down my body and sat on my feet. "There you are, every inch for me tonight." He stroked my hips.

A lazy thought drifted through my hazy post-orgasmic mind. Pre-orgasmic? Because I was hard again. "You're gonna break me."

His chuckle was wicked. "Yeah, maybe." He was up and crawling, but this time to claim a condom and the lube. "But I'm good at putting stuff back together."

The rip of the foil rolled over my body, and sparks tingled at the back of my head. "Better be. Gotta work tomorrow." By Ian's side too. I was so fucking lucky.

Lube next, and he made a nice show of slicking his dick before he circled my hole and pressed a finger inside me. "Fuuuuck." Another long moan for Ian. I loved being breached. The sting, the intimacy, the rise of pleasure that curled in my balls. I spread myself wider for him. I wanted a hell of a lot more than his finger. "Can we—skip the prep?"

"My bed, my rules." His smile alone made me twist on the sheets, then he finger-fucked me fast and I arched for him, any curses lost in the groans at the back of my throat. "Besides, I like seeing you like this."

Bet he'd like seeing his cock in me, but I was shuddering too hard, my tongue too tied to try to say it. But it must have been true, because he pulled his finger out of me, pressed his dick against my asshole, and pushed in.

I bit my lip against my cry, then let it out because Ian wanted the sound. Probably wanted the sparks of light and the tears that stung the corners of my eyes. The pleasure was laced with pain and I couldn't free my shaking arms from the cloth that bound them. Helpless. His. There was no better feeling.

"Yeah, like that, Si." He moved inside me, slowly pulling back and pressing in until I was sure he'd split me in two if he managed to get all of himself in. "Fuck, you're so tight."

When I opened my eyes, he was above me, eyes shining. I wanted to reach up and kiss him, but I was tied to the headboard. Still, I tried, lifting my head as my body strained against his.

He tangled his fingers in my hair, took my mouth, and kissed me until I made helpless noises. When he relented, he had the gleam of a devil. "Look at me." Soft words, but iron with his will. "Don't you dare take your eyes off me. Not for one moment, Si."

"Yes." A single word, straight from my soul.

Ian fucked me hard, deep, and relentlessly. Rougher than I'd ever imagined he could, each stroke a glorious burn of pleasure. And oh, God. He *was* going to break me. Split me open and spill my heart and soul out on the bed. I couldn't turn away, because in that instant, I was the only thing in Ian's life . . . and I knew it.

I came first, hot jizz pouring out over his hand and my stomach, my cry echoing off the ceiling. Then he was there too, his face a joy to watch, and his shout as loud.

There were tears in my eyes when he was done and I ached everywhere. Concern marred his contentment, and he pulled at the sash. The fabric slipped off, and I was able to catch his head in my hands and kiss him.

He obviously hadn't expected that, because I swallowed a yelp. He might have had his rules, but right now, I didn't care that this was his bed—I had my own rules: if someone fucks you that grandly, you thank them. So I did, with my tongue and my lips and my mouth, then finally my words. "I loved every second of that."

He huffed a laugh, then settled next to me on the bed as we caught our breaths. He drew circles on my chest and kissed my shoulder and whispered words I didn't understand but knew he believed. "You're perfection, Simon."

I wasn't. Not nearly. But that didn't stop my heart from tumbling over and over.

CHAPTER NINE

IAN

Morning came too damn soon, but I could forgive the sun, since Simon was in my bed, sleeping hard against the mattress. He looked like a goofball, hair every which way, mouth slightly open and face pressed against the pillow. A sexy, wonderful goofball, who I'd fucked into oblivion.

God, last night had been wonderful. He . . . I. He'd given me so much, as if I were the only person in his life. Which was weird, because I wasn't.

Still, Simon had been wholly mine last night. I peered at the clock and sighed. Nope. No time for a replay—not if I wanted to get to End o' Earth and back to work on the miniature set. We still had all the little details to put in so it would seem as real as the life-size one. Wednesday was one day closer.

No idea how Simon would react to being woken up. I guessed I would find out. "Si? Simon?"

A flicker of movement behind his eyelids, then he blinked them open. A deep breath and those blue eyes meeting mine. His smile was sunlight. "Hey." Gravelly voice. Did he know what that did to my insides?

Before I could tell him he should probably get out of bed, he pulled me to him and kissed me. For a guy who was pretty submissive in bed, Simon could be awfully damn dominating. Though, eventually, I ended up on top of him, our cocks sliding together, like during the previous night, except this time Simon's hands were free to wander and roam and clench my ass when he thrust up against me.

"Don't have much time." I spoke between kisses and groans.

"For this we do." A sexy whisper in that morning voice of his.

My bed, my rules—right out the window. I gave in and we tangled, thrust, and moaned into each other until we both came hard against each other. What a hell of a way to wake up.

After a fast shower, we were back in my car and heading toward town. I'd drop Simon off at his place so he could grab a fresh set of clothes, then head to the shop. Except . . . Simon's bike was at End o' Earth. "Hey, how are you getting to work? Your bike's at the shop."

"I'll grab Lydia's bike—we ride the same model. She's got a bike rack on the SUV, so we can get both home." His voice was lethargic, but so full of joy. "We need to do this again."

I focused on the road, because if I gazed at him, I'd run into a damn tree. "Yeah. We hardly ticked anything off my list."

His chuckle was soft. A moment later, he sat up. "You'll want to take the next right."

Simon gave me directions that bypassed the main drag of Bluewater Bay and had us over where a bunch of craftsman-style two-stories had been built not too far out of town, probably from the heyday of the logging industry.

"That one there, with the blue trim."

Bright blue, against a gray that reminded me of rain. It seemed like the kind of house a nice happy het couple would have, except Simon wasn't het at all. While I didn't know how I felt about being the third wheel to this not-het couple, after last night, I wanted to have as much fun with Simon as I could until I did know. "Nice house."

"Mmm-hmm." He leaned in, and I met him in a kiss that would probably raise the neighbors' eyebrows. "See you in a few." With that, he hopped out of the car and headed up the path to the front door, and I pulled away from the curb.

Before I got to End o' Earth, I stopped at Stomping Grounds, got myself a coffee, and picked up Lydia's favorite drink again. It was the least I could do.

The barista probably still thought I was buttering Lydia up. If she only knew. "Is that all?" Her hand was paused over the cash register.

"Umm." She'd been the one to tell me the other day that Simon liked his coffee super hot. "Do you have a travel mug or something that'll keep a cup hot enough for Simon?"

She lowered her hand and peered at the mugs. "You know, there's this new one that's supposed to keep drinks blazing hot for up to four hours."

"Let's give it a try."

I left Stomping Grounds with a little paper carrier for mine and Lydia's coffees, and a bright blue high-tech travel mug full of the hottest coffee they could legally sell me. Couple minutes later, I rang the doorbell at the back of End o' Earth while standing where Simon had knelt and sucked me off last night.

Weird. So weird. Stranger still when Lydia opened the door and beamed at me. "God, Ian, you don't have to bring coffee every day!"

"I really do." We were both laughing as if everything were normal and wonderful . . . and maybe it was. She took the carrier and eyed the travel mug while we walked out to the front of the store. "It's for Simon," I said. "The barista said he likes it hot."

A sly smile. "Yeah, he certainly does."

I nearly tripped. "Uh— Well." The heat in my face was intense. "Yeah."

Damned if Lydia's smile wasn't sunshine too. How the hell did they do that?

"I asked Jesse to come in a little earlier if he was free, to give you and Simon additional time this afternoon. I know you need to get that finished." She nodded over toward the set.

That was nice of her. "I do. Thank you for that."

She took a sip of her coffee. "Dude, I understand deadlines. Probably more than Simon does."

I put Simon's mug down and finally scored a pull of my own coffee. It was warm and earthy and wonderful. "How's your work going, anyway?"

"It's good." She fiddled with her cup. "I wish I could show you, but . . ."

"Hey, I know all about intellectual property and non-disclosures. The only reason I can build the set here is that everyone's seen the grove already. I do wish I could see some of your stuff, though."

She stood straighter. "Really? I could show you my comic. Or some fan art."

I perked up. "Sure!"

A few minutes later, I was in her studio at the back of the shop and wow, Simon hadn't been kidding about the comic. What I saw of it was awesome. Lydia had an incredible sense of story and layout, and the art was top-notch. "You *need* to get that out in the market."

She grinned up at me.

Since I knew her not-so-secret passion, I smiled back. "Got any Wolf's Landing stuff?"

Blush to high heaven. Bingo. I knew she had to have some fan art of the show.

She cleared her throat and spoke. "Yeah." She was using one of those drawing tablets and the pen slid across the surface. "But don't tell anyone."

"Eh, they're okay with fan stuff, as long as no one sells it, you know?"

She nodded, and a moment later I was looking at an image of the characters of Wolf's Landing done up in the style of an '80s movie poster. Yeah. Lydia could *draw*. She had the actors down pat. I saw those folks pretty often and what was before me was *them*. Then my eye honed in on something else and I croaked. "There's a rune on the altar."

"Yup. It was added at the end of last season, during the mid-season finale." She peered up at me.

Oh shit. There wasn't a rune on my altar. Or on the plans. Or the photos the production manager had given to me. "You . . . sure?" My voice sounded shaky. I took a sip of coffee and hoped she hadn't noticed.

Of course, she had, given the concern in her voice. "I can show you screen caps . . ."

She navigated to Fandom Landing, the most popular of the Wolf's Landing fan sites and logged in. In a forum dedicated to screen caps, she brought up a thread—and there it was. Proof my set's altar was wrong. "Shit."

"I mean, if it's not on yours, you can add it, right?"

"Yeah." I could. That was easy. But the fact that it wasn't on the plans or the photos meant there'd been a larger fuckup along the line. "But if it's not on mine, it's not on the full-scale set they've been filming with."

"Oh." Lydia stared at the screen. "Shit."

Exactly. "I need to make a phone call." I wandered back out into the shop and over to the model to recheck the plans. They were the correct ones for the season and episode we were shooting. No rune. Both relief and horror ran through me. I *knew* I hadn't fucked up, but I'd kinda hoped I had, because this was worse. Anna would *not* be happy. I knew some of the schedule, and I was pretty sure they'd been filming on the full-sized set for a while now. Someone would get chewed out. Badly.

Fuck. I had no choice, though. A continuity error like that was *super* bad. Better to raise the flag now than let the mistake get all the way to post. How they fixed it wasn't my job to figure out. But calling it in? That was. I scrolled through my contacts and found the number for the production manager.

His gruff voice answered on the other end. "Yeah?"

"Hey, it's Ian Meyers. I'm working on the sacred grove miniature."

"Yeah. You nearly done?" Papers were shuffled in the background.

"Getting there. But, um. I noticed something. And I think it might be a problem."

Silence. Probably because he knew if there was a problem with my set, I'd fix it and not bother calling. "What is it?"

"There's no rune on the altar."

More silence. I cleared my throat. "During the mid-season finale last season, there was."

The sound that came out of my phone was one long hiss of a word. "Shit!" That was followed by "Fuck." Then he sighed. "Keep working on your set. I'll check this out and get back to you."

The line went dead before I could say anything else. I didn't take it personally. He was pretty damn busy and I'd dropped one hell of an issue into his lap. But it was done. I let out a breath before plunking myself down on my chair to drink the rest of my coffee. After all, I still had a set to complete, with or without a rune.

Lydia Derry's fan art may have saved *Wolf's Landing* from a whole lot of egg on our faces.

I was mounting a few of the smaller items to the set when I heard Simon's unmistakable voice murmur through the store, then Lydia's. Couldn't make out the words, but I knew he was heading my direction from the thumps on the carpet before he appeared.

"You bought me coffee? And a mug?" He held the bright blue travel mug up.

"The barista told me you like your coffee hot, and well, those paper cups wouldn't cut it."

"You didn't have to." He turned something on the top, took a sip, and it was almost as nice as watching him come under me. "Oh." It came out as a delighted sigh. "That's *good*."

"Worth every penny."

He chuckled. "I think I can make sure you get your money's worth from me."

Bet he could. I still wanted to bend Simon over a piece of furniture and had no doubt he'd let me. It dawned on me that I could probably have him about anyway I wanted to. The expression on my face must have been something else, because Simon's breath caught. He set down the mug on the table, took my face in his hands, and kissed me hard. I gripped his arms, mostly to keep from falling over. Simon was sex on ice when he kissed like there was nothing in the world but us.

"Later." He spoke against my lips. "I'll pay later."

"Yeah, you will." I stole a kiss back and bit his lip in the process.

He groaned. "Gotta open the store."

And I had to get back to working on the set. We broke apart, both breathless. I wanted to say something else to keep him here for another moment, but my phone blared out the theme from *The Good, The Bad, and The Ugly*, and I jumped. That was Anna's ring. "Shit." I grabbed the cell and answered. "This is Ian."

"I don't know whether to thank you or kill you," Anna said, "but the altar rune was a good catch."

Simon stood next to me, his curiosity making him damn sexy. Unfair. "Is it going to be much of an issue?" I asked.

A sigh from the other end. I could almost see her brushing strands of her hair out of the way. "We're reshooting a few scenes. For the others, we'll do CGI in post. Going forward, the rune will be there, so make sure it's on your set."

"Will do. But I'll need to swing by to pick up some photos."

Simon fiddled with his coffee.

"Already on their way to you," Anna said. "Fresh ones. So if there's anything else you spot . . ."

I was starting to feel a little guilty, because the catch wasn't mine. "Well, I only saw the rune because of one of the shop owners here. She knows the show." I met Simon's gaze. "Likely better than I do."

He raised an eyebrow, and I shrugged. It was true. I'd watched episodes and knew the storyline, but the continuity stuff was beyond me. There were producers and assistants and writers for that. I'd never have caught the error if Lydia hadn't shown me her art.

"Fans always do," Anna said. "Which is why it's good you pushed it up the chain, or we'd have been in a world of hurt in a few months. It was the right call, Ian, and I appreciate it, even if it fucks things up."

"Thanks. I think."

"Those photos should be there, soon."

I told Anna I'd watch for them, and we hung up.

"Problem with the set?" I couldn't nail down Simon's expression. Worried. Giddy. Proud. Who knew?

"There should be a rune on the altar." I shook my head. "Everyone missed it. Probably pulled the older plans of the set when they were getting ready for the season. Lydia showed me some of her art and *bam*, there it was."

His eyes got wide. "Oh my God, I should have noticed, too." A little crinkle formed on his forehead. "I mean I *repaired* the thing, and I didn't notice."

I waved my hand. "No one did. It happens. Thanks to Lydia, we caught it."

He nodded slowly, his attention on the model. "So, what's the plan for today?"

"Finish the bits, then dig into the details." This is where Simon would come in handy. "It's a lot of paint work."

His smile said it all: He *loved* to paint. I did too. But he was vibrating with glee. Or maybe that was the coffee.

Simon peered at his watch. "Nearly opening time. I'll be over when I can." He took another swig of his coffee. "This *does* keep it hot!"

"You like it hot." I tried not to grin, but I was lousy at it.

That grin of Simon's put all kinds of heat into my body. "So do you." With that, he headed up to the front, enough spring in his step to bounce his ass oh-so-nicely. I chuckled and got back to work.

The photos arrived about half an hour after the store opened, and were brought by Anderson. I set down the moss I'd been attaching to the grove and stepped in front of it. "They have you playing courier?"

He made a sour face. "More like doing penance." He peered around me. "Looks good!"

"You touch it, I'll mash your fingers." I kept my tone light.

He laughed. "Dude, I'm not gonna go any farther than this." He handed over an envelope. "And Natalya already mashed every part of me during training."

Yeah, the best way not to piss off the director's girlfriend was to not piss off the director. He'd failed at that. I pulled out the photos. "Thanks, Anderson."

He nodded and headed out while I studied the photos and my model. Not a bad replica. A few tree parts needed to be adjusted, but overall, my set was pretty much like the life-sized one. Tingles ran from my toes to my head, and I caught a breath. Sometimes this happened, those moments when I realized I worked on *Wolf's Landing*, that I'd made it this far in my oddball career, and that I was damned good at my job.

But not perfect. I studied the photos again, and picked up the moss. Still needed to glue on a few fiddly parts, then we could get down to painting.

Around lunch, Simon reappeared with two sandwiches in his hands. "Beef or chicken?"

My stomach growled, even though I desperately wanted to keep working. But if I waved him off, I'd only end up eating the sandwich after some lengthy argument that Simon would rightly win. "Chicken."

I took the time to wash my hands, though. Moss and glue and paint—not crap I wanted to ingest. By the time I got back, Simon had brought chips and two bottles of water. We chowed down, and I felt a lot better after putting food into me.

When we finished, Simon leaned back in his chair. "You have me for the rest of the day."

So very tempting not to return to working, but set before sex. "Good. I'll put those fingers to work." My hands were now greasy from the sandwich. His too, so we headed to the employee area to fix that.

I didn't want to be away from the model too long, but the privacy gave me a chance to pull Simon close and sample his lips. He gave a huff of laughter as we kissed, slow and sweet. When we broke apart, he licked his bottom lip. "Here I was going to go in for that."

"Great minds."

When we returned to the grove, we found Jesse planted in front of it with his hands up. He was surprisingly intimidating in a purple and pink striped shirt and his skinny jeans. "I can't let you any closer."

He was blocking a scowling woman in one of the newer Wolf's Landing T-shirts and a pair of jeans. She had a curl of distaste in her expression. "You shouldn't have that. You're not allowed to have Wolf's Landing merchandise! I'll be taking it."

Whoa. What? "Excuse me?" I put myself between the woman and my set. "You're not taking shit."

"It's not merchandise, Marlina." Simon joined us. "It's a miniature set."

Simon knew this woman?

"Simon Derry, you know you're not supposed to have any Wolf's Landing-licensed items." A little crowd was forming behind her, with people peeking over shoulders to get a better view. Great. Just what we needed, a spectacle. Who was this woman? A moment later, two and two mashed together in my brain. She must be from Howling Moon, the shop next door. "It's not licensed. It's official."

"Ian—"

I ignored Simon. "It's official *Wolf's Landing* property." I stepped forward. "And if you so much as touch it, I'll call the police."

"Ian—"

Marlina crossed her arms. "Who the hell are you?"

"I'm Ian Meyers, and I'm the miniature set designer for *Wolf's Landing*."

That stopped her in her tracks. She gaped at me for a moment. "You work for *Wolf's Landing*?"

I took another step forward, forcing her to retreat. "Yup." I dug out the badge I used to get on the lot from my wallet.

She retreated farther and flicked her eyes to the miniature set, then focused on me. "But—"

Simon slid up next to me. "Look, I'm helping Ian out. Long story, but I've got the space and supplies he needs in a pinch—"

"He does," I said.

"—And we need to get back to work." He peered past her shoulder. "If you want your very own Sacred Grove figurine set, I'm sure Marlina will be happy to sell one to you"—he focused on her—"over at Howling Moon." Simon spoke the last bit hard and clear, with anger underneath.

Marlina turned and walked away. Some of the crowd dissipated. Others lingered—probably to catch a glimpse of us working. As long as they kept out of our hair, I didn't care. I clapped Simon on the shoulder. "Come on. Let's get back to it."

He glanced at the stragglers. "We're going to get a crowd now."

Jesse sighed. "I'll do what I can to keep the hordes down." He shooed a few people away as he worked his way back to the counter.

"Better some people watching us do boring shit with paint than it vanishing next door and being completely ruined."

Simon scrubbed his neck. "I'm sorry, Ian."

God, he looked adorable when contrite. But this wasn't on him. "Don't be." I nodded to the set. "Let me show you what's next."

For the next few hours, we studied the photos, put bits of the grove into place, painted, and I carved a rune onto the altar. We ignored the people watching us. Occasionally, Jesse or Lydia would come and gently redirect people to buy something or take their leave of the shop. "They're on a deadline, you know," Lydia murmured to someone.

We were. Or rather, I was. But with Simon helping, the set was becoming more and more like an actual *set* and not a pile of broken shit. I'd been right about his painting too. Absolutely professional quality. He made the parts of the grove he was painting match the photographs, and our styles blended well. You couldn't tell what he'd done and what I had.

It was damn nice to have someone to work with too. I ended up on my own when doing the miniatures, since *Wolf's Landing* could be so prop-heavy at times. When I wasn't in the prop shop alone, I was lending a hand on a full-scale set, or crafting a one-off. I should talk to Anna about getting additional help for the miniatures. She owed me one now.

Of course, I owed Lydia too.

I stole a long gaze at Simon. He was so intensely focused on the model, he didn't register me ogling him. God, he was hot down to his shoes, hotter in the throes of creativity. I couldn't wait to get him naked again. My mind drifted back to the previous night and the comment he'd made while he was blowing me.

Maybe there *was* a way to give Lydia her due.

We worked straight through until closing and had people watching us the whole time, which felt odd. There'd been questions about the set and *Wolf's Landing*, and I answered them as best I could, employing the whole, "I can't talk about that" shtick more than once. There *were* things I couldn't talk about. There were also things I didn't know.

Like always, everyone wanted to talk about the stars of the show.

"I don't see the actors all that often, to be honest," I said to one guy. "Mostly, I'm hip deep in production people."

By the time we were putting our supplies away and cleaning up, I was both hungry and slightly annoyed at being the center of attention. Granted, I'd announced exactly who I was and what I was working on, so it was my fault . . . but not entirely.

End o' Earth's next-door neighbor was on my shit list, even if she did sell the stuff that partly paid for my employment.

The thought of my set in her store chilled me. What the hell would she have done to it? "Is there any way we can cover this without getting the paint all fucked up?" Because draping a sheet over it seemed a bad, bad plan, but I wanted it hidden from prying eyes when we weren't here. Yeah, the store had a lock and alarm. Still.

Simon rubbed his chin and studied the model and the work tables. "Grab your chair and put it over there." He gestured to the right side of the table. I didn't get what he meant until he hefted his chair and put it on the left side.

Duh. Yeah, that would work. I lifted mine and mirrored Simon's placement, but on the right. "I take it, you have something we can use as a cover?"

He did. A painter's tarp, one that wasn't too heavy. We were able to drape it over the chairs and with some additional taller boxes, make sure that it didn't touch the grove at all.

My stomach growled again and I winced, glad that Simon had made me eat lunch. "Guess I'll get a sandwich somewhere." It was after nine.

Simon seemed like he might say something, when Lydia and Jesse joined us.

"You guys ready to get out of here?" Lydia nodded toward the back of the shop.

"Yeah," I said. Not brilliant, but I wasn't firing on all cylinders. Tired, hungry, and I still wanted Simon. I wished this set wasn't exhausting us both. There were lines of weariness around his eyes too.

We trooped to the back, Simon had me grab the extra bike, and Lydia set the alarm. Jesse said his goodbyes, and I dutifully followed the Derrys to Lydia's SUV. As Simon had said, she had a bike rack. They strapped the bikes on, and I stuffed my hands in my pockets.

This was awkward. Saying goodnight to your new lover with his wife present, even if she did approve. "I should go find dinner."

Lydia dusted her hands together. "I'm making some spaghetti when we get home. Want to join us?"

Should I? Shouldn't I? I glanced from one Derry to the other. "Um . . . it's late."

"Not *that* late." Simon shrugged. "You still gotta eat, right?" He had a grin that slipped past all my defenses and lit me up like a Christmas tree. All sparks and tingles and wants. "Hop in." He gestured at the SUV.

"What about my car?"

"Eh," Lydia said. "No one will bother it. It'll be there in the morning."

Oh. *Oh.* I let out a breath. "Okay." Shaky, but maybe that was the hunger and not the way my head was spinning. Lydia was inviting me over to spend the night. Undoubtedly, given his smile, with her husband.

I could get used to this type of polyamory. No lies. No jealousy. I didn't get how *that* worked. But tonight? I jumped in the SUV.

Dinner was nice. Nothing special about spaghetti and pasta sauce from a jar, but it was warm, fast, and went well with the red wine Simon had opened. We didn't talk much while eating—all too ravenous. But once the meal was done, Lydia leaned back and swirled the wine in her glass. "I can't believe the nerve of Marlina."

"Well, at least we know she's still sending people to check up on us." Simon shrugged. "She made a fool out of herself today."

I broke in. "Wait, she sends people into your store? To make sure you're not selling Wolf's Landing stuff?" Their large longhaired cat brushed against my leg and I scratched his head before he wandered off.

"Yup." Simon's *P* was exaggerated. He pushed his plate away and crossed his arms. "All the damn time."

Lydia sipped her wine. "She's very stern about the licensing." A sly smile. "Jesse said you cut her down to size."

Before I could say anything, Simon chipped in. "He can be quite commanding when he wants."

Lydia studied Simon for a moment, then seemed to turn that focus on me. "Oh *really*?"

Amazing how loaded two words could be. Heat rose from my toes up to my skull. I picked up my wine glass, sipped, and plotted how best to exact my revenge on Simon. "You ever drop your keys in the alley behind the shop?"

Simon sat up bolt straight. Lydia looked puzzled.

"Uh," Simon said. "Officer Merrick—"

Lydia clasped her hand over her mouth and laughed. She was shaking enough she had to set her wine down. "Oh," she said. "Why, yes. I have." Another chuckle. "Simon told you about the rule, eh?"

I felt a bit like a James Bond villain smiling over the top of my wine. "Yes, he did." Before I could suck them back in, words tumbled out of my mouth. "He said you'd like to watch."

Simon put down his wine. He seemed to be holding his breath. Lydia met my gaze. Talk about somewhat evil grins over wine—she beat mine. "You offering?"

Was I?

"Please say yes." Simon's voice was a whisper and he squirmed in his seat.

Oh hell, yes. I was. "Maybe we should take this elsewhere?"

We all rose, and I suspected we were all in a daze. The glasses and the wine remained on the table.

"Stairs." Simon pointed, and he seemed as breathless as I felt.

I caught his arm, pulled him to me and claimed his mouth, relishing that sexy groan in the back of his throat. He melted against me like before, surrendering, wanting. Every part of me needed him moaning and gasping under me.

"Wow." Lydia's voice somehow added to my desire. "You're serious."

I broke the kiss and spoke against Simon's lips. "Yes, I am."

Didn't know how we all made it upstairs, but we did and I found myself in a bedroom that was a little too small to be the master bedroom, but still had personal touches to it. I stroked Simon's cheek. "Lube and condoms?"

A huff that was almost laughter. "In the bedside table, where they belong."

I stole a kiss before checking. Yup, as promised. And a few other items besides. Vibrator, a scarf similar to the one I owned, leather cuffs, a small paddle and a gag. *Someone* liked sex on the kinkier side.

Lydia lowered herself into a chair against the wall opposite me. That would give her an excellent view of the bed.

Of *course*. Swingers. I wondered how many times Simon had sat there and watched Lydia. "Ever seen your husband be fucked?"

She shook her head, eyes wide, cheeks as flushed as Simon's. Being gay, I'd never paid too much attention to what women look like when turned on, but I guessed Lydia was there.

Simon's arousal was easy to spot, that nice hard ridge in his jeans as he stood at the foot of the bed. "Today's your lucky day," I said. Didn't know which one I was talking to. Probably both. I pulled out the lube and a condom and hesitated before closing the drawer. "Whose cuffs?"

Simon swallowed. "Um. They fit both of us."

Oh good. I pulled them out, then slid the drawer shut. Simon was practically vibrating, and I met his stare. "Strip. Now."

He did, first kicking off his shoes, then unbuttoning his shirt to reveal his chest and stomach, before letting it fall to the floor. Jeans next, unbuttoning and unzipping. Both those and his underwear joined his shirt.

His cock was full and pointing up, tip already beaded with pre-come. *Someone* wanted to be fucked badly. I glanced casually at Lydia, expecting her attention to be engrossed with her husband, but she met my gaze, mouth open slightly, as if I were a complete surprise. Maybe she was turned on by me. I couldn't tell. I gave her a smile, then focused on Simon, who'd taken off his socks and now stood naked at the foot of the bed.

Good. "Step back a pace."

He did and I tossed the condom, lube, and cuffs onto the bed, and sauntered to stand in front of him. Simon's attention was entirely on me. He was hard for *me.*

Heady, always, this feeling of power. Utterly intoxicating with Lydia in the room. I'd never been naked with a woman present, or taken out my aching dick and stroked myself. I did the latter now, and watched Simon shiver in delight.

The chair creaked and that sent a tremble up my spine. "Get on your knees, Si."

He knelt and peered up, blue eyes so intent on me. I took a seat on the bed and stroked my length while Simon leaned forward with anticipation.

Lydia gave a little sigh, probably because Simon was so damn hot. Hell, I sighed too.

I stroked myself once. "Suck me."

A sly smile from Simon, then that lovely mouth closed around me. I twined my fingers in Simon's hair but let him lick and suck and go down on me to his heart's content. At least for now. I loved the way his mouth felt, how he used his tongue to tease, and how far he could swallow me. It was unbelievable. "You're such a good cocksucker."

He moaned around me and started stroking himself. I tightened my grip in his hair until the moaning turned sharp. "Did I say you could touch yourself?"

A whimper, but Simon left his dick alone.

Lydia was obviously trying to be quiet, but the chair squeaked and her breathing gave away how turned on *she* was. The deep gasps of need and pleasure were pretty universal. I snuck another glance, and yeah. Lydia had her hand down her unzipped pants.

She was allowed. Simon? His orgasm was mine to give. I gripped his head, stilling his motion. His tongue and lips didn't stop, though. I leaned down and whispered, "I'm gonna fuck your face while your wife watches."

His groan and tremble were things of delight. Dirty man.

But then, I was too. Knowing Lydia was there, knowing I was sliding my cock in and out of her husband's mouth while she watched—that turned me inside out. I could control both of them, give them what they wanted and needed. Both Derrys were in my hands—even if I wasn't touching one of them.

I fucked Simon's mouth gently at first, then with force until he was moaning and gasping and tears formed at the corner of his eyes, trusting that he would tell me if it was too much. Or Lydia would. They both seemed versed enough in kink.

My own desire was swirling and rising, and if I didn't slow down, it wouldn't take me long to come down Simon's throat.

I had other plans . . . so I backed off and pulled Simon away. "You like that, don't you?"

"Yeah." Simon licked his swollen lips and met my gaze. His voice was gravel and joy. "Love any way you fuck me."

Not only a cocksucker, but also a lovely, subby bottom. How perfect was that? I stood and grabbed the cuffs I'd thrown on the bed. "Get up. Turn around."

I'll give him credit, despite his shakiness and the wince I saw when he climbed to his feet, Simon obeyed quickly. Lovely back, delectable ass. I smacked each cheek, and he rose up onto his toes with a little cry.

That turned into a moan when I hooked the hand with the cuffs over his stomach and dragged the index finger of my free hand up his crack.

That got me a moan from Lydia as well, and sparks went off at the top of my head and down into my balls. *Got you too.*

Leather needed to be around Simon's wrists. I drew one of his hands back and fit the cuff snug around it, then around the other. They clipped together with a handy tiny carabineer.

There. Wrists nice and shackled. Simon's shoulders rose and fell with each breath, and I kissed the nape of his neck. "Do you trust me?"

He relaxed under my lips. I nipped at his skin. "Yes." The word was a breathless groan.

Good. The tension in Simon's body was from anticipation, not fear. I swung him around until he faced the bed. "I want you kneeling there." I pointed to a spot on the bedspread.

As before, Simon did as I ordered. He folded his beautiful long limbs, and his hard cock jutted out. His skin was flushed from his chest up. I moved the condom and lube out of the way, pressed a hand against his back and spoke into his ear. "Forehead against the mattress."

With an intake of breath and a grunt deep in his throat, he lowered himself. I pushed his knees apart until he was on the edge of straining to hold the position.

Glorious. Prostrate on the bed, ass in the air for me.

I didn't play these games often, but oh how I loved them. I ran my hand over Simon's flesh. "You really want my cock, don't you?"

He shifted from knee to knee. "Yeah."

"Tell me." I wanted to hear it. I wanted Lydia to hear it.

She had her hand down her pants now, rubbing circles. Mouth opened with an amazing expression. When she met my gaze, she smiled and her face took on greater color.

"I want—" Simon's voice wavered. He took a breath and started again. "I want you to fuck me. Hard. I want your cock in me so deep I can't see or breathe or speak. I want you to tell me when to come—or not." He paused. "I want what gets you off the best."

Everything about Simon in this moment got me off. Part of me wanted to slap the condom and lube on and fuck him rough and fast until we both collapsed, but the other part thought teasing would be fun. Making him beg. I got the lube and coated my fingers and his crack, skimming across his hole and his taint. Rolling his balls and pumping his cock until he was squirming and panting, and desperate sounds were pouring out of him.

He was damn close to the edge already.

Lydia was biting her lip, her gaze on my hand and where it stroked and slid. Some additional lube, and I gave them both what they wanted—a finger deep in Simon's ass.

The groan he made was exquisite. "Yeah, yeah."

Lydia's breath caught.

I finger-fucked him deep and hard, each stroke shaking Simon's body. Hot. Tight. I wanted more than my damn finger in him. Didn't take long to get a condom and lube onto my dick, or kneel on the bed behind Simon.

Simon trembled, but the hiccup of a groan that sounded in the room was Lydia's. I couldn't help looking over. I didn't know why, but the sight of her there, waiting, wanting, so obviously enjoying— flipped something in my head and my chest. Maybe it was the trust she was giving me . . . us. I liked her watching.

"Want me to fuck him?" I murmured.

A tiny nod and that sweet smile again, as if to thank me.

"Please," Simon said. "Please, Ian. I need—"

Whatever he'd been going to say became a guttural moan when I drove my dick into his ass. I went as deep as I could, slid out, and slammed back in, burying myself to the root. "You were saying?"

He replied with whimpers. I loved those sounds and the way Simon shook and rocked as I held myself in him. Mine, at least for the time being. I pulled out and fucked him with long, slow thrusts, savoring his breath and the sexy sounds he ground out when I raked over his prostate again and again. Simon pushed back to meet me, joining in the tempo I set, and our bodies moved in tandem, slick and hot. My own grunts followed his moans and I dug my fingers into his slender hips. The chair squeaked and under all that was Lydia's breath—fast quiet huffs.

"Oh, God." Simon's voice was a shaky mess. "I wanna come."

So did I. Everything was heady and powerful. Simon beneath me. Lydia watching. I grabbed his cuffed wrists—to punctuate how much he was mine—and growled, "Not yet."

The sound he made, one born of surrender and need, set desire down into my core and up into my head. I broke our gentle rhythm and turned it into something wanton and harsh. I drove into him fast, but still deep as I could manage, each thrust pressing his head into the mattress. "You'll come when I say. Not before."

Simon gave a hiss and a throaty cry. But he kept up with my thrusts until we were slamming against each other and I was too damn close to tease this out any longer. Sparks flew up my back, heat descended in my center, and my balls ached. I wanted to feel Simon's pleasure as much as hear it.

Only needed one hand to hold his cuffed wrists. The other I wrapped around his cock and stroked him as furiously as I fucked him. Simon gave an anguished cry that hung between pleasure and pain. "I gotta . . . please let me come. Please, please . . ." His words fell away into moans and gasps.

Light was everywhere. "Yeah, Si. Come for me."

He did, coating my hand and tightening around me, and I was gone too, soaring off into a heaven of light and bliss and heat. As a counterpoint to our own release, Lydia groaned deep and long and I knew I'd taken her there too.

Perfect. So fucking good.

Took a while to come down—for all of us, I think. When I could move again, I slid free of Simon and he fell sideways, stretching out his torso and pulling in deep breaths. I wanted to join him, but his hands were still bound together, so I crawled up next to him and unhooked the cuffs from each other. "You okay?"

Simon gave a choked laugh. "Oh yeah." Another breath. "So much better than okay."

Relief flooded over my post-orgasmic glory. "I should get cleaned up." Except I couldn't move. Fucking Simon like that—coming like that—it made me want to lie there and stare at the ceiling for a while.

Soft footfalls, then louder ones on tile, then Lydia handed me a towel and held out a trash can.

I should have been embarrassed by her seeing me spent and softening, but hell, she'd watched me fuck Simon. Modesty was so two hours ago. I took off the condom, threw it into the trash, and grabbed the towel.

Once I'd cleaned my hand, I offered the towel to Simon. He wiped himself up best he could, then rolled close to me. Funny angles, but hell, we'd move later. Maybe.

There was a gentle *clink* as Lydia replaced the trash can in the bathroom, then she was back. "Night, guys," she whispered, and kissed us on the foreheads, me first, then Simon.

Then she was gone, and the door to the room clicked closed.

Something fluttered in my chest, but I didn't want to figure out what, so I curled up around Simon and pressed my cheek against his warm chest. He smelled of salt and musk. Sex and lube and leather.

After a while, he stroked my hair and spoke, sounding far more together than me. "Maybe I should ask if you're all right?"

"Yeah, I am." I tasted the truth there. "Very all right."

He drew a finger over my cheek. "Come on. Let's get under the covers."

In short order, we were nestled in each other's arms, in the dark, under a sheet and a light blanket. Somewhere along the line, Simon had taken off the cuffs. He brushed a thumb over my lips, and kissed me, slow and sweet. He spoke against my lips. "Thank you for that. You have no idea. But thank you."

I kissed him back. Didn't trust myself to speak. I didn't have a clue what was going on in his head. Didn't know what was going on in mine, only that here and now, Simon was in my arms, I was in his, and that was enough.

CHAPTER TEN

SIMON

Thank goodness we opened the shop later on Sundays, because all three of us were dragging in the morning, though the sex had been so very worth it. I was sore in every glorious way I loved.

Mr. Purrbody waltzed into the guest bedroom while Ian was in the shower and jumped on the bed. He sniffed the covers with a disdain only cats manage, and stared at me.

"Yeah, well, it was fun, Flufferbutt. Don't give me the stink-eye."

He swished his tail, then flopped down near the end of the bed, next to the clothes I'd found for Ian to wear. A fairly innocuous T-shirt and jeans, since no one needed to know he'd spent the night here, though honestly, I was beginning not to care so much. Something I should talk to Lydia about.

A few minutes after the water shut off, Ian exited the bathroom, wonderfully naked, towel drying his wet hair. I must have been staring, because he shrugged. "Figured everyone's seen it."

Yeah, but I could gaze at his body for ages, the way his hips moved, the trail of hair from his belly to his cock. Those delicious nipples. His glorious tattoo displayed for all the world to see. "Mr. Purrbody hasn't."

He eyed the cat and slung the towel over his shoulder. "Purrbody? You called him McFluff last night."

"He's got lots of names. Officially, he's Lawrence Purrbody, but also Flufferbutt. McFluff. Larry Fuzzbottom." I laughed. "He's our judgmental feline overlord."

I swear, if any cat could give me a raised eyebrow, my cat could. "Love you too, sweetheart," I said to him.

"Aww." Ian tossed the towel on the bed. "Is he making fun of you?" Only took a few scratches on the head, and Lawrence demonstrated his surname by purring up a storm for Ian.

"There's some clothes you can borrow." I'd already dressed, as had Lydia. Not that Ian was slow or lazy, I'd just decided to go down on him before he crawled out of bed.

"Thanks. I'm okay with wearing my stuff from yesterday, but if we're going to get an audience in the shop . . ."

Someone might notice he hadn't changed and I didn't want to hand Marlina another reason to give us grief, even if I was less worried about being out. I closed the distance and kissed him. "It's fine." He tasted of toothpaste and smelled of my woodsy shower gel, and I wanted more than his mouth. I craved the heat and passion of him fucking me until I couldn't breathe.

He must have sensed my mood, because he placed a finger on my lips. "Don't. We have to work." He backed away and grabbed the jeans. "Bad enough that I'm going commando in your pants. Gonna be thinking about you all day."

Oh, as if that would cool down my blood. I scratched Purrbody under the chin and was granted a deep rumble and a display of a tummy of white floof.

"Is it a trap?" Ian pulled on the simple black T-shirt and eyed the cat's belly.

"No. Actually likes his stomach rubbed." I demonstrated and those purrs got louder.

There were thumps up the stairs. "You guys about ready?" Lydia leaned against the doorframe, and my heart did a little flip. She was glowing and seemed happy, if a bit tired around the edges.

God, last night had been spectacular. The memory sang through my veins. Ian. Lydia. The cuffs. Her getting off. I had to be the luckiest guy alive.

"Yeah," Ian said. "I have to get my shoes on."

"Larry's been distracting us." I gave him a final pet.

"Poor neglected baby." She pursed her lips at the kitty. "I should spend a few nights with him. I've nearly finished my freelance work, so I can take some time at home."

A shuffle as Ian tied his shoes. He stood up and there was trepidation and worry in the line of his back. "I'm sorry I've disrupted everything in your life."

"No, no." Lydia strode into the room and took Ian's hands. "God, no. You haven't done anything. You've been nothing but a joy."

He had, both in the shop and in bed. The sex had been wonderful, but I was also getting to live a piece of my dream working next to— and learning from—a real live Hollywood miniature set artist.

"I—" Ian seemed at a loss for words. Then he laughed and caught my eye before focusing on Lydia. "You two are something else." He gave Lydia's hands a squeeze, then dropped them. "We should probably get going."

We left Mr. Purrbody lounging on the bed, trooped out to the SUV, and Lydia drove us into town. I sat in the front, and Ian in the back.

As the businesses started appearing along Main, Lydia asked, "Any objections to swinging by Stomping Grounds?"

"No!" Ian and I answered emphatically, practically at the same time, and Lydia laughed. Soon enough, we were in the shop and ordering our drinks. The barista gave Ian a raised eyebrow. "So now you're bringing 'em in for coffee?"

Oh man, Ian blushed nicely at that. "Well . . . yes." His smile was coy. "Figured it's easier to carry their coffee this way."

"As if I'd let you pay . . ." Lydia slapped down a twenty on the counter.

Ian and Lydia jostled and laughed over the bill, but Ian gave up gracefully to Lydia in the end. My heart melted in my chest. I— This. This was what I'd always wanted.

It had been less than a week. *Slow down, Si. Don't get too attached.* This kind of relationship, with all its complexity, could always fall apart. But my soul tied itself up in knots at the potential for so much more and I clung to that hope.

Coffees in hand, we drove the extra couple of blocks to the shop, parked in our spot in the alley, and clambered into the back rooms of End o' Earth. After Ian headed into the main part of the shop to check on the set, Lydia bumped me with her shoulder. "You okay?" Concern there, and love. Always love.

I nodded. "Trying not to get ahead of myself." I studied the path Ian had taken. "But he's— Well, you said it yourself."

A joy. Utterly. That was the problem.

"You're worried it's too good to be true."

"Pretty much." I knew myself, how fast I fell and how hard it hurt when the seemingly inevitable happened.

She kissed me and tasted of cinnamon and java. "I love you, Si. Go spend the day with that lovely man."

Now, that was an order I could follow. I headed out into the store. Dexy would be in soon and Lydia would do some restocking. Everything was in hand, except for my heart, which I could never corral. Maybe I'd get burned. But Ian seemed happy too, so maybe I wouldn't.

Only one way to find out. I stepped out into the store and found him by the set, which he'd already uncovered.

A breathtaking smile greeted me. "Let's get to work."

"I'm all yours," I said, and meant every single word.

According to Ian, we got a shitload of work done that Sunday, despite answering questions from *Wolf's Landing* fans. It'd been pleasant, actually. I fielded a few inquiries about painting, model building, and miniatures. Some folks said they'd seen me working before, but never had the courage to come up and ask about model construction or miniature painting.

We must have been getting people coming over from Howling Moon, because I kept spying some Wolf's Landing T-shirts I hadn't seen before. It was about the time of year they put out new ones. I'd have to look at the newer designs sometime.

During one of the lulls, Lydia wandered back with some bottles of water, and I set down my brush. "Do you think maybe I should teach a workshop on miniature and model painting?"

"Yes," Lydia and Ian answered in the same tone, one that had *duh* rather than a period at the end of the sentence.

Huh. Okay. I put that on my mental to-do list.

"I should give you one of my sculptures to paint." Ian shoved some strands of hair out of his face with the back of his wrist. "I bet it'd be stunning."

I didn't know what to say to that. Luckily, Lydia spoke. "Wait, you sculpt?"

And they were off, Ian filling in Lydia on his sculptures and her offering shop space. My heart did a dance in my chest, seeing them animatedly discussing his art.

Please. A silent prayer. I wanted this to work.

By the time that night rolled around, we were all exhausted. Once the shop was locked up, and Dexy had waved her goodbyes, Ian took a breath. "I think I need to go home tonight." There was trepidation in his words. He met my gaze. "As much as I love this, I'm so worn out." As if to punctuate the statement, he yawned, then looked completely sheepish. "Sorry."

I held back a yawn of my own. Barely. "No, totally understand." Mostly because I was also beat-ass tired. I pulled him close and stole a kiss. "Besides, having energy is good for other things."

Lydia nearly held back a snicker and that turned into a yawn. She'd been burning the candle too much lately also.

Ian drew me back in and his lips and tongue took my breath away. As did the feel of his body against mine. "Just you wait." Then he broke the kiss and smiled. "I'll see you guys bright and early tomorrow."

Still, there was a pang in my chest when he sauntered down the alley to the walkway that took him back to Main.

"Hey, come on," Lydia said. "Let's go home."

I climbed into the SUV. Lydia was kind enough to leave me to my thoughts during the ride home, and as we went through the evening. She knew me well, especially after all this time. When we settled into bed for the night, I pulled her to me. "I love you so much." Her hair was soft against my lips and her skin warm.

"Oh, Si, I know," she whispered, as if she'd heard all the words I hadn't said. The fears. The worries. All the what-ifs. "I know, I know. It'll be okay, whatever happens."

On some level, I knew it would. I had her. I would always have her.

But I wanted Ian too. For the first time, I wondered if that made me greedy.

Monday came and went much as the other days with Ian in the shop. We worked and laughed and fielded questions from customers and *Wolf's Landing* fans. I soaked in as much of Ian's presence as I could: his long limbs and stunning smile. Everything. Time was ticking on, and the set looked better than ever. Soon, he wouldn't be working his magic in my shop. He'd be back on the *Wolf's Landing* lot, and life would return to normal at End o' Earth.

I wasn't ready. Seemed like he wasn't either, given the sometimes-mournful glances he gave the shop.

My fear was that whatever lay between us would end the minute he and the set left. Was this a fling to him? Or worse, a way to repay me? I had no idea. We should talk about where this was going, but there wasn't time or the privacy we needed while we were working. Lunch in the back didn't afford us the space, not with Dexy and Lydia in and out. While they both knew what was going on, I didn't want to spill my guts in front of Dexy, and I wasn't sure Ian wanted to have this conversation while Lydia was in the room.

We'd eventually all talk, but that was putting the cart miles before the horse. So, I'd see if he wanted to get a beer tonight.

As it turned out, it would be a celebratory brew, because about half an hour before closing, Ian eyed the model and said, "I think we're done."

"Really?" To me, the model could've been mistaken for the photographs of the set, but I wasn't the professional.

A slow nod. "Yeah. I'm at the stage where I keep wanting to touch up my touch-ups . . . and that means there's nothing left to do and my perfectionism is taking over."

I set my brush down and leaned back in my chair. It was beautiful and so very *Wolf's Landing*. "Wow. We did it."

His smile set my blood on fire, as did his warm hand on my shoulder. "That's right—*we* did it."

Tingles surged up and down my back. I helped build a set for my favorite TV show. And I'd met—and slept with—Ian. Life didn't get much better.

"Now I have to figure out how to get it out of here and back to the lot." Ian laughed. "It's not gonna fit in the Mini."

Not anymore, it wouldn't. Oops. It was also going to be damn tricky getting it through the door. "We can use the SUV." It *would* fit in the back of that. "But I think we're gonna need everyone's help to get this out of the front door. Or the one in the back."

Ian's eyes got wide. "Oh, shit. I forgot about the door."

Though there were people around, I grabbed his hand. "Hey, we'll get it out. Promise. You said you were good at squeezing things into tight places."

There was that reddening I loved. "Yeah. Okay."

We tidied the area and covered the set one final time. Ian looked around. "I'll pack up my supplies tomorrow."

Good, more time for us tonight.

We got the rest of the store cleaned up, I let Jesse out the front, and Ian and I headed out the back. Once I set the alarm and locked the door, I turned to him. "Up for a beer to toast our success?"

Ian stuffed his hands in his pocket. "I'd love one. But I need to take a raincheck tonight. There's a meeting on set at five-thirty tomorrow morning and Anna wants me there. We're going over the shooting schedule and plans for Wednesday."

Well, shit. There went having a conversation, or anything else. "Okay."

I must have failed to keep the disappointment from my voice, because Ian stepped forward. "Hey." His voice was soft and his fingers cupped my face. Heat from his body radiated against mine.

He brushed his thumb over my lips. "There's nothing in the world I want more than a beer with you." His mouth met mine, and our tongues tangled until I moaned into him. Our bodies brushed, dicks rocking against each other.

Oh yeah, he was still into me. Ian broke the kiss, and that was sensual and breathtaking, the slow pull apart, the way he sucked on my lower lip. "I want you so bad."

"Same," I whispered.

He slid his hands down my back and pulled us together tight. "I can tell."

Couldn't help the hiss as he ground into me. So fucking good.

He backed off. "Come on, I'll drive you home."

When we reached my house, he wrapped his hand around my neck and claimed my lips again. Still so hot and demanding. His fingers traced the length of my shaft in my jeans until I was squirming in my seat and incapable of anything but throaty whimpers.

"Yeah." Ian palmed my cock. "That's what I like."

"Me putty in your hands?" My whisper filled the car.

"Mm-hmm. Exactly." He heaved a sigh. "I'd blow off the meeting tomorrow, but truth is, Anna scares the shit out of me."

I'd heard that about the director, that she was good, and fair, but exacting and she'd call you on the carpet if you screwed up. "Don't get in trouble on account of me." I brushed his cheek with a shaky hand. "I'll be here tomorrow. And the next day. And the one after that."

I couldn't get a read on the emotions that flickered over Ian before he kissed me again. This one was sweet, though, and he'd finally relented on my cock. "I want you to do something for me," he said.

"Anything."

A chuckle. "Tell Lydia I want her to use the cuffs on you." His grin was wicked as he let me go. "Good night, Simon."

When I'd caught my breath, I murmured, "Good night," and somehow managed to get out of the car and not trip over my own feet on the way to the front porch. My blood burned so hot, it was a wonder I didn't light the way up the path.

Ian pulled away and drove off into the night, the bastard. *God, I think I'm falling in love.* Hell, I knew I was.

Terrifying. Astounding.

When I got inside, I must have looked eight different kinds of turned on, because Lydia stared at me from the kitchen doorway.

"Um." I put my wallet and keys on the entry table. "Ian told me he wants you to use the cuffs. On me." It had been years since I'd been nervous in front of Lydia, but tonight I was, and out came my dorky giggle.

"Well," she said, her smile as deviant as Ian's, "I suppose we shouldn't disappoint him." She stepped forward, took my hand and drew me upstairs.

Yeah. I was totally in love. With both of them.

CHAPTER ELEVEN

IAN

The bad thing about my career in television was that sometimes meetings happened at the ass-crack of dawn. I rubbed my face and took a swig of the coffee I'd gotten from the catering trailer. Ugh. They tried, but food service drip into a huge vat wasn't a decent cup. Pretty sure the stars got better coffee, but us crew? Na.

Still, it had enough caffeine to get my sluggish brain moving and take the edge off the fact that I was here and not in bed with Simon.

I hoped he'd enjoyed last night. One of us should've. I'd beaten off to the thought of him tied up, helpless, and loving it, but the orgasm had left me oddly unfulfilled. I wanted Simon in the flesh, needed his voice and sighs. Hell, I'd have been happy sleeping next to him, but I knew myself better than that. There'd have been no sleeping if I'd stayed with Si or taken him home. So, a night alone and a morning of crappy coffee for me.

Several of us from production were milling around outside Anna's trailer. We were early, which was fine. Better that than late. I took another swallow of joe and missed my daily dose of Stomping Grounds. Town was out of the way from my place to the studio lot, so I hadn't bothered. Besides, Stomping Grounds opened at six. Not even they got up for a five-thirty meeting.

As much as I tried not to let my thoughts turn toward the Derrys, I found myself mulling over Lydia's smile and how she'd assured me that I hadn't blown apart their normal life. I *liked* her. Really liked her. Had the suspicion that if I'd been attracted to women at all, I'd feel what Simon undoubtedly felt for her. I supposed that was why I'd suggested Simon tell Lydia to use the cuffs. He'd given so much to me, and she'd let him, I'd wanted to give her something back too. I didn't know if it had worked, and I didn't want to know the details of their kinky escapades.

When I thought about Simon, everything was crystal clear. But when I thought about Simon *and* Lydia, my emotions got murky. Their marriage, despite being open, made me stumble. Lydia was his *wife*. What was I to Simon? I was so damn confused as to how things were supposed to work between all of us.

Anna appeared in a whirlwind—well, not really—but it felt like it. One minute, we were all sipping coffee and moving like slugs, and the next, she was breezing across the lot to her trailer and talking, and we were listening and following and scribbling notes as we piled in after her. She started in on the shooting plan for Wednesday. Day shots, night shots. Extras. Wrangling. Somewhere along the line, she spotted me.

"Ian, please tell me that set of yours is finished, because we need to get pyrotechnics on it."

"It's finished." Man, the relief that crossed Anna's face. I breathed out and my muscles unclenched. "Should be on set today. I just need to pick it up and bring it over."

"You're a miracle worker."

I'd actually managed to impress Anna Maxwell. Who'd have thought? But I couldn't take all the credit. "Well, I did have help," I said. "And I'll need a pass for him, since we're going to use his SUV to get it here."

Anna waved the concern away. "I'll talk to security after this."

My part done, the meeting swirled around me and then was over. But before I could escape, Anna called my name. "A minute, please."

Shit. She always made me so anxious. "Yeah?"

When everyone had filed out, she turned her laser-sharp focus on me. "I'm very impressed with how you handled this situation, and your innovation in finding a solution to your supply problem."

I swallowed. "Thanks. I knew you needed it fast." Hell, with help, I hadn't gotten myself into too much of a panic. "Though, what saved my ass was having an extra set of hands. If Simon—the store owner—hadn't been a model and miniature painter, I'm not sure I would've finished it in time."

She studied me. "Are you trying to tell me you'd like an assistant in your shop?"

The woman was psychic. "Yeah. I mean, I know the budget—"

"*I* know the budget, and yes, we can afford it." Her gaze changed, softened, and my cheeks heated. "I don't suppose your shop owner would be available?"

Wow. What? Simon? I stumbled over my answer. "I—I don't know. He owns End o' Earth. I don't think he could up and drop it." And as much as I loved working beside Simon, I wasn't sure I wanted him as my *assistant*, especially if we kept this—whatever it was—up. "I can ask, but—"

She nodded, and stood straighter, her business posture back. "Let me call over to security to get him a pass for the day."

I rattled off the information they needed, at least as much as I knew, and scurried out of Anna's office once she dismissed me. It was too early to go over to End o' Earth, so I headed to the prop department and my shop. Hadn't been there in nearly a week and it felt weird to walk in. As if I'd taken a long vacation. There were a few boxes piled inside the door—the supplies I'd ordered. A note from Toby, one of the prop guys, said they'd arrived yesterday—far too late to help with the sacred altar set.

If nothing else, I could pass some time putting the supplies away and getting my shop ready for the next set. I fired up my laptop and poured over the shooting, prop, and set production schedules. It was about nine when I finished, and now I had a good grasp for what was on my plate for the next few weeks. Nothing major, though they wanted a flashback scene on one of the streets in town. That was fairly easy to do with some fancy camera angles and vintage car models. I might have the ones we needed here.

If not, I had an inkling of where I could find a few.

Couldn't help whistling as I left the shop and sauntered back to my car. I even gave Anderson a wave when I saw him. Hell, if he hadn't fallen on my set, I'd have never set foot in End o' Earth. Now it was going to be hard to keep out of that shop.

End o' Earth didn't open until ten, so as normal, I slipped around and rang the delivery bell. And, as normal, Lydia opened the door, all smiles and charm and light. "Hey! Meeting over?"

I entered, and followed her to her studio. "Has been for a while. But I doubted you guys would be here at seven, so I got some work done in my shop."

She laughed. "Unlike Si, I'm an early riser, but I was still munching on toast around then."

So domestic. *I guess when you have a house and a kitchen and a partner* . . . I shook the thought away. Wasn't going to happen. "I'm gonna check on the model. I need to measure it to see if we can get it out of here."

"Oh shit. I hadn't thought of that!"

"Didn't cross my mind, either. I have a garage door on the shop."

Lydia followed me out to the model and I pulled a tape measure from my tackle box. We measured, then measured again, then checked both doors. I breathed a sigh of relief and rubbed the back of my neck. We'd have to tip the set ninety degrees, but it would make it through either door.

"Si said he'd drive me over in the SUV, 'cause this isn't fitting in the Mini."

"Yeah, he mentioned he'd need the car." She bumped me with her hip. "I'm a little jealous he's gonna get to go to the lot. I've been on the tourist tour, but . . ."

Wasn't the same. "I'm sure I can get you a pass." She'd saved our bacon, after all.

Red appeared on her cheeks. "No, it's okay. Someone needs to mind the store." She gave a helpless shrug. "Besides I'd be too embarrassed."

"Embarrassed?"

She took a breath. "Some of the fan art I draw—it's not exactly safe for work. I guess I feel bad about it. Sometimes."

Because the main actors lived here, in town. And were married to each other. "No one's gonna hold that against you. I mean, Hunter Easton and Kevyan Montanari live here too, and they write the stuff."

"Yeah, but they don't write them boffing."

I wasn't too sure about that, but I bit my tongue. "I get it, though."

As I dropped the tape measure into my tackle box, Simon came into the shop. "Hey! I didn't expect you until later."

And I didn't expect the kiss he gave me, sweet and sensual, right in front of Lydia. My pulse beat in my ears and my heart flipped in my chest. God, I couldn't get enough of him.

But a kiss was all we had, because a moment later, Jesse rang the bell on the back door, and the work day started.

Once the shop was ready for the day, and with a little help from Lydia and Jesse, Simon and I maneuvered the model behind the counter, down the hall, and out the back. It fit nicely in the SUV. I dusted my hands off on my pants. "I should pay you for the stuff I used."

Simon shrugged. "Na. Think of it as payment for teaching me about Hollywood model set production." His smile dropped away. "And for making some of my dreams come true."

Were his dreams about us or working on the set? "You know, Anna asked if we could hire you."

Simon laughed as if I'd told a joke. "Right."

"I mean it. She did."

His humor fled into something serious. "I have a job." He peered toward the register and the back office. "This is a dream come true, too."

Now I wasn't sure if he was talking about the shop or Lydia. Both, maybe.

"Regardless, I should pay you for the supplies. It's for studio bookkeeping, and all that."

He twisted his face, but in the end, I had an itemized list of what I'd used, and the pricing. "Besides," I said. "You'll get this nifty check from the studio."

That brightened him up. "Really?"

I had to laugh, mostly because I still had the stub from the first check I'd gotten from a studio framed on my wall. "Really."

After all my supplies had been packed into my car, we got into his and headed to the studio lot. I let him drive, since I'd been driving my Mini too long to make the switch from little and nimble to large and lumbering. I'd probably take a side mirror off this behemoth if I were behind the wheel. He drove carefully, which I appreciated, since there was no time to repair the model.

The guard at the gate recognized me and with Simon on the books, Simon got his bright shiny temporary visitor tag, and the car got another. I directed him around the lot to my shop and had him park in my spot. When he turned off the car, he exhaled like he'd been holding his breath the entire time.

"What's up?"

Simon's self-deprecating laugh was followed by a shy smile. "I can't believe I'm here, that's all. Like— *Wolf's Landing*. And not the tourist tour."

Yup. Smitten. Hell, same thing had happened to me the first couple of times, and—like the other day—the amazement lingered. "Come on. Help me move the set into the trailer and then I'll give you a non-tourist tour."

We maneuvered the set inside. It had survived the trip fine and didn't need any touch-ups, thank God. "I should let Anna know it's here." I pulled out my phone and sent a quick text, since I wasn't sure if she was filming right now.

A second later my phone rang.

"Where are you? Where is it?" Anna's voice was brisk and the sounds of gravel crunching meant she was on the move.

"In my shop. We just got here."

"I'm on my way," she said, then the call ended.

I stared at my phone. "Change of plans. Anna's on her way to see the set."

"The director of *Wolf's Landing*?" Simon's voice squeaked at the end of that.

Poor guy. Starstruck already, and he hadn't *seen* any of the stars. "Pretty sure that's the name of the show, yeah."

He exhaled. "I'm being horrible."

"You're being cute." I waved his stricken look away. "It's all right. Everyone who isn't an actor goes through the same thing. And some of the actors do, as well."

He had a dubious expression, but that vanished into shock when the door banged open and Anna marched in.

She stopped in front of the grove and breathed out an audible sigh of relief. "Now, that's an impressive week's worth of work."

Hearing that was a booster shot straight to my pride. "Thanks."

Anna bent down and examined the set from a different angle. "I dare say, this is better than your original." She stood and turned to me. "Especially considering the issue with the altar."

Guess that was a silver lining in the whole stuntman crash— we caught an error that the fans would have roasted us over. "I had excellent help." I gestured to Simon, who stood gaping at Anna.

He had the wherewithal to close his mouth before she turned to him.

"Anna Maxwell." She held out her hand, and Simon took it. "Thank you for supporting Ian. I suspect becoming a workshop wasn't what you envisioned when you opened your store."

"Simon Derry." And wow, all hint that Simon had been a nervous wreck had vanished. "I was grateful to be able to lend a hand." There. Color touched his cheeks. Not much, but a little. "Bit of a dream to work on a real set."

She nodded, and examined the grove again. "It's almost a shame we're going to blow it up and burn it down."

Simon blanched. I'd never told him the final fate of all our hard work. I gave a light shrug. "Better than the forest."

"Especially since the EPA would close us down if we tried that." She turned to Simon. "Would you like to watch the shoot, since you helped make it happen?"

There was the kid in the candy store vibe. "Um. Yes? I mean—" He took a breath. "When is it?"

"Tomorrow night." Anna's phone buzzed and she whipped it out. "Yes? Oh hell, I'm on my way." She headed for the door, still talking into the phone, but paused for a moment. "Ian can fill you in on the filming." Then she was gone.

Simon blinked a few times. "Wow. She was nothing and everything like I thought she'd be."

Pretty much. I scratched the back of my head. "Can you come tomorrow night? They're filming at eight."

Simon nodded slowly. "It's comic book day tomorrow, but that only means an early morning. Evening should be fine. I'll double check with Lydia."

While I didn't want to suggest it, I felt I had to. "She can come as well, you know." I was almost certain Anna wouldn't object, given that Lydia had been the one to uncover the altar snafu. But this had been mostly mine and Simon's project. I wanted to keep it to ourselves.

Something in Simon's rueful expression told me he'd heard the hesitation in my voice. "I'll ask, but I suspect she'll want to stay at the shop."

Good. I liked Lydia a ton, and I was grateful she was sharing Simon, but this was ours. Mine and his. I wanted to have this memory once I couldn't have Simon anymore. Since we were alone, I took his hand and pulled him to me. "How about that tour?" Before he could answer, I claimed his mouth and breath and his lovely moan.

Such sweet surrender every time I kissed him. When I relented, his smile lit his face. "Sure," he said. "I'd love a tour."

That could wait a little bit. We had enough time for me to take those lips again, feel his heat against me, and his dick press against my own. We were both pretty hot and bothered when he murmured against my lips, "If this is a way to make me less nervous, you're doing a good job."

I laughed. It hadn't been. "I can't get enough of you, that's all. But if it worked . . ."

A grunt. "Well, now I'm turned on."

We didn't *exactly* have a no-sex-at-work rule. It was a *keep-it-discreet* rule. Still, going down on Simon here, right now seemed a bad plan, so I stepped back. "Sorry."

"No, you're not." His grin was sly. "But maybe save it until later?"

Yeah, he was right, though something about the conversation after Anna had left niggled my brain. I ushered Simon outside, and started down the path to one of the main outdoor sets. It was a recreation of part of Main Street—or rather our version of Main Street. No one was filming there right now. As we got closer, Simon muttered, "Holy shit. It looks exactly like it does on TV."

Well, at least from the front. "Let me show you inside one of the houses." We walked in and that's where you could see it wasn't real. Oh, there was furniture and some of the walls were decorated, but above, there was no ceiling, despite the steps that led up—only a walkway and racks of lights. Other areas were bare bones, since those angles would never be filmed. I explained it all to Simon, and he took it in. Up and down. Everywhere.

"Can I . . . touch . . . the couch?"

"I don't see any harm in that. Just don't move it."

His splendid fingers brushed over the fabric. "I can't believe I'm here."

"There's more to see." I took him around to one of the sound stages, but the light was on. "They're filming, so we can't go in."

"I didn't think they did tours on Wednesdays," a voice behind us said. We both turned and Simon went sheet white.

Carter Samuels stood there, holding a cup of coffee that definitely hadn't come from the crew service van. In costume and everything.

"They don't." I nodded to Carter. "Ian Meyers from props."

"Oh, the miniature guy! I heard about your set." He twisted his lips. "Bad break. Literally."

"Well, I fixed it, with a lot of help from town." I gestured to Simon. "So, I'm giving him a small tour."

Interest flickered in Carter's eyes, and he held out his hand to Simon. "Carter Samuels."

Simon was still pale and somewhat wide-eyed, but he took the offered hand and shook it. "Simon Derry." Soft, wondrous voice. He let go. All of Simon's movements were careful. Yeah, starstruck.

"He and his wife own the comic and games place in town," I said, as Carter took a sip of his coffee.

"End o' Earth." Simon's voice sounded stronger now. Less overwhelmed.

A nod from Carter. "I've wanted to go in. Miss comics something fierce, but I wouldn't know where to start with all the new stuff. I should research—" His wave encompassed the sound stage. "But I'm a little busy."

I saw the gears grind in Simon's head and watched the fear vanish—this topic he knew. "Well, if you tell me what you like, what you used to read, I can put together some books for you to try."

A raised eyebrow from Carter. "Like a comic book sommelier?"

"Exactly." Simon's smile was stunning.

I wanted to drag him behind the sound stage and have my way with him.

Carter rattled off a few titles and why he liked them, and Simon whipped out his phone and jotted them down. I was trying hard not to laugh. Starstruck to salesman in no time flat. My lovely sexy Simon.

That's when it hit me, a bit like a boom lowered too far. I was in love with Simon. Except I shouldn't—couldn't be. Not *love* love. Not long term. He was married—there wouldn't *be* a long-term anything. I swallowed the gnawing lump just before the sound-stage door opened. "Mr. Samuels, we're ready for you."

"That's their way of saying *get your ass in here*," Carter said. "Nice to meet you, Simon. I'll stop by your shop next time I'm in town." A quick nod to me. "Ian." Carter threw back the rest of the coffee, then tossed the cup in the trash as he headed into the sound stage.

Once the door had clanged shut, Simon deflated. "Wow. Did that really happen? Did I just meet Carter Samuels?"

"Yup." I stuffed my hands in my pockets and pushed away my churning thoughts. "And charmed the socks off him so he's gonna come in and buy comics from you."

Simon turned red. "Oh, shit." Then he laughed. "Lydia's gonna kill me."

I clapped him on the back. "Let me show you the rest of the place."

Took a good part of the day to walk around the lot. We watched Natalya working with the stunt actors, and meandered through a few of the other outdoor sets. One of the sound stages wasn't being used, and turned out that was the one where the sacred grove had been built.

"This is weird." Simon walked around the altar like the floor was covered in eggshells.

It *was* eerie to be here after working so hard on the miniature version. "It kinda is." But also wonderful. "You know, we did this." I gestured to the set. "In a week!"

His grin took my breath and did nothing to ease the worry in the back of my mind. But damn, I was going to enjoy Simon while I had him, so I let it go. We were both here, now.

He must have seen something in my stare, because a moment later, we were tangled in each other, hands in hair, and kissing like we hadn't made out in my shop. "We shouldn't do this here," I said, between taking his mouth and making him moan.

"Probably not." He was breathless and hard against me.

"Because what I want is to fuck you on that altar, and I would get in so much shit if I did that." I cupped his package and he rocked into my palm.

Simon groaned. "Killjoy."

Oh hell, that only intensified my desire to bend him over the altar. But logistically—and professionally—so not a good idea. "Let's go back to my shop." At least there I could lock the door.

We hurried out of the sound stage. Simon seemed determined and sexy and vulnerable all at once and I wanted him so bad. If I focused on *now*, then I wouldn't have to think about the future and the churn of my emotions. Lust was so much easier to unravel.

So, of course on the way back to my shop, we ran into Anna. She was walking with the assistant art director and the head of pyrotechnics. "Ian. *There* you are. Come with me."

I checked my phone, and there was a text I hadn't felt. Shit. "Sorry, I didn't—" But Anna was already marching off. I started after her, but realized Simon wasn't at my side. "Si."

"I—" He seemed spooked.

I got it—we'd been about to fuck, and now Hollywood had descended in all its non-starry glory. "Hey, come on. I can't leave you and I gotta go." I tugged at his arm. "Plus, I think you'll like this."

His lips twisted, but he followed. Thank God.

We had to jog to catch up. "I didn't see your text," I said to Anna.

She flipped her wrist as if to brush the thought away. "It's fine."

We ended up back in my shop, gathered around the model. The art director grunted. "You were right. Better than before." He eyed me. "We should put you under pressure more often."

I must have blanched, because he got that gruff grin that let me know he was joking.

Except Simon hadn't seen it, since he strode forward. "Hey, he worked damn hard for you people. Give him some credit."

Anger had tinged his face red. I tried to stop him. "Si . . ." Now was not the time to go protective on me.

"No, I mean— You were there before opening every fucking day and worked straight through until after closing and we had to pry you away for lunch and dinner."

I tried again, heat in my cheeks. "Si—it's okay."

"They ought to appreciate how lucky they are to have you." He crossed his arms and leveled his gaze at me. "That's all."

The shop fell silent. Then Anna huffed a laugh. "We do, believe me." She studied Simon. "Your passionate defense of his talent and work ethic, notwithstanding."

The art director, who was normally pretty damn crotchety, wore the same smile as before. "I was poking fun."

"Oh," Simon said, and the anger slipped straight into horror. "I— Uh . . ." He loosened his arms.

The head of pyrotechnics merely seemed puzzled as she took Simon in.

Anna nodded at Simon. "Mr. Derry helped Ian during the week. And noted the problem with the altar."

"That was my wife," Simon said. "She's better with the details. I'm—" He waved his hand.

"Plot focused?" She grinned.

Simon scrubbed the back of his head. "Something like that."

Suddenly, I realized Anna was enjoying herself. Not at putting Simon on edge, but with the whole event. Like somehow the destroyed miniature set had made her week. "He paints better than I do," I blurted out.

"I—"

"Do. And I'm the pro, so there."

That quieted Simon down. He gave a helpless shrug.

"Wouldn't happen to need a job?" That came from the art director.

Simon started and stared. "Wow. I own a comic book store. I can't. But I would, if I could." He glanced at me. "You weren't kidding."

"No," I said. "I wasn't." About anything.

Anna raised an eyebrow at me, but after a moment turned back to the model. "We should figure out how we want to blow this up."

I pulled Simon closer so he could overhear the discussion, and after a few moments of listening, he relaxed and leaned in. Most of it was jargon, but he remained enwrapped. When they finished and had a plan, they all stepped back from the model.

The pyrotechnics head rubbed her hands together. "I'll have my people come over and start rigging it here, unless Ian objects. This is the closest building to the shoot."

"My trailer is your trailer," I said.

"Good." Anna glanced at her watch. "Break time's over for me." Her shoes clipped a fast pace out of the trailer. She was followed by the head of pyrotechnics, but the art director lingered.

He pulled out a card and handed it to Simon. "Look, if you have any free time— If Ian says you're good, then you're good." Then he too, was gone.

Simon stared at the business card and flipped it over in his hands. "Shit."

"Hey, you okay?" I asked. He seemed a little green around the edges.

Simon fingered the card. "I want this. But I love End o' Earth." He took his wallet from his back pocket and slipped the little rectangle inside. "I need to think about it."

I could imagine. I'd not had anything on my plate when *Wolf's Landing* had called, but I knew friends who'd agonized over their career choices. And this was Simon's store we were talking about—not any old job. "If you want to talk it over . . ."

He took a breath. "Not right now." His smile was small, but real. "Have I told you lately that you're amazing?"

Warmth flooded through me. Not lust—no, this wasn't hot passion but a mix of heady happiness and flickering hope. "Not in the last few hours."

A bigger grin, and he pulled me to him and wrapped his arms around me. Comfortable. Familiar. "Ian Meyers," he said. "You're absolutely *amazing*."

My chest hurt and the corners of my eyes. No one, not a single one of my lovers, had ever said those words, not the way Simon had. He *believed* it. No lie in his soulful blue eyes. "Thanks." My voice was a mess. "You are, too."

A lackluster response, but maybe he didn't care because he held me tighter. No kissing, no groping. This wasn't the frenzy of lust we'd had before.

Nope. This was love, and I was doomed.

Simon drove me back to End o' Earth and we were both damn quiet in the car. My mind churned, flitting from lust to fear to anger at myself for having gotten into this mess, to sadness because eventually I was going to lose Simon. I'd never had him, to begin with. From the very start, he'd been on loan. I couldn't be mad at Lydia. Hell, if she'd been a guy, I'd have suggested a threesome.

Though in some ways we'd done that, even if we hadn't all been in bed together. I scrubbed my face.

"You okay?" Simon spoke softly, his concern so evident, so loving.

I should say something. Maybe break it off now, but I didn't want to. I hated lying. Did anyway. "Yeah. Tired. I think the past week is catching up with me." Well, that was *partly* true. My stomach twisted.

He didn't say anything and remained focused on the road. Soon, we were parking behind End o' Earth. He shut off the car, and we both climbed out. I met his gaze and the worry was still there. I hoped he didn't ask how I was again, because when he looked at me like that, I couldn't lie.

"Gonna come in?" He nodded toward the shop.

This time, the truth came out. "No. I think I need to go home and decompress for a while."

He studied me. Maybe he saw through to the despair I was trying to hide. "Do you want me there at the shoot tomorrow?" Those were the words he used, but I swear his tone said, *"Are you breaking up with me?"*

My lungs and head ached. I had no way to process the pain and hurt buried in Simon's voice, except I *knew* I didn't want him upset. "Of course I do!" I wanted Simon to see the end result of all his hard work. He deserved to be there. I took his hands in mine. "Please come tomorrow."

His smile undid me every time. This one was no exception. That flip in my chest, that zing down my limbs. He gave my hands a squeeze. "Pick me up at the shop? Still need to check with Lydia, but I'm a hundred-percent sure it's fine."

"Of course I can pick you up." My fear slid away. If I stared at Simon, at those deep eyes and that lovely grin, all the what-ifs vanished. "Is seven okay? It's a busy day for you."

"Oh yeah. All the hard work's done in the morning. By evening, the new comic rush has petered out."

"Seven it is." I stepped in and kissed him. Like always, the way he opened to me, those little noises, the warmth of him set my heart racing and lit my nerves. Simon wrapped his arms around me. We fit together like two puzzle pieces, his body molding to mine. Perfect. Always so right—until we parted—which we always did.

Simon stepped back. "I'll see you tomorrow."

It was a ridiculous thing to do, but I grabbed his hand and kissed his knuckles like some kind of weird-ass knight. "Tomorrow."

I didn't think his grin could get wider, but I was wrong. Our hands slipped apart, and he backed toward the door to End o' Earth. I gave him a wave and headed around front to my Mini, still stuffed with my supplies and tools. I should take them back to work.

Wolf's Landing. My job.

But End o' Earth had started to feel like home, just like Simon had started to feel like my boyfriend, not a friend with benefits.

My head was too screwed up, so all I did was head back to my place. Maybe I needed sleep. I hoped I only needed some rest.

How did you tell a married man you were falling in love with him? And what would that mean for him? For Lydia? For me?

Yeah. I was fucked. I didn't know what to do.

CHAPTER TWELVE

SIMON

Around six-thirty in the evening, I headed in back to check on Lydia. Dexy had the register and the burst of new comic day traffic had died down. Had people stopping in and asking about models too. Probably the after-effect of having an honest-to-God Wolf's Landing prop sitting in the shop. Was good to see other folks interested in that side of the business besides the hard core gamers and model builders.

Lydia sat at her computer, her drafting tablet resting at an angle as she drew. On the screen was another one of her fandom creations—this one Wolf's Landing. After this week, it was all on our minds. This was a silver wolf running beneath the moon, with the two men silhouetted against the wolf's bright fur: Gabriel Hanford and Max Fuhrman. "Oh, now that's nice!" I stopped right behind her chair.

"Thanks!" She leaned her head back and beamed up at me. "New composition. Like one of those old '80s-style wolf T-shirts."

I knew the ones she meant, though the '80s were slightly before our time. We'd been born by then, but missed out on the era. Lydia loved the retro stuff, however. All of the music and movies. "This is better. Streamlined. Modern."

"Not too cheesy?"

I laughed and kissed her forehead. "You never do cheese."

When I pulled back, she glanced at the time. "You getting ready to head out?"

"Yeah." Off to watch the model I'd help build get destroyed for the greater good of *Wolf's Landing*. And to see Ian. I was concerned about the latter.

Lydia knew my moods. She put her pen down and rotated her chair. "Is something wrong?"

I fiddled with my watch. "I think something's bothering Ian. But I don't know what."

She chewed on her lip. "I'm assuming you asked."

"I did. He said he was fine." And then he'd kissed me. "And then he *was* fine, but . . ."

She caught my hand. "Si. I've seen the way Ian looks at you. I don't think you have anything to worry about."

Heat to my face. "I hate this part, you know." The awkward fumbling stage when all the emotions come out.

She gave my hand a squeeze. "You're in love with him."

Yeah, there it was. "I'm in love with him. He's—" I gave a little sigh. "Well, you know."

She laughed. "I do."

"I love you. More than ever."

"Know that too." She stood and wrapped her arms around my neck. "You're not very good about hiding your emotions."

Heart on my sleeve. Pretty much always. "What if—"

She pressed a finger to my lips. "None of that. You go have fun with Ian and see your work set on fire. Spend the night and connect. Tell him how you feel."

"Okay." I spoke around her digit. Seemed like a reasonable plan. Except for the part where I was sure Ian would tell me he wasn't interested in anything as complex as a long-term partnership in a poly arrangement.

Lydia shook her head, and replaced her finger with her lips. A warm, sweet kiss. "Go. Because if I know Ian, he's early and already waiting for you."

My heart flipped, both because of the thought of Ian already being here, and that Lydia loved me enough to push me out the door when I was being weird and insecure. I went, and she had guessed correctly. Ian stood in front of the new comics racks, peering at the titles and pulling at his shirt sleeve as if he didn't know what to do with his hands.

I gave Dexy a nod and rounded the counter to join Ian. His smile as I approached was shy—hesitant—and all my fears poured in.

He gestured to the rack. "I have no idea where to start again."

"You know, I could be your comic sommelier, too."

His shyness vanished. "You'd do that for me?"

God, if we hadn't been standing in the middle of the shop, I would have kissed his expression right off those lips. "Of course I would!" For him above anyone else.

"I'll have to think about the comics I liked way back when. I read a lot, but some were closer to my tastes than others."

Yeah, that was pretty much true of everything. "You get older, and there's less time to separate the wheat out." That's where I could help. Tailor a sampling to a person's—to Ian's—tastes.

"Exactly." Ian pulled out his phone and checked the time. "We should get going. Anna won't hold the shoot for us, even if we did make the set."

"Lead on."

We took his Mini and he sped along the winding roads almost like he'd lived here forever, but then he must have driven this path too many times to count. Soon enough, we were pulling up to the gate, where I got a visitor's pass. Ian drove in, parked in his spot, and we got out. It was still light—summertime after all—but the sun had nearly set and evening was creeping across the sky as we headed toward where Ian said they'd be shooting.

"They can use filters to make it seem like night, but Anna likes to use as much natural ambiance as possible with these kinds of shots."

"Hence the rain in the episodes."

Ian barked a laugh. "Well, that's because this *is* the Olympic Peninsula. If they'd stayed in Hollywood to do *Wolf's Landing*, we'd have used up all the water in California while filming the first season."

Someone nearby chuckled, and I jumped. Then started again, because Hunter Easton was grinning at us. Holy shit. Hunter lived here, and I should've been used to seeing him since it wasn't like he was a hermit. Came into town with his husband, like everyone else, but I still got tongue-tied around the guy.

Hunter shrugged. "Be glad it isn't raining tonight."

"Oh," Ian said, as if running into Hunter Easton was normal, "believe me, I am."

Up ahead, there were people milling about a clearing in the woods, setting up a bunch of equipment. Toward one end sat our model on a stand. A woman crouched beneath it, playing with some wiring, and a guy stood nearby with a big fire extinguisher.

Maybe that's what made it real to me, the dude getting ready to put a fire out. My pulse ticked up and I stared at the nozzle on the extinguisher. "They're really going to burn it down." All that work.

Ian gripped my shoulder, his fingers warm and familiar, and his thumb stroked against my shirt. "Yup. It'll be okay. And it's gonna look great on the screen."

Hunter rubbed his hands together. "I've been waiting to see this happen for ages." He gave me a glance, his gaze zeroing in on my visitor's badge, and held out his hand. "I'm Hunter Easton, by the way."

"I know." I choked out, and somehow I shook his hand. Unlike with Carter Samuels, my throat closed up completely and my mind went blank. What do you say to a guy who wrote the books you love and got lost in? He *made* Wolf's Landing.

Hunter raised an eyebrow, obviously expecting conversation. Probably my name, but I couldn't get it out.

Ian came to my rescue, thank God. "This is Simon Derry. He helped me build the miniature set, Mr. Easton." His hand didn't leave my shoulder, and his thumb continued its soothing circles.

"Call me Hunter, please." He offered Ian his hand. "You're Ian . . . oh damn it. M-something. We met at the holiday party, but my mind's a sieve."

"Meyers." There was a wonder in Ian's voice I'd never heard before. "I'm surprised you remembered." A touch of red in his cheeks. "I mean, you had to have met a billion people that night."

He chuckled. "A couple hundred. But you had an interesting job." He gestured at the set. "Tell me about it."

I trailed along, still tripping in the clouds, as Ian showed Hunter the set and launched into the story of its destruction and rebirth, including how I'd helped him.

Hunter glanced at me. "So wait, you own that comic book shop next to Howling Moon?"

Oh, is that how we were known? A touch of anger unstopped my brain. "End o' Earth, yes." I cleared my throat of its gravel. "And we were there before Howling Moon moved in."

"Si . . ." Ian's eyes got wide, but Hunter laughed.

"It's fine." He had a sly smile. "Little rivalry there?"

I shrugged. "No, not on our part. We have limits on what Wolf's Landing stuff we can carry, though."

Like Ian, Hunter seemed taken aback by that. "Really?"

"Yup." I tried not to let my laugh get bitter. "Howling Moon's owner almost laid claim to Ian's set, because she thought I was building official merchandise."

"Well," Ian said, "to be fair, it *is* an official reproduction. But not *at all* merchandise."

Hunter rubbed his chin, and I couldn't read his expression. "So what Wolf's Landing stuff do you carry?"

"Comics and books."

"That's it?" He lowered his hand. "Not the collectable card game?"

I winced. "No—it caused too many issues." Mostly Marlina giving us grief over selling it, though we could.

"Wait," Ian said. "Are you allowed to carry it?"

"Technically, yes." They carried it at the big box stores after all. And in supermarkets. "But sometimes you learn that the best thing isn't always what you want to do."

Hunter had his unreadable face on again. "*Obviously* not on your part," he muttered.

I wanted to ask him what he meant, but Anna breezed into the middle of the set, rapidly firing orders to clear the scene and get everyone where they belonged. Even Hunter moved, obviously not ready to catch hell from *Wolf's Landing*'s director.

I hadn't realized how much jargon was in the film business, because half of what Anna said made no sense. Eventually, the cameras were positioned correctly and the lighting was right and she stepped back from the monitors she was viewing, then peered through all of the cameras themselves.

"Do you see how low the cameras are?" Ian whispered into my ear.

I nodded slowly. "They're level with the set." I kept my voice low. Other people were conversing as quietly as we were.

"Almost. They're at what would be eye-level. Trick is, the forest behind—the real trees and ferns—also seem like they're part of the model now."

I pulled back and peered at him. "You're shitting me." Not as quiet.

"No," Hunter said. "It's how it works. Optical illusion."

"Gentlemen?" Anna crossed her arms and stared at us.

"Sorry," Ian said. "I was explaining the angles to Simon."

Now *everyone* was staring at me. Great. Maybe the earth would swallow me up like that guy in Season Four. Anna's stance softened though, and she beckoned me to join her. Both Ian and Hunter nudged me, so I went.

She led me to a bank of monitors that had been set up under something similar to a camping popup. "These are all the camera angles. They show what the cameras see."

And there it was, the sacred grove in the middle of the woods, looking exactly like it had the last time I'd seen it on the show. Except I was standing in the middle of a clearing, surrounded by equipment, and I knew that the set was a model. "That's . . . It looks like the real thing."

"It *is* the real thing," Anna said. "You were always working on an actual Wolf's Landing set." Her words were mild, which made me meet her gaze, because that was so not the image of Anna Maxwell that I was used to. "It's magic, but it's also real. And you helped Ian build it."

I stared over at the miniature on its stand and my head felt stretched thin. "This doesn't happen all that often, does it?"

"Random people from town finding themselves mixed up in our crazy Wolf's Landing life?"

I suppose I was a random townie. "Well, helping out with sets and shit."

Her chuckle was more in line with the hard-ass director I'd seen before. "You'd be surprised." She nodded over to Ian and Hunter. "If you wouldn't mind, I do have a set to destroy."

I headed back. They likely only got one take on something like this. "Um. What happens if—"

Ian leapt at me and covered my mouth. "Don't. Don't say it. The shoot will go off without a hitch."

I couldn't help pressing my tongue against his fingers. His breath caught and there was the flutter of eyelids that meant I'd turned him on a little. He took his hand away. "Later," he muttered under his breath.

"Picture's up!" I didn't know who yelled it, but everyone shifted to watch the model and Ian pulled me close. "Here we go . . ."

I hadn't realized all the stuff they show in movies about films was real, but we got *Roll Camera* and *Camera Speed* and the guy with one of those boards that claps down—though after he read out the scene, he didn't snap it shut—his hand was in the way.

"Watch the model," Ian said into my ear.

"Set."

"Action!" Anna's voice.

At first, there was nothing, then a sizzling pop and the whole set exploded spectacularly, with sparks and flames and fire licking everywhere. Elation and sadness rammed into me. There were the torches I'd painted and the moss I'd glued on and the trees I'd helped piece back together—all gone.

"Cut!" Anna yelled. "Print it."

The guy with the extinguisher hosed down the burning set and a collective sigh moved over the crew. A few people clapped. I must have had quite the expression, because Ian stroked the back of my neck. "It's all right. This is what we built it for."

"But—" I hadn't expected the anguish of loss, the stab of hurt when I peered at the ruined remains. "How do you do this all the time?"

Ian pressed the side of his body against mine and rubbed between my shoulder blades. "I don't. A lot of the sets aren't blown up, but they are taken apart eventually. I'll need pieces elsewhere, or there's no space or—any number of reasons." He gave my arm a squeeze with his other hand, and I realized he was holding me because I was shaking. "It's all ephemeral. Except for what ends up in the final product on film."

I didn't like *ephemeral*. I wanted things that lasted. "I don't think I could do that, watch the work . . . vanish."

"But it doesn't." Ian let me go enough to walk me toward Anna's tent of monitors. "Excuse me, Anna?"

She turned and focused on me and whatever Ian had been going to ask was waved away. "Come take a look at the scene," she said.

I watched it again, from multiple angles; the sacred grove being destroyed, just as it had been in the books.

"In less than a year, a whole hell of a lot of people will gasp and cry at that," Anna said, "because you helped make it possible to put it on their screen."

"And they'll buy the Blu-ray," Hunter said, "and make gifs that will play forever." He'd come up next to us.

I choked out a laugh. "We're gonna be a meme!"

Hunter's smile turned serious. "How'd you feel when I destroyed the grove in the book?"

I thought back to that. "Horrible. I mean, you'd been hinting all along." I sighed and peered at the debris they were now dumping into a big trash bin on wheels. "I get attached to stuff."

"Everyone does." Hunter got this weird smile. "We writers like to exploit that and make you suffer for it."

Anna snorted. "Writers are sadists."

"So are directors," Hunter said. "That's why we get along so well."

Anna gave him a look that would have scared me to death, but only made Hunter grin. "Anyone have any questions?" Her voice said she expected all of us to say no, but one question still prodded at my mind.

"I do."

They all stared at me, and Ian gave my arm a gentle squeeze.

"That guy with the clapper-board thing—"

"Slate," Anna said.

"It's supposed to snap shut, right?" I mimicked the motion. "But he had his hand in the way. Why?"

Anna blinked. "Oh!" Obviously, that was not a question she'd been expecting. "To indicate we weren't rolling sound. The clap of the slate is to sync the sound in production, but with this, we'll mix the explosions and music in later."

That made sense. "Thanks. I didn't mean to hit you with film 101 questions."

She rubbed her forehead. "That was somewhat refreshing. But if you'll excuse me—"

Ian pulled me away. "Thanks for everything, Anna."

Hunter wandered off toward another group of people, and Ian led me down the path back toward the car.

"I'm sorry I'm such a fucking dork," I said. "I shouldn't have gotten upset or asked stupid questions." Probably embarrassed the hell out of him.

He shot me a smile that melted my bones. "You're not. And you didn't." He was still holding onto my arm and his grip tightened marginally. "If I didn't know that we'd have people tromping up this path behind us, I'd do something very wicked and improper to you up against a tree."

I gulped.

"But we kinda have a no-sex-at-work rule, *especially* where people can see you."

Oh, yeah. Ian wanted me. Just like Lydia had said. "I have a solution for that." We reached the parking lot where Ian's Mini was sitting.

"Yeah?" He was breathless and close and still had a grip on my arm.

"We could go to your place, and you could have your way with me." After seeing our work blown up for the greater good, what I wanted most was oblivion, heat, and the tactile knowledge that someone gave a damn about me. I knew it logically, but sometimes, I needed more than words.

Ian's hold on me loosened, but his gaze held me like a collar. "Get in the car, Simon."

CHAPTER THIRTEEN

IAN

There was something about a vulnerable, submissive man that turned me inside out. That it was Simon tripped up my heart and mind. I drove down the darkened road toward my apartment, my hand on his over the emergency brake handle when I didn't have to shift gears.

He'd been pretty close to tears after watching our miniature get blown up, even though that's exactly what it had been built for. Couldn't blame him. Intense work for an intense end, and I'd gone home a wreck the first time one of the sets I'd painstakingly built to perfection had been destroyed for the sake of a film. Sorrow still lingered on his features when I glanced his way and light from a stray streetlamp shone on his face.

I wanted to take the pain away, replace it with pleasure and obedience and love. I knew I could get from him two of those—the third he already had from his wife. No matter how much I cared for Simon, how much I loved him, I would never have the permanence he had with Lydia. Oh, I could love him for the long run—I was sure of that—but he'd given that commitment to someone else. *We'd* never have it. On that drive to my place though, I let myself believe we could.

I parked, we got out, and I beckoned Simon to me. He came, and though all the light we had was from a dim bulb above the garage door, I saw the focus in his eyes and how he parted his lips. He was giving every bit of himself to me tonight.

I drew him in and kissed him, a sweet press of lips followed by a taste that could only be described as wanton. I claimed his mouth and pulled his body tight against my own.

I loved his moans and the way his desire trembled through his body. Hard muscles, harder dick, but so soft and pliable. My Simon. I relented, and he was breathless. "Upstairs," I ordered.

He went first, and after we reached the top, I pressed him against the door while I unlocked it. "Let's see how many of my fantasies I can fulfill tonight."

Simon sighed, a sound of sheer surrender. When the door opened, he practically fell into my apartment, but my arm around his waist kept him standing. Soon after, my mouth was on his again, where it belonged, and my fingers bunched his shirt. I hauled Simon across the room until we were at my bed. "I want you to stand here for now. Nothing more." I spoke against his lips. "No sounds, no roaming hands, only you here, for me."

He met my gaze and nodded slightly.

A thumb against his lips got me a flicker of eyelashes and what looked to be a swallowed moan. Control and obedience. We'd see how long that lasted. I traced fingers down his neck to his collar and worked the first button of his shirt. Then the next, and another, until his button-down hung open, exposing his sweet flesh to my hands and mouth. I pushed the shirt off and freed his hands from the cuffs so that it fell to the floor. A press of my palm over his pecs made Simon waver. When I caressed, then pinched his nipple, he bit his lip and closed his eyes, but he didn't move much, and he didn't utter a sound aside from his quickening breath.

"You know, this makes me wonder if you were ever in a formal D/s relationship." I met his gaze, but he gave nothing away. "You're so obedient. Too bad I'm going to break you in the end."

A touch of a smile at that, as if he took my words as a challenge.

We'd see. I stepped in close, my hands on the top of his jeans, my lips grazing against his. "I'm gonna make you scream, Simon."

His Adam's apple bobbed as he swallowed. I unbuttoned and unzipped his jeans, and pushed them down over his hips until they dropped around his legs.

A twitch of his arms and legs, as if he wanted to help the slide, to give me access, to thrust against me. The heat from his skin was delicious, as were his shallow huffs of breath. Cracks in that passive face, with so much lust and desire spilling out from beneath the stillness.

Passionate, hard, needy Simon. All mine. I'd savor every breath and inch and moan. I'd break him until I had him all, until I consumed him and he stole my heart and we burned like the model we'd made.

His cock was tenting his underwear and brushed against my thigh. I stroked the flesh above the elastic band before slipping my hands inside to push those off his body too.

Still not a murmur. His breath caught, but no sound, not even when I held his hips and rocked against him.

How he fought to stay silent was a fucking masterpiece. His flush face, his eyes screwed shut, and his teeth pressing indents into his bottom lip. Huffs of breath through his nose, and every muscle trembling.

"You know I'll win in the end, Si. Might as well give up."

He opened both mouth and eyes at that. A smile formed. He was clearly enjoying the game, thinking he was clever and capable, which he was.

Simon was perfect, but I was an evil bastard at heart. I pressed a kiss to his chest, then slid down his body until I was on my knees before him. When I gazed up, I knew I'd won.

Shock, elation, and resignation on Simon's face. Oh, he'd continue to fight, and did, as I took the head of his cock between my lips and tasted the salt in his slit. His thighs trembled when I licked his length and mouthed his balls. Little catches of breath each time I rolled a nut in my mouth. I teased his taint with my fingers and worked lips and tongue back up his length, then swallowed him as deep as I could before I drew back and took him down my throat again.

Simon moaned, low and guttural, as if I'd drawn the sound out of his soul. His fingers caught in my hair and he rocked into my mouth. "Oh fuck, Ian."

I had him, but I'd give him this. We found a rhythm, him pressing in and me savoring the taste and texture of his dick until both of us were moaning and my scalp was tight with pain and tension from Simon gripping my hair. I'd make him pay later, but for now it was enough to hear his groans and feel the quaking in his legs as I brought him closer and closer to ecstasy. My only warning was the thickening of his dick before he was shouting out and shooting ribbons of semen down my throat. Like he had that night behind End o' Earth, I swallowed every drop. My first and last full taste of Simon Derry.

He loosened his grip on my hair and grunted when I sucked him clean. "I'm going to pay for that, aren't I?" He didn't even seem mildly concerned.

Didn't know exactly what I'd do, but yes. "Sit down on the bed."

He did and I scooped up his clothing and tossed the bundle on a nearby chair, then stalked over to where he was sitting. "What's the opposite of Simon says?" I nudged his knees apart and stepped in until I hovered over him.

He craned his neck back to meet my gaze. I adored the length of his body and his unashamed nakedness. "Simon does exactly as *you* say?" Amusement in his voice.

I cupped his chin with one hand, and toyed with a nipple with the other. "Only you didn't." I pinched the nub of flesh between my fingers. Simon gave a sharp intake of breath. "Did you?"

"No," he whispered.

I leaned down and took those lips before grinding his nipple between my fingers. Oh, how I loved the struggle and the taste of Simon. He squirmed against me, his throaty groans music as he surrendered his mouth. When I relented, he sucked in a breath and looked down, his cheeks flaming and his dick hard again. He'd grabbed hold of my shirt. I was sure that was what kept him from tumbling onto his back, especially given the way I leaned into him.

"You like pain." At least on some level, given his reaction.

Simon wet his swollen lips with his tongue. "No, and yes." He gazed up, his eyes wide and beautiful. "Pain and I have a complicated relationship."

"Don't we all." I hadn't let go of his chin, and stroked my thumb against his jaw. "You did say anything, once upon a time . . . that still true?"

"Wasn't too long ago." Simon's smile was slight. "And yes, I meant what I said."

That was a heap of faith to hand me. "You *have* done this before."

A chuckle. "Once upon a time." The smile fell into seriousness. "I trust you, Ian."

"How do you feel about gags?" There'd been one in their guest room drawer.

His pulse quickened under my grip and his fingers shifted against my shirt. "I have a complicated relationship with gags, too."

Those words sent heat into my blood. "Good." I enjoyed his obedience, his discomfort, and how he gave me his body. "Lay yourself out on the bed."

He closed his eyes and let himself drop to the mattress. While I undressed, Simon repositioned himself neutrally on the comforter. No assumptions that I would tie him up, but none that I wouldn't either. I stroked myself as I contemplated Simon's limbs and his surrender. He'd loved the sash and the cuffs. I loved him in strips of leather. What to use was an easy enough decision to make. I got what I needed and returned to the bed.

He eyed the cuffs with interest, but when his gaze fell on the gag, he tensed. Not much, but it was enough to send a little bolt of desire through me.

"It has a dildo." His voice was breathless.

I dropped the cuffs next to Simon and turned the gag over in my hands. "It does." Not a very large one. It wasn't meant for anal penetration, after all. The idea was to fill the mouth, not to choke the wearer—much like a ball gag, but . . . specific.

Simon swallowed.

"I want you to understand that your lovely mouth belongs to me tonight. Since I can't fuck you in both your holes at the same time—" I held up the gag.

"Okay." Trepidation there.

"You can say no, Si."

Annoyance crept into his expression. "Yeah, I know. I would if I wanted to." He paused. "I know the risks. I'm consenting."

Yes, he'd played before. Maybe not in a *what's your safeword* type scene, but there were other ways to do kink. "Just checking. You need some kind of signal if things get too much?"

He rolled his eyes. "You'll know, believe me."

Well, that was that.

I gagged him first, slipping the end with the little cock between his lips and buckling the straps around his head so it was secure. His mouth and throat worked against the intrusion, but his breathing was fine—if a little fast. He shifted on the bed, his hips rocking ever so slightly. He might not like the gag, but it obviously turned him on. I wrapped a hand around his shaft and stroked a few times. "Good?"

Simon moaned and gave me a look that was both a *yes* and an *are you fucking kidding me*? He thrust his dick into my hand, and I laughed. I let up on his cock—he'd come once already. The next time, I wanted to be buried to the hilt inside him, with his tears on those cheeks. Pain and pleasure.

I took each wrist and kissed his pulse points before buckling leather over them. Simon's chest rose and fell, his grunts muffled by the gag and his limbs shaking under my touch. Once they were circled with leather, I pulled his arms up to the headboard, clipped the cuffs together, and used my sash to tie him down to the slats.

Simon moaned, and I stroked his throat. "I'm tempted to tie your ankles up there, too."

I'd never seen his eyes go wider than at that moment. White around his pale blue irises. Could be fear, could be desire. Either way was fine with me. "I suppose we could see if you're flexible enough."

Simon whimpered as I wrapped the cuffs around his ankles. His moans were exquisite when I folded his legs up above his head. Yes, indeed, he was flexible enough and vibrating as I tied him down.

Such a lovely view, Simon trussed up and exposed for me. Eyes closed and mouth working against the dick I'd shoved into it. I savored every tremble and groan as he waited for whatever I wanted to do next. I ached to bury myself in him, take all that I could and bring him off harder than I'd managed before—and I was done with waiting. Some lube on my fingers opened him enough. I rolled a condom on my dick and slicked myself up, then knelt over Simon, the head of my cock pressed against his ass. "Want this?"

Don't know how he managed it, but he rocked up and took me inside a fraction. My breath caught, and he seemed to smile around the gag, as if to say *Simon says fuck me*.

Two could play that game. I pulled back and slammed into him as far as I could. Hot, tight, and deep. Simon moaned and struggled and rolled his head back against the pillow. "My bed, my rules, Simon."

His reply was the sexiest, deepest moan I'd ever heard in all my times fucking men. It pulsed through me and played over every part of my body. I drove forward over and over to hear that sound again. My hands gripped Simon's shoulders and our bodies rammed together. The tears I wanted rolled from the corners of his eyes, but he met my strokes and my gaze. Both demanded more from me, so I gave Simon everything I had, taking him hard and fast. Making him moan and cry and tremble. All my breath. All my soul.

Unfair that I had only this night, but with how deep I'd fallen, I couldn't go beyond that.

I wanted too much of Simon. Not only nights of passion, and the days of friendship. I wanted—needed love. A house. Cats. All of what he *already had* with someone else.

I wished to God I was jealous of Lydia, but I *wasn't*. They were twined in my mind. Losing Simon meant losing her too, and I choked at the thought. But what choice did I have?

Though I burned with desire, I ached with sadness. Pain and pleasure indeed.

Cuffed to my headboard, moaning around my gag, Simon thrust himself on my cock as I fucked him within an inch of his life. When my balls tightened and sparks threatened to blur my vision, I gripped Simon's dick and jerked him off until he yelled around the intruding gag and pumped his jizz over my hand and his chest. That sight, his abandonment, and how he tightened around me stole the last of my vision. I rammed into his ass and spilled my balls until I'd emptied myself. I held myself there, deep inside him, desperate to remember every movement and breath and the glorious seconds that hung between us where no cares in the world existed.

Simon's whimper was joy. He pressed his body against mine and we lingered, joined as one.

Time has a way of marching on, though. Before I softened too much, I pulled out and tossed the condom, then dragged myself up near Simon's head and freed his ankles, carefully lowering each leg back down to the mattress.

His eyes flicked closed for a moment and he sighed.

Before I unbuckled the gag, I kissed away the tears on his face, tasting a different kind of salt. When I freed his mouth, his lips were swollen, red, and wet with spit. Simon took several deep breaths and

I let him rest before I trapped him again, this time with my lips and tongue.

He uttered a throaty groan, then relaxed and opened to me. We kissed lazily, and I traced my hand over his chest, memorizing the texture of his flesh and the contours of muscles and bones.

My Simon, my joy, at least for a little longer.

When we broke apart, I reached up and freed his wrists from the headboard. A moment later, he caught my head between his hands and kissed me. A gentle, sweet and loving taste that tumbled my heart in ways his submission and ecstasy never could.

"Thank you." He stroked my hair and held my gaze. "For everything. For coming into my life. For the model, the shooting. The sex. This, right now."

God, my chest ached like it was full of burning stones. I laid my head down on Simon's torso so he couldn't see my expression. Maybe he wouldn't guess that the choking in my voice was from despair and heartache. "You're most welcome."

"I love you," he whispered, and I wanted to cry.

"Love you too." Because I did, and that was the problem. What I needed from Simon and what he could give me were two very different things. "Simon, I—" I didn't know how to end this. Not gracefully, not kindly. I was so fucking confused because my heart needed what I knew it couldn't have. I longed for forever, but I only had now. Tonight. "I'm glad you're here."

I closed my eyes and listened to Simon's heartbeat. I didn't think he was lying when he said he loved me, but I knew that he couldn't love me like I wanted. Long-term, committed love. A true partner.

In the end, I knew what I had to do.

I woke and found myself alone in my bed, and cold panic washed through me until I spotted Simon over by my fantasy sculptures. He'd put on his underwear, but nothing else. Lovely. I'd never tire of looking at him.

The smell of coffee filled the apartment, and I rolled onto my back to stare at the ceiling. Guilt gnawed at me. I'd gotten spooked by the empty bed, and yet I was about to walk away from the man I'd fallen for. But I didn't know how else to do this. Simon had a full life. I wanted to be a significant part of it, not a side fling.

He must have heard or seen me moving—the drawback to a no-bedroom apartment. "Do you want some coffee?"

For someone I'd fucked into oblivion last night, he sounded way too chipper and awake. "Yeah." I struggled to sitting, my head a mess and pain pounding against my temples. If I hadn't known better, I'd have said I had a hangover.

Drunk on Simon. Hopefully, the coffee would help.

He handed me a mug and sat on the edge of the bed. "I didn't want to wake you. But I needed some caffeine."

I breathed in the aroma from the mug and took a sip. The headache remained, but it was fading. "It's fine. My place is your place and all that." My heart bled as I drank my coffee. "What time is it anyway?" There was a clock on the nightstand, but that would mean turning away from Simon, and I didn't want to do that yet.

He glanced there for me. "Just after eight."

Not too late. "I should get to the lot by ten. They do consider evening shoots and all, but I have a bunch of stuff I didn't do while we were rebuilding the model." Sounded reasonable. Normal.

I didn't want to leave.

His smile was achingly beautiful, and I tried to write it into my bones.

"Enough time to get ready, then," he said.

I nodded. "And drop you off." It came out as a whisper.

He leaned down and kissed me. It was tender and kind. The kiss of a lover. "You know where to pick me up again."

God, my heart.

His gaze drifted toward my sculptures. "I hope you didn't mind me looking at your art."

"Not at all." That came out honest, and I followed it with a laugh. "I wish other people could see them."

"We could help you with that . . ."

We. End o' Earth. Simon *and* Lydia. The offer tugged at me in so many ways. I'd love to sell the sculptures to people who'd care for them, but that would mean continuing on with Simon. To cover my confusion, I sipped my coffee and stared into its dark depths. "Let me think about it?"

He chuckled. "Of course. I don't mean to be overeager. I'm like that with Lydia's work, too."

"She's a pretty amazing artist." A wonderful human too. Fuck.

"She is." He breathed out the words like a man totally in love. But his expression didn't change when he focused on me. "So are you."

"Thanks." I didn't know what else to say. I wanted to tell him what was churning inside me, but that wouldn't change a damn thing. "I should get my ass showered and dressed."

He patted my leg and stood. "Let me get out of your way."

I lingered in the shower longer than normal. Simon cared about me, that was obvious. I loved him—obvious as well. I wanted all that I couldn't ask from him. A lifetime. A commitment. A home together. He *had* those with someone else.

I'd known him exactly one week. That was far too soon to be this in love. I'd crash and burn. We'd both get hurt. Better to nip this off now. Cold turkey.

Nothing left to do. I got out, shaved, and dressed. Simon was over by the sculptures again, wearing the clothes he'd had on last night. He smiled as he handled a dragon I'd yet to paint. Such a simple expression, so honest.

"Would you like it? You can have it, if you want." I'd give him the moon, if I could.

He looked up, both gratitude and shock written on his face. "I couldn't."

"Sure you can." I collected my wallet and keys. "I want you to have it." A little piece of me. "Paint it. It can be . . ." It could be a memory of us.

"All right." His voice was reverent and soft.

I packed the sculpture in bubble wrap and a random cardboard box, and Simon carried it down to the car. Bliss when he looked at the contents. Adoration too. Simon seemed to have an infinite capacity to love. I didn't understand it.

On the way to his house, we held hands when we could, and I succeeded in not letting out any of the tears in my throat or the ones lurking behind my eyes.

Simon touched my thigh. "What will you be working on next?"

At least I could talk shop without cracking. "A flashback scene. Have to recreate the ambiance of Bluewater Bay from the seventies. It uses trick photography and angles, so I'll be building individual miniature pieces, rather than a big set."

"Sounds like fun."

My smile came easily. "Yeah, it should be." My humor fled when I turned onto Simon's street. In moments, I pulled over in front of his house. *Their* house. "Say hi to Lydia for me?" My throat felt tight. I'd miss her too. Dexy and Jesse. My temporary little family.

"Of course." He laughed and pulled me into a hug that turned into a kiss, which turned into me indulging in a last taste of those lips and that mouth. I swallowed one of Simon's delightful moans.

"God," he said, when we broke apart. "You're too much." He stroked my cheek. "Call me?"

"Sure." I was so damn good at lying. "I'll see you around, Si."

"You better." He opened the door and climbed out into his life.

I pulled away from the curb and headed back to mine. "Goodbye, Simon," I said to his reflection in the rear-view mirror. Once I was back on familiar roads, I let the tears fall.

CHAPTER FOURTEEN

SIMON

My feet felt like they weren't touching the ground. I was sore in all the right ways and I had a gift from Ian in my hands. When I got into the house, I made my way into the kitchen—if Lydia were home, that's where she'd be. And she was, sitting at the kitchen table, her Kindle in front of her and a mug in her hand. Purrbody occupied the chair next to her, looking regal on the light blue cushion. The whole place was white and blue and yellow, and our royal kitty somehow knew he was as pretty as a model sitting there.

Lydia grinned at me over her coffee. "Wow. Looks like you had a good time."

Hell, yes, I had. I set the box down on the island and crossed over to her. "Overall, yeah." I gave His Royal Fluff a scritch on the head, and he presented his cheeks for me to scratch as well. "The filming was a bit rough. Hard to see something you worked so intently on go up in flames, but it came out great on camera, and the director explained the camera and the shot to me." I sat down across from Lydia. "And I met Hunter Easton."

Her coffee mug clanked down on the table. "No, you didn't!"

Purrbody seemed downright disgusted at the outburst, but he didn't move his fluff, just swished his tail.

"I did! Honest! I should've gotten a photo, but I didn't want to ask . . ." I mean, it isn't every day you meet an idol, but . . . he also was a local.

She sat back. "Yeah, I get that. I wouldn't have asked, either." Probably for the same reason.

"Right? Anyway, after that, I was pretty out of it, so Ian took me to his place."

"And you had a blast." Her sexy sly smile was back.

I shivered from the memory of Ian's hands over my body and the press of the gag's cock in my mouth. His grin when he cuffed me to his headboard. "He's . . ." I spread my hands, helplessly and met her gaze. "I'm *really* in love with him."

"Si, I *know*." Her smile didn't diminish when she took another sip of coffee. "I'm so happy for you."

"I think . . . I think we need to talk about long-term." Me and Ian. Her and me. All of us.

This time, she set the mug down slowly, but there was no shock on her face. "Figured we'd get here soon, too."

Sometimes Lydia knew me better than I knew myself. "When?"

"When he came to dinner the other day. The way you looked at each other." She stretched out her hand across the table, and I took it. "You looked at Ian the same way you look at me when you're under the impression I'm not noticing you."

Oh. I guess that *would* give it away.

She squeezed my hand, and her smile was open and real. "We'll make it work, Si. I love you and want to see you happy." Those were an echo of the words I'd spoken to her when we'd first talked about her and Dexy's dad, Vince.

"I love you so much." She was my compass and my star. And so was Ian. "Let's find some time when we can invite him over for dinner."

"We can do that." She slipped her fingers from mine. "*After* you shower."

I laughed and pushed back from the table. "Hint taken."

"Wasn't a hint, Simon Derry." Humor there and love. So much love.

I was the luckiest man alive.

After my shower, I discovered Lydia had unpacked Ian's dragon from its box and had set it on the marble countertop. Now she was pulling dishes from the dishwasher. "Isn't that amazing?" I gestured at the sculpture.

"It really is. One of Ian's?"

I nodded and grabbed a banana out of the basket on the island. "He wants me to paint it. Sort of a symbol of . . . us." Saying those words left me giddy. Us. *Ian.*

"I'm guessing you haven't a clue what color to use yet."

I started in on the banana and contemplated the piece. "I'm not sure I can do it justice."

A dish towel hit my chest. "You spent a week working on a *Wolf's Landing* prop. You're a pro now."

Maybe. That art director's card was still on my nightstand upstairs. Lydia had urged me to call when I'd told her about it. See if they had any part-time gigs. Or weekends. Something.

But it would be weird working with Ian for real—not as a favor. Especially if he agreed to become a permanent part of our life.

Lydia crossed the kitchen. "Si . . ." She rubbed my arm.

"I got used to thinking of myself as a hobbyist. It's a bit of a shock to find out I've got talent."

"Talent and hobby aren't opposites, you know." She took the dish towel back. "Do I have less talent when I do fan art?"

"No!" I blew out a breath. "God, I know I'm being an idiot."

"Good." That was followed by a kiss. "Then stop it."

I wrapped my arms around her and murmured against her lips. "You win."

"I always do."

Pretty much, but that was fine by me.

Two days later, I moved the dragon from the kitchen island to my workstation in the basement, where I wouldn't see it every time I walked through the house.

Ian hadn't called me back. Or replied to my texts.

I couldn't catch a breath for the constriction in my chest. Had I been wrong about Ian wanting more? Had I done something? No way of knowing, short of showing up at his place—and I had long ago vowed never to be the clingy ex who did shit like that. Especially since I'd once had to fend off a fling who wouldn't take no for an answer. Wasn't about to do that to anyone else.

But Ian wasn't a fling. Unless . . . unless *I'd* been the fling. "Fuck." I stomped back up the stairs from the basement and slammed the door.

Lydia jumped at the stove and Purrbody's claws scraped against the tile as he took off for the stairs.

"Sorry."

Lydia tapped her spoon against the pot and set it aside. Lines of worry ringed her eyes. "Give him some time. People can get spooked when relationships move fast. I don't think he'd just . . . drop you."

I had my doubts, and from the depth in Lydia's voice, I knew she had hers too. "Yeah well, maybe I'm the wrong guy for him." The married guy, good only for a few fucks, but nothing else. Moisture prickled at the back of my eyes. "It's fine. I'll live."

Her fingers entwined between mine. "I know what I saw between you two. I'm sure he'll call."

God, I hoped she was right.

Another week went by without any sign of Ian and my heart was in pieces. Why had I been so foolish? Hot, horny guy walks in, and I'm the dupe who falls all over himself, for what? A taste of cock? I should stick to hookups on Grindr. Except I hated hooking up.

Ian hadn't been a hookup. We'd talked. Hell, we'd fucked in front of Lydia. That last night at his place had been astounding. I'd trusted him. Let him tie me up. Gag me. Take me.

The figurine I'd been trying to paint for the last hour tumbled out of my fingers, smearing what little work I had done. I bit back a curse. Not good to swear up a storm in front of customers. Painting wasn't helping my mood at all, so I set the brush down and packed up my bottles and figures. I'd be able to salvage the warlord I'd dropped, but that would wait for another day.

I burned with sadness, anger, and humiliation. Every day the rock in my stomach grew. I tried to hide it, but Jesse had his worried face on when he watched me. Dexy brought me chocolate and Lydia—

God, I didn't deserve that woman. Here I was married to her and pining over a guy I'd known a week. Slap *asshole* on my forehead and be done with it.

Lydia held me when I cried. She listened when I'd ranted and made love to me when I'd needed someone to remind me I was worth loving. But I knew what a strain it was for her to see me like this.

Once the paints and figures were packed up, I headed in back to clean my brushes.

I didn't know how to get over Ian. Mostly because I didn't understand *why* I was getting over Ian. We should have had dinner, talked about how we were going to do a long-term poly arrangement. Or broken up properly if long-term turned out not to be what he wanted.

But this? Being dumped without warning, without a fucking word? I shaped the ends of the brushes and set them out to dry. I couldn't handle this.

I deserved better than that. Lydia deserved to have a husband and a business partner who wasn't being eaten alive by the pain of what could have been.

"Hey, boss?" Jesse called from the front. "There's . . . someone to see you."

I froze and my heart pounded in my chest. Oh fuck, please let it be Ian. *Please.*

When I emerged from the back room, my heart sank, but my brain did a double-take. It wasn't Ian—it was Carter Samuels. Pretty much everyone in the shop was watching him, even if they were pretending not to.

"Oh, hey," I said. "You came!"

His smile was rueful rather than Hollywood. "I said I would."

At least someone kept their promises. I leaned over the counter. "Don't take this the wrong way, but my wife will kill me if I don't tell her you're here."

He chuckled. "No, it's fine." He shooed me away and I headed in back.

Today, Lydia wasn't working on her art, but on inventorying our back issues to put up online. "Um, honey?"

"Yeah?" She cocked her head, frowning, and I wondered about my expression.

"Carter Samuels is here to buy comics."

She slapped a hand over her mouth, but nothing kept the giggles from spilling out. "Really?"

"Really. Come meet him."

I thought she'd hide in the back, but she didn't. Maybe it was the shock of him being *here* in our world. She kept her cool through the introductions and the handshake. Additional people had wandered in—probably from Howling Moon given their Wolf's Landing T-shirts, but Marlina couldn't lay claim to Carter as property of her store, though I bet she wanted to.

I had a small pile for him, based on our earlier conversation, but over the next half hour, Carter rattled off more titles he'd liked back before he'd become famous and we pulled newer comics we thought he'd love. In the end, he had a nice stack of diverse books. Not a single one was Wolf's Landing, though he did eye the graphic novel of the first book, with a comic version of him on the cover. "It's still so weird. You'd think I'd be used to it." He shook his head and focused on the stack in front of him. "Thank you for this."

When Carter handed me his credit card, I waved it away. "On the house."

He drew himself up a little taller. "Nope."

We haggled for a bit, but Carter won in the end. "Dude, I have the money. Save the kindness for someone who doesn't."

Heat rose to my face, but I nodded. "I will, promise." Because I kept my word.

The rest of the day was intense. Suddenly, everyone wanted to know what Carter Samuels had bought and what he read. We sold out of a couple of issues and some of the graphic novels we'd recommended, and people were combing through the older comics to find titles Carter had mentioned.

"Welcome to fandom." I bumped Lydia with my hip.

She snorted. "We're already in fandom."

I laughed and the ache in my chest loosened, but it didn't go away. Unlike Ian, it looked like my heartache would stick around.

CHAPTER FIFTEEN

IAN

The only problem with avoiding town so I didn't run into Simon was that outside Bluewater Bay, there wasn't very much at all. I could drive all the way to Port Angeles, but that felt too much like I was hiding.

Even though I was.

I made trips after midnight to the few twenty-four-hour places nearby, so I ate okay and had some supplies, but damn I missed good coffee. I'd run out of decent ground at home and the swill the studio provided was a poor substitute, especially since it was weak as fuck.

The day after I'd been pulled into helping on a particularly late-night set-building spree, I decided to chance a trip into town to visit Stomping Grounds, both for ground coffee and a nice hot cup of joe. Since it was about three in the afternoon, Simon would probably be working, so there'd be little chance of running into him.

I parked my car far away from End o' Earth, and headed into the coffee shop. The same barista that had served me those mornings three weeks ago was behind the counter, along with another barista. I didn't recognize anyone else in the shop, thank goodness.

The morning barista eyed me. "Well, hello, stranger."

My laugh was hollow. "I guess it's been a while."

She nodded. "I suppose you won't be ordering for the Derrys."

The other barista ran the coffee grinder and I had to wait to answer—everything else was drowned out by the racket. When it died down, I spoke. "No, only a simple large cappuccino for me."

She jotted something down on the cup and handed it to the barista behind the machine before ringing me up.

"Actually, I'll pay for Ian's coffee." Lydia's voice sounded behind me. "And a small cinnamon latte, please."

My heart dropped straight to the floor. Shit. *Shit.* She should have been at the shop too. But no, she slid up next to me and I was caught.

"It's the *least* I can do," she said. Clipped speech, and when I hazarded a glance, her eyes bored straight through me as she handed the barista her card.

"Thanks." I pushed the word out through a dry throat.

Her smile didn't reach anywhere near her eyes. Hell, it barely touched her lips. "Got a minute to chat, Ian?"

After a night like last night, I didn't have to be back on the lot at any particular time. I didn't want to sit with Lydia, but at this point, I couldn't exactly run away. The barista handed us our drinks and gave me a long look that included quite the frown.

"I— Yeah. I have time." Maybe coffee hadn't been the best plan. My hands were shaking already.

Lydia pointed at a table set back away from everyone else, and I was grateful for that. I slinked after her and took a seat. She sat after I did and placed her coffee down in front of her and watched me. Her stare went on forever.

I squirmed. "Lydia—"

"No." She lifted her chin and there was fire in her eyes. "I don't care about your reasons, or about how sorry you are, or any of that shit. I care about Simon."

My cheeks heated while everything else grew cold. "I care about him, too."

She barked a laugh. "Really? Because you have a horrible way of showing it."

"I—" All the logic in my head churned and whirled and collapsed.

"No." She held up her hand this time. "I don't want to hear it. I'm not the one who *should* be hearing it."

I chewed on my tongue. She had a point there. A fucking good one. Shame clamped onto me and pierced my skin.

"I watched Simon go from floating on cloud nine to dragging around a cinderblock of agony that has *your* name written all over it. I'm done with seeing him being unable to breathe or think because you don't have the balls to break up with him properly. So, you're going to talk to him like a goddamned adult and tell him all the shit that's ready to spill out of your *caring* mouth."

Lydia's voice hadn't risen one bit, but it cut through me like high-velocity shards of glass. The coffee shop had gone very, *very* quiet.

"Well?"

Her tone brooked no argument and required an answer. I nodded because my throat was too tight to speak.

"You free this evening?"

I wanted to say no, wanted to run, but the creeping icy tingling all over my skin told me I couldn't. This town was small. I was pretty sure everyone in Stomping Grounds had a good idea of what was going down and I was on track to become the town pariah. *That* would follow me to work too, and justifiably. "I—can be." I had to put in a few hours today, but no one would blink if I left at my normal time.

"Then be at our house at seven." She rose, picked up her coffee, and walked away.

It took me a moment to remember to breathe, and when I did, it was shaky and full of pain. In my throat, in my head, and behind my eyes. Oh man, I'd totally fucked up. I could ignore what I'd done when I thought—or didn't think—about Simon. I could lie to myself. Believe I'd backed away because it was the best thing for Simon. Being face-to-face with Lydia was another matter entirely.

Worse, I *understood* her anger so much. If our roles had been reversed and she'd been the one to hurt Simon? I'd have been livid and ... probably a lot less level-headed.

Seeing her anger and hearing her describe Simon's misery had shaken me to the bone. Doubt crept over me, clawing deeper than the shame of my cowardice.

A man who didn't want more than a fuck buddy wouldn't be brokenhearted, nor would his wife ream me a new one for breaking his heart.

I didn't like the conclusion bearing down on me like a freight train, because it said something pretty awful about the person I was. Not knowing what to do, I sat there until my coffee went cold and my hands weren't shaking so much. After that, I drank my tepid cappuccino, stood, and made my way out to my car, pausing to toss the cup into the composting bin.

Apropos, that, since I felt like dirt.

The rest of the day flew by. I tried to bury myself in work, but painting model cars reminded me too much of Simon. Every second was one closer to facing the music. Around five-thirty, I gave up and headed home to shower and change. Jeans. A nice shirt. I had a bit of scruff, but I left that. This wasn't a date.

But it was dinner. I had no idea if I was supposed to bring something. What do you take to a "grow a pair and talk to your boyfriend" meal? Ex-boyfriend? Technically, we hadn't broken up, but I'd pretty much killed the relationship.

I hadn't wanted to, but I also hadn't seen any other way not to have my life crack apart. *That* hadn't worked so well.

In the end, I swung by the grocery store and found a nice bottle of wine—pricier than I usually went for, but I owed Simon an apology. Or at least an explanation. I also wanted to thank Lydia for pulling my head out of my ass. She'd been right about me needing to talk to Simon, though the idea filled me with dread.

A few minutes before seven, I stood on the Derrys' stoop and rang their doorbell.

Lydia answered. "Hello, Ian." Her eyes were a little wide.

"Hi." Walking in felt tender and sharp, as if I were both welcome and unwelcome. I handed her the bottle of wine. "Did you think I wouldn't show?"

Lydia studied the label, then appraised me the same way. "You told Simon you'd call."

I winced. Yeah, I'd earned that. I followed her into the kitchen. Whatever she'd been cooking smelled fantastic—beef and something with garlic and the delightful odor of caramelized onions. My stomach would have been growling if it hadn't been tied up in knots.

Simon wasn't there. Lydia nodded at a partially open door on the other side of the kitchen. "He's in the basement."

Oh. I fidgeted for a moment, but I couldn't put this off any longer, so I went. The stairs were plain wood, and the basement wasn't finished—there were concrete floors and rafters of under flooring and supports. The gentle sound of running water filled the space. Simon stood at a utility sink by the washer and dryer, cleaning a brush. His shoulders were tight, and when I set foot on the floor of the basement, he glanced over, frowned, and went back to work.

I didn't know what else to do, so I came a little closer and watched him. Black—he'd been painting with black, given the rinse water and the stains on his fingers. Simon took his time, until the paint was gone and the water ran clear. He set the brush down, cleaned his hands, then shut the water off.

The basement fell into silence. Simon shaped the end of the brush, then put it down on a paper towel on top of the drier. Finally, he turned to me and crossed his arms.

He didn't say a word. Not one. Anger. Contempt. Sadness. I recognized all those emotions in his body and in the downward pull of his lips.

"Hi," I whispered.

Simon tilted his head and snorted.

Yeah, that wasn't going to be enough. I swallowed the lump in my throat. "I'm sorry."

"You damn well better be." Fury there, cold and hard. Simon lowered his arms. "Two weeks, Ian. You wouldn't *be* here if Lydia hadn't run into you."

My heart ticked up a notch. He was right about that. "Eventually—"

"Eventually?" Simon ground the word out. "I don't know what the hell I did for you to treat me like shit."

Man, that was a punch to the gut. "You didn't—you didn't do anything." I'd been dumb enough to fall in love.

"Then what the hell, Ian?" His voice pitched up, both in volume and tone, and he waved his hands in frustration.

I looked away. I couldn't take the pain in his eyes, the crack in his voice. Mistake, that, because what I found was my dragon, the one I'd given him. He'd painted it, the entire sculpture, the darkest shade of black I'd ever seen. Not one spot of white bisque remained. If I thought his words had hurt— This was far beyond that blow. I took one step and then another, until I was leaning over the table, my heart in my throat and my lungs too tight to breathe.

There'd been so much detail there, now covered over. The dragon that leapt toward the sky wasn't the one I'd painstakingly created. Something else sat there now, ugly and twisted and false.

"Our relationship." Simon's words were cold and low.

Simon didn't think himself an artist. Oh, he was. Only a fellow artist could have rammed the blade in and twisted it so neatly.

"That's unfair," I said.

"No, it's not, and you know it."

I couldn't argue, because in the end, Simon was right. I hadn't wanted to face this. Tried to avoid it. I'd run. I'd been caught. "Look." I stared at my hands. "It's not you—"

"Don't you dare, Ian. No platitudes. I'm thirty-five years old. The 'It's not you, it's me' routine got old in high school." He'd come closer. I pushed myself off the table. God damn him. I was *trying*. I didn't want to hurt him more or make this harder than it already was.

"You want the truth?"

"I *always* want the truth." He met my stare. "Always."

"I can't do this." I gestured between him and me. "I tried, but I can't be this side fling you have."

He stepped back, his expression shifting to confusion.

"I mean, you've got the perfect life, Si. A beautiful wife who understands you. A great community. An adorable snotty cat. I don't fit into that picture. It was like a dream being with you. This wonderful, incredible time we had. But it's not real, you know?" My heart hammered against my ribs and I couldn't keep the tears from slipping past. "I'm not a part of your life. I can't be a part of it. But I want to be and— I didn't know what else to do."

The anger had drained away from Simon like blood, leaving him pale and watching me. He scrubbed his face. "Wait. What are you trying to tell me?"

Everything tumbled in my head. I glanced at the dragon, its glory covered, and tried to find the words. "I know we just met, and everything moved so damn fast, and you're fucking amazing . . .

and . . ." I swallowed and met his wide-eyed gaze. Simon had his hand over his mouth. "I fell in love. Which is stupid to do in a week."

Simon didn't move, so I kept going.

"Thing is, I want to *be* with you. Not be a fuck buddy or a friend with benefits or whatever the hell we were. But that's impossible because you *have* a life already. So I . . . ran. Which was dumb. And cowardly. And I'm sorry. But I couldn't take the thought of you dumping me when our time ended, so . . ." I wiped my eyes. There. That was all I had. The tears were gone and I felt hollow.

"Oh." Simon breathed out the word. "Damn it, Ian." No heat. He backed up and leaned against his washing machine, and took a deep breath. "I wish you'd told me some of this. I should have asked too, which is my fault."

"Would it have made a difference?"

When he met my gaze this time, some of the Simon I'd known from two weeks ago gazed back, not the furious man, but the hurt and yet understanding one. "Yes." Another huff of painful laughter. "Did you think I was lying when I said I loved you?"

"Yes . . . and no." Man, the pain on Simon's face. "I mean, I'm sure you meant what you said, but it's not like you love me like you love—" I glanced up to where I'd last seen Lydia in the kitchen.

Simon closed his eyes and twisted his lips. "Oh, for fuck's sake," he mumbled. When he opened them again, he sighed. "Do you know how long it took me to realize I wanted to spend the rest of my life with Lydia?"

I shook my head.

"Three days. We were married a month later, and everyone said it would never last because it happened so fast."

I didn't know the point of this. "But it did. You guys are perfect together."

He let out a laugh. "Oh, we're not. No one is, Ian. We love each other to pieces but we also *talk* to each other. We've always been poly, so we knew all the pitfalls of relationships since we'd been through them. You *have to* communicate if you have any hope of surviving. That's true of every relationship, but up the number of people, and it's *essential.*"

Still didn't get where this was going. "I don't understand."

"Yeah, I know. I thought you did, and it's my fault for not checking to make sure. We could have avoided all of this if I had." He waved his hand around, then dropped it back on his thigh with a slap.

I stared at him.

"I'm guessing that you think polyamory is all about sex, right? Fuck a bunch of people with permission and have guilt-free flings. Yes?"

I hadn't thought about it. "I suppose so? I mean you said you were swingers. All the poly guys I dated were into it for the sex, so ... yeah."

He nodded. "Well, to be honest, it *can* be that. But it doesn't have to be. It's not what I enjoy, because flings exhaust me. I need the emotional connection beyond the sex."

I studied him as his words sank into my brain. A wash of calm flowed over me. "Si, what is it that *you're* trying to tell *me*?"

"That I absolutely can love you like I love Lydia. I want that. I'm not in it only for the sex, Ian. I want a relationship. With you."

All those words scuttled around my head. I took them in and tried to pry them apart. "You ... have that already. With Lydia." I couldn't be a part of that, could I?

"Yes, I know." The smile I so loved surfaced for a moment, but seriousness stole it away. "I want that with you, too."

"But—you've been married ten years!" So much history there. I could never hope to match it. "You know her so much better, and—" I shrugged helplessly.

Simon crossed his arms again, but it didn't seem standoffish, since he was lounging against the washing machine. "Love's not a competition, Ian. I've known Lydia longer, yeah. Doesn't mean I can't love you. With a little time and a hell of a lot of communication, we can make things work."

The calm I'd found vanished into a buzzing in my veins and heart. He meant every word. He loved me. Wanted what I wanted—had wanted that all along. I had so many questions, though. "How does it all work? Between you and me and Lydia and ... all that." This wasn't just us. It had never been just us, but emotionally a relationship was far different than a fling.

"Well, after our last time together, I *had* been planning to invite you over to figure that all out. Or at least start the conversation to see if you'd be interested in something serious."

But I'd up and vanished on him. I shoved a hand through my hair. "Is it too late to say I'm sorry and I shouldn't have disappeared like that?"

A chuckle. "No." He pushed himself off the washer and beckoned with his index finger. "Come here."

As commands went, it was mild. Still, warmth tingled through me, and I was moving before I'd thought about it. When we met, he wrapped his arms around me and pulled me close.

God, I'd missed him. His heat, his scent. The beating of his heart. I pressed my face into his shoulder, and he stroked my back. I didn't realize I was crying until he murmured, "It's okay."

I laughed, then hiccupped and pulled back enough to wipe my eyes. "I have no idea what you see in me."

"You're charming, insufferable, talented, witty, and fucking incredible in bed." He caressed the back of my neck. "You're a certified geek and you like comics. You're not going to hate me for getting lost in painting. Plus, Lydia thinks you're adorable." He paused. "I could keep going, you know."

I was already flushed with embarrassment. "Maybe later."

A huff at that. He cupped the side of my face and kissed me. His lips were warm and sweet, and he coaxed mine open with his tongue. I'd been the aggressor before, and he didn't kiss like I did, but he possessed me nonetheless—my soul, my heart. I was terrified and elated and I had no idea what was going to happen.

Only that Simon wanted me like I wanted him. We could figure the rest of the complicated picture out. I melted against him and let him kiss me into oblivion.

Eventually, he pulled back. "We ought to go upstairs."

Lydia had been cooking. No idea how long we'd been talking, but it had to have been long enough to overcook about everything. I winced. "I bet I ruined the meal."

He caressed my jaw with his thumb. "Doubt it." He nudged me toward the stairs.

I turned and caught a glimpse of the dragon. "What are you going to do now?" I nodded toward it.

"Wait and see." Amusement graced his voice. I'd missed that so much. "Sometimes black is a fantastic base to build up the most brilliant work."

Hope bloomed inside me and something far warmer and deeper too. The love I'd felt before—tempered this time with caution and understanding.

Lydia waited upstairs. The final piece of this strange puzzle we were building.

CHAPTER SIXTEEN

SIMON

When Ian and I emerged from the basement, Lydia's whole body softened and a smile lit her face. "Better?"

Ian answered before I could. "Yeah, I think so." He glanced my way for confirmation, and I nodded. "We have a lot to talk about," he said. "The three of us."

"Oh, good." Her exhale was one of relief. "Why doesn't one of you open the wine, and the other can help me put dinner on the table?"

Practical. That was Lydia. She knew tasks smoothed over awkwardness. I took the wine so Ian would have a few moments alone with her.

While digging the corkscrew out of the kitchen drawer, I studied the label. Quite a nice bottle, and another indication Ian had been hurting. You didn't bring a forty-buck bottle of wine to someone who was only a fuck when his wife asked you to dinner.

Lydia and Ian would never be lovers—Ian didn't blink at women and that was fine with both of us—but the fact he'd come here because *she'd* asked, with the bottle of wine in my hand, and that *he'd* invited her to watch us have sex back then, meant he cared about her too. Quite a lot, I suspected.

I certainly needed that. So did she. And if this were to work in the long term . . .

Oh my God.

The reality of the situation crashed down around me, and my hands stilled. I let out a breath and stared at the wall across from the island. We were going to try to make this work. Not at all the outcome I'd expected when Lydia had told me she'd run into Ian and pretty much ordered him to dinner. I'd figured we'd yell, he'd storm out, and it would be over. Guess I didn't know everything.

Here I was, the one who hated miscommunication and I hadn't bothered to verify Ian and I were on the same page. Too blissed out of my mind with sex and submission. When I'd whispered "I love you" to him and he'd replied, I'd not followed up, not told him it was more than sex.

This was *so much more* than sex.

"Si, the wine, please." Lydia's voice.

Right. I finished uncorking the bottle, grabbed three glasses and headed to the table.

She'd cooked chili. Easy enough to hold on the stove for a while, and if Ian had stormed out, the leftovers would have frozen well. Ian sat, his hands tucked under his thighs, and seemed entirely overwhelmed and uncertain again. I poured his wine, filling his glass. Not proper protocol to serve him first, but fuck that. He was our guest.

He stared at the level. "I have to drive home, you know."

"Do you?"

Lydia swallowed a laugh. Ian raised his head. "I— Do I?"

I gave a shrug and started filling Lydia's glass, but she halted me before it reached half-full. "I have deadlines, so it's back to work for me after this."

Which would leave me and Ian alone, if he wanted to stay. Before I filled my own glass, I spoke. "I can take half your wine, Ian, if you'd like."

He swung his attention to Lydia. "Are you heading back to the shop so Simon and I can have makeup sex?"

She did laugh at that. "I *do* have deadlines. Haven't gotten as much done as I've wanted to recently." Her gaze shifted to me. "Simon needed me."

Ian studied his plate.

She cleared her throat. "But, I also want to give you two the space to work out whatever it is you have to work out." A sly-ass smile.

Ian nodded, and his lips lifted to match hers before he wet them with his tongue. "Then I'll keep the wine."

Someone thought he was getting laid tonight. I poured my own glass. Whether Ian got his wish was yet to be seen. I wasn't *quite* over being pissed.

We passed around the chili and bread and settled into eating.

Ian relaxed after the second sip of wine. When he set down the glass, he looked between Lydia and me. "How does something long-term between us"—he gestured between me and him—"work for *all* of us?" Another wave, this time including Lydia. "I mean, we're not lovers," he said to Lydia. "And I'm still gay."

She set down her fork. "Well, you'd be Simon's partner and I'd be Simon's partner and we'd be metamours."

"Wait, there's a word for it?" Ian's voice wobbled.

"There's a word for *everything*," Lydia said. "But mostly, we'd be friends." She paused. "I *hope*. I like you, Ian. You're a dumbass sometimes, but so is Simon."

I chuckled. "I am, it's true."

"Okay." He pushed the chili around. "That makes sense." He took a bite, another sip of wine, and seemed to steady himself. "Lyds, if you were a guy, I'd totally be into you." He reddened to his ear tips. "If we're gonna be honest."

Lyds? I raised an eyebrow to Lydia—who'd never had a nickname in all the years I'd known her.

She gave me a smile and a shrug. Okay, I guess Lyds would stick then. Something for her and Ian. Tingles in the back of my skull. This might work. This could work. "Honesty is the best idea in a relationship like this," I said.

A thoughtful glance at both of us from Ian, but he didn't say anything. He was obviously chewing on something other than dinner.

I nudged Lydia's leg with my foot. "How do you feel about all this?"

"Fucking relieved," she said. "You two are great together when you're not being dipshits."

Ian started at that, and I snorted. I loved my wife.

She polished off her wine. "Si, the week you two were together was the happiest and most centered I've seen you in *ages*. It's a *good* thing."

My turn to have a warm face.

"Don't fuck it up again, guys? Please?"

I couldn't tell if it was laughter or embarrassment Ian was trying to hide. He took a long drink of his wine and sat back in the chair. "I—So what happens next?" Quiet words. "If Simon and I stay together, and I'm in his life and yours, then what?"

Lydia pushed her plate away. "Well, last time we got near this point, it was me and Vince."

"Dexy's father?" Ian asked.

Lydia nodded. "We'd been seeing each other for eight or so months . . . and yeah, we were in love." She pursed her lips.

"We were ready to fold our families together, ready to take that next step," I said.

"So, what happened?" Ian reached across the table and almost instinctually, Lydia took his hand. I held my breath, because there it was. Might not have been sexual, but damned if that wasn't love too.

"We'd talked about getting a big place together, the four of us, and figuring out what we were going to tell the town and all that. Started discussing some legal things and maybe having a commitment ceremony. Then, he went down to Seattle for a couple of days to meet up with some old college buddies. While he was there, he met a woman at a hotel bar."

"Just . . . like that?" Ian sounded incredulous.

She sighed. "More or less. They'd talked for a while—they both shared an interest in nineteenth-century scrimshaw, and it's rare enough they exchanged numbers. Texted back and forth while he was there, and met at the Seattle library to pour over books. He didn't realize he was seriously crushing on her until he was halfway back to Bluewater Bay. By the time he got home, he was shell-shocked and worried and came here."

I picked up the story. "Eventually, we all decided if he was *that* torn up, maybe it wasn't time for him to commit to Lydia—or to blend our families."

Lydia gave Ian's hand a squeeze. "Six months later, he proposed to her."

"Holy shit." Ian slipped his hand from Lydia's and picked up his wine. "I'd be livid."

"I was . . . and I wasn't," Lydia said. "After he came back from that trip, I knew it wasn't going to work, no matter how much I loved him and when I met her, I understood." She folded her hands on the table in front of her. "She was, in fact, exactly the right woman for him."

Ian took that all in, his eyes narrowing, as if he were thinking. Considering. I saw his next question when he turned his gaze to me. He didn't have to ask it.

"I wanted whatever made Lydia the happiest. Always do." I rubbed the stem of my glass between my fingers. "Vince is straight, but we were friends. Still are, all of us."

"So," Ian said. "I guess what's next is you and me figure out our shit, and if we're still here in a couple of months, all of us talk about the future?"

Give us the time to get over this bump and make sure there weren't others. "I think that's an ideal plan."

"So do I." Lydia stood and grabbed her plate. "I'll clean this up, then head out. Why don't you guys go watch TV or something?"

Very much a dismissal. We both stood, but Ian followed Lydia to the sink. When she put her plate and glass down, Ian muttered something low, and Lydia turned. A smile, then she wrapped Ian in a hug, before pulling back and patting him on the cheek. She spoke as well, but again, I couldn't make out the words.

My heart soared. I picked up the remaining plates and glasses and took them to the sink.

"Netflix and chill?" I said to Ian.

He got a wicked grin. "Sure."

I guessed that when we hit the couch, we'd figure out how much of a euphemism *that* was.

"Holy hell," Ian said. "This couch is huge!"

I fought back a laugh. "Yeah, well. Sometimes you want furniture that holds a bit more than two."

"This would hold an orgy of people." His hand lingered over the back cushions. He hadn't walked around either of the ends of the L-shaped sectional to sit. "Have you had an orgy on this?"

"Here? Nope." I gave him a wicked grin and waited to see if he'd ask whether I'd had an orgy at all. Which I'd had back when I was younger. It'd been a horrible disaster, but hey, it was a checkbox on a sex quiz somewhere.

Ian swallowed, stroked the couch, and didn't say a word. I rounded one end and took a seat. "Simon says, 'get your ass over here and sit down, Ian.'" I patted the cushion next to me.

His eyes widened, but he did as I'd said and planted himself beside me. "Isn't this backward?" He gestured between the two of us. "Usually I'm the one giving orders."

"Mm-hmm." I cupped my hand around the back of Ian's neck and drew him close. He seemed off balance, his lips parted and cheeks tinged, whether with wine or desire. Didn't matter. "So here's the thing, Ian. Tonight, I'm going to say and you're going to do."

"Simon says."

"Exactly." I pressed my thumb lightly against his throat. "I fucking love surrendering. Being submissive. But only in bed. Not all the time, and certainly not after you've been a jackass." I didn't give him time to answer before I kissed him the same way he'd kissed me so many times—forcefully and demanding, opening him with my lips and tongue.

Ian melted against me and I pulled him closer and tighter, until he straddled my legs, and every breath was a moan. I let him go, but only inches.

His pupils were huge. "I— Si—" Fear there, though he'd been content to be manhandled and kissed.

He seemed to need room, so I shifted back. "Not something you're into?"

"I don't—can't—bottom." It came out as a whisper.

Was that all? I exhaled a laugh. "I don't need to put my dick in your ass to be in charge."

It was like that concept had never passed through his mind. Ian blinked, then blinked again, then focused on me. "What?"

The kiss I gave him was long and hard. Then, I nipped his jaw before I whispered in his ear. "I don't need to fuck your hole to tie you up, gag you, and make you come."

He shivered in my arms. "Oh." It came out as a sexy sigh. "I've only ever been—" His breath caught. I could guess the rest, though. Bad experience with anal while being dominated. Happened a lot.

"Do you trust me?" I slackened my grip on Ian. "I want to turn you inside out—and I think you'll enjoy this."

Ian pulled back enough to look me in the eyes. He traced the contour of my face with his fingers. "After what I've put you through, I owe it to you to trust you."

"You can always say no."

His expression turned rueful. "I *know* that, Si. Yes. The answer's yes. Take me upstairs and do whatever you want with me—that doesn't involve me taking it up the ass."

Well, that was pretty explicit consent, with pretty explicit limits. I chuckled. "Cock in your mouth fine?" Yeah, he'd gone down on me before, but I hadn't been the one in control then.

"Oh God, yeah. I love giving head."

"Good. We'll start there." I tightened my grip on Ian and stood. He yelped and clung to me, wrapping arms and legs around my body.

Nice side-effect of hauling boxes full of paper? They were heavy and gave my arms a good workout. Ian wasn't a burden as I walked from the living room and headed for the stairs. I caught a glimpse of Lydia in the hallway and she gave me a thumbs-up before slipping through the front door. Or maybe that was for Ian, because I felt him laugh and relax.

A quick climb of the stairs and into the guest bedroom, and I dumped him on the bed. He was flushed and out of breath and sporting quite the bulge in his jeans. "No one's ever carried me anywhere before."

I stood over him and smiled. "Simon says, 'Lose the shirt and jeans.'"

A gulp that bobbled his Adam's apple, then he was shucking his clothes. I hovered too close for him to stand, but he managed fine, shimmying off his pants until they were pooled around my feet. He tossed his shirt off the side of the bed.

"Sandals, too."

Ian kicked those off. All that was left were his nice white briefs, tented big-time by his hard-on. Part of the tattoo on his stomach curled under the waistband, just waiting to be exposed. Heat raced through me. Ian was on his back, half-propped up on his elbows. I crooked my finger and beckoned him to sitting. When he sat up, he was an inch away from me and at exactly the right height to stare at my belt buckle.

I took my time undoing the belt. *My* turn for a little fun. Ian's turn to give himself to me. To finally trust *me* for a change.

"I'm still a tiny bit pissed at you." Turned on at the moment, sure, but *fuck*—two weeks of his avoidance shit, when all he'd needed to do was talk to me? I slid the belt free from my pants.

His voice was a whisper. "I guess 'I'm sorry' isn't going to cut it?"

I tipped his chin up with my free hand and savored his shiver. "Not entirely." I fingered the belt, let Ian go, and stepped back. "Stand up and turn around."

A flash of fear, but Ian rose and turned.

Lovely. I could get used to this. I nipped the nape of his neck, not hard, but enough to make him shudder and groan. "You're delicious." He was too. All worry and willingness. I took his wrists, crossed them over each other, and used my belt to tie them together.

"Oh, God." A moan of pleasure.

As I suspected—Ian was enjoying this flipping of the tables. Probably as much as I was. I rotated him around again. "Sit."

He did, and every line of his body quivered. His dark eyes stood out from his flushed face. Took me only a second to undo my jeans and free my dick.

I wanted his mouth on me and his groans in my ears as I fucked his throat.

Ian let out a happy sigh. Didn't bother telling him to suck my cock—he didn't deserve the order. I cupped his chin and forced the head of my dick between his pouting lips.

Took all my concentration to remain standing when Ian opened himself like a pro and went to town. Holy hell, Ian did like giving head, and he fucking excelled at it. I moaned and his hot mouth and talented tongue took me places I'd never been to before. I curled my fingers into Ian's hair and pressed in deeper. "I should have had you on your knees that first night."

Ian's groan vibrated my shaft.

"Like that, huh?" I held his head still and fucked his face. "I'll wait until it's rainy and dark, and this time I'll let Officer Merrick catch us with my cock down your throat." I slid in deep and damned if Ian didn't let me. No gag reflex. "Just like this."

Groans and whimpers and tremors as I thrust in repeatedly. When I finally pulled out all the way, Ian licked his lips, his eyes watery. "Yes, please."

I wiped away the tear that slipped down his cheek, and slid my dick between his lips again.

So fucking good. At this rate, I'd come hard and fast, and this wasn't how I wanted to get off. I had *plans* for Ian tonight. Retribution. Absolution. So, after a few moments of Ian mouthing and licking my shaft, I stepped back.

A spot on the front of his white briefs was translucent where his cockhead was straining against them. All of Ian struggled forward, for my cock, for my orders, for me.

Thank God Lydia had found him and he'd gotten his head on straight.

This time, I knelt, but only long enough to pull his underwear off. They joined his jeans at the foot of the bed.

"Simon says"—I reached around him and freed his wrists—"get on your back with your hands at the headboard."

Ian rubbed his wrists for a second, then scooted his butt up the bed and splayed himself out as ordered. "I really want to make you come, Si," he said. "Tell me what to do!"

"Oh, Ian." I pressed a finger to his lips. "I did. I will." His breath was warm and ragged.

What I needed next was in the nightstand. I pulled out the ball gag and let it dangle from my fingers. "Remember when I said I had a complicated relationship with gags?"

Ian nodded, flushed from his chest up. His eyes never left the gag.

"It fucking turns me on hard to gag someone else, way more than it does to be gagged."

He squirmed on the bed. "So—"

I pushed the ball between Ian's lips. "So, Simon says, 'Shut the fuck up.'" I buckled the gag down and Ian groaned.

Yeah, *someone* liked being gagged too. I stroked myself as Ian shivered and swallowed. His dick bobbed against his stomach. Next, I pulled out the cuffs he'd used on me, and in no time had him trussed up to the headboard. Nice. So *nice*. Mr. I'm-Dominant all owned by subby me. I trailed fingers down his chest and abs. He kicked his legs and struggled against his bonds.

"Is someone ticklish?" I tapped my fingers against the side of his torso and he let out a high-pitched whine.

I couldn't help the evilness of my chuckle, or running my nails over his skin, tracing the ink over his stomach, until he was twisting and rolling on the bed, held down only by his wrists. He glared at me.

I kissed his forehead. "You wiggle too much."

Even though he was gagged, I got the distinct impression his two grunts very much meant *Fuck you.*

"Later," I murmured. "Right after I do something about your legs." I took out another set of cuffs from the drawer.

Ian's groan was long and low, but he let me shackle his ankles. His eyes did get a little wide when I pulled out the rope that was always attached to the bottom of the bed frame.

"Told you I'm not always a sub. I'm prepared for switching." I pulled his legs over and tied them down spread-eagle to the bed. Heat blazed through me when I stood and inspected my handiwork.

Ian had pressed his head against the pillow and closed his eyes. Deep breaths. Quaking body. *Perfect.* I ran a hand up his leg and cupped his balls. He pulled against all the cuffs, throaty deep moans pouring from beneath the gag, and I imagined there was a staccato refrain of *fuck, fuck, fuck* running through his head.

"Different when you're not in the driver's seat, huh?" But he was hard and flushed and while he might dislike aspects of this, he'd given me no sign he wanted me to stop.

When he peeled open his eyes, he managed a shrug of sorts, and relaxed completely into the mattress with a soft grunt.

I'd never seen Ian so placid or trusting as in that moment.

Finally. Finally. Every nerve in my body sang and I was so damn turned on. "Watch me."

Ian's gaze never left my body as I painstakingly unbuttoned each button on my shirt, then stripped the fabric off my torso. He muttered something against his gag, and I tossed the shirt over him and onto the chair on the far side of the room. My jeans and underwear followed and I stroked myself while inspecting Ian, a mirror of the first time he'd fucked me.

He must have remembered that as well, because he tensed—not much—but enough. "Trust, Ian." I drew circles on his foot with my finger and he curled and flexed, trying to get away from me. "I'll torment you." I repeated the circles on the other side. "I'll make you moan and struggle and curse at me." I found his ticklish spots again. He thrashed against the mattress, the whine back, his voice louder.

"But I won't do anything you ask me not to." This time I cupped his balls and bent down to take the tip of his dick into my mouth.

His deep groan of pleasure nearly had me coming on his thigh. I'd done this to him—turned him into a whimpering mess—and he'd let me. To see him helpless—his mouth spread around the gag, limbs bound and stretched—sent my pulse high. I wanted to devour him, ride him, and make him come so hard he forgot his own name.

When I stood, there were tears in Ian's eyes . . . and something profound. Not fear. Not desire, though that was written into every twitch of his body.

Trust. Surrender. Love.

God, I wanted to spend the rest of my life with this man.

I got a condom and lube out of the drawer, rolled the first down Ian's cock and used the second to slick him—and myself. Then, I straddled him and gazed down into those deep, dark eyes. "Thing is, I love your cock up *my* ass. So, I have no problems fucking myself on you until you can't see straight."

When I sank down, Ian's eyes nearly rolled into the back of his head. His exhale around and through the gag was one long deep sound of pure lust.

I loved having him inside me, stretching me, hitting me exactly right. A little pain, but so much pleasure. I pulled that same sound out of Ian each time I rose up and slid down, taking him deeper until his thighs met my ass, and he arched his back and attempted to thrust deeper into me.

"God," I murmured, and closed my eyes, savoring the moment— Ian tied down and buried in me, unable to take what he wanted. He was *mine*. "I fucking love your cock."

He grunted appreciatively, but that turned into a whimper when I started to ride him in earnest, taking my own pleasure from him. I found his pecs and thumbed his nipples. Stroked my cock to the sounds he made. Ian shook and thrashed beneath me, and I loved every second of owning his body and mind. Heat raced through me and I fought against the rising tide of my desire.

I knew he was close when his moans grew deeper and more guttural. I wasn't far behind, the fire in my blood rising and rising, ready to burn through me until there was nothing left. I fucked Ian's cock, ramming him into me as I beat myself off. Part of me wanted him to come first, but I also knew he'd lose it when I shot all over him. Didn't matter—only that I'd be the one making him come.

In the end, I broke first. One moment I was riding Ian and jacking off, and the next I was yelling his name and shooting jizz all over his chest and throat. He shook beneath me, eyes wide, then he screwed them tight as he moaned and yelled around the gag, thrusting and twisting until he whimpered and stilled. There were tears in his eyes and semen on his chin.

A come-soaked Ian had to be the most glorious sight I'd seen in a long time.

When I could breathe, I rose, stripped the condom off him and found some tissues to clean my hands.

I left my jizz on Ian's chest and chin. I liked it there. Hell, I loved seeing him well fucked and still helpless, all bound up on the bed. I contemplated leaving him like that—a last touch of punishment—but that seemed unfair, so I removed the gag. I left him tied down while I kissed him, though.

Didn't have to give him all freedoms back at once.

He devoured my mouth as ravenously as I kissed him. If we both hadn't just come, we'd have probably been hard by the time we came up for air.

"That," he said, "was something else."

"Did you like it?"

"I hated it. I loved it. Please tie me up and fuck me again."

I chuckled. "As often as you like."

He leaned his head on the pillow. "And you've given me *so many* ideas for the next time I fuck you."

I took my sweet time kissing him, drinking down his lips and tongue before I whispered against his lips, "As often as you like."

He sighed and his limbs went slack. "Oh God, Si. I love you so much."

This time, I knew he spoke the truth. "I love you too."

We kissed and nipped and Ian fought against me and the cuffs a little longer, until we were both high on each other and totally exhausted. Eventually, I untied him and took the cuffs off. After we both cleaned ourselves up, we slid under the covers.

Ian wrapped shaky arms around me. "Do you forgive me?"

His cheek was hot against my palm and my heart tumbled over and over. "Yes, of course." I found his lips and pressed a finger against them. "But next time, talk to me, Ian. Don't run."

"I won't. I promise."

His words were like glittering gold in the dark. I sighed against him, warm inside and out. "Good." So good.

CHAPTER SEVENTEEN

IAN

I woke up to the slight scent of coffee and the beautiful sight of Simon sleeping next to me. All the worry, all the pain of the past two weeks was gone. I wasn't an afterthought, nor a fling. No idea if we'd make it to forever, but that option shone through our lives now.

Simon Derry was in love with *me*.

He was also out like a light. "Si?"

No response. I shifted in the bed, but Simon didn't wake. He was breathing deeply, and utterly relaxed. While I wanted to curl up next to him, other physical needs motivated me to get out of bed. Simon snuggled deeper under the covers.

Sadly, I was completely awake by the time I exited the bathroom. I didn't want to wake Si, so I snuck out of the room and headed down to the kitchen in search of the source of the lovely brewed coffee smell.

Lydia was perched on one of the stools at the kitchen island, bent over a thin laptop, her head in her hands. Her rounded shoulders shook, and I stopped short, because she was crying. Not loudly, but unmistakably.

Shit. Was it me? No. Couldn't be. Not after the conversation over dinner. Still, nervousness etched itself into my bones. "Lyds?"

She started and glanced up. Yup, wet eyes. She wiped her tears away with her hands. "Oh, God, Ian. I'm sorry. Did I wake you?"

"No." I covered the distance between us and stood by her side. "You okay?" Next to the laptop was a crumpled T-shirt. Looked like one of the new Wolf's Landing ones.

"Um, yeah." She hesitated. "Well . . . no. But it's not you!"

Good. I knew. But good. "Sweetie, you wouldn't have left me with Simon if it was."

That earned me a chuckle and her smile, though another tear slipped from her eye.

"Let me get some coffee—then tell me about it?"

She nodded. "Okay—yeah. Maybe you can figure out how not to have Simon lose his mind over this."

That didn't sound so good. I found the coffee maker and took a chance the mugs were stored in the cabinet above. Yup. Bingo. There was cream in the fridge and every movement of pouring myself a cup in this kitchen felt perfect. The only thing that didn't was a distraught Lydia. I pulled out one of the stools and sat next to her. "So, what's up?"

She blew out her breath. "Well, last night, I walked past Howling Moon and saw this shirt." She smoothed out the T-shirt, and yup. It was one of the new Wolf's Landing designs.

I studied it, not quite understanding what she was getting at. Then my heart dropped. "This . . . kinda looks like that poster you showed me."

She nodded slowly, then turned her laptop. The poster was on the screen and the top right corner, the one with Gabriel Hanford and a wolf, was *exactly* the same as the T-shirt image, albeit mirrored.

Ice washed over me. "You didn't submit the design."

"No." She wiped her eyes again. "I never would . . . or could."

"Wait—why couldn't you? Your art is great!"

She twisted her lips. "Well, one, it's fan art. And two, remember, I've also drawn some . . . explicit . . . stuff of the actors. You know, the ones that *live in my town*."

Oh. Yeah. She'd mentioned that before. Could be embarrassing. "So, no one knows it's you?"

"I use an alias online, and I only post on Fandom Landing."

One of the big *Wolf's Landing* fan sites. I think I was about the only person at work who *didn't* have a covert account. "Someone stole them from there?"

Another nod. "Or someone posted them elsewhere or something." She crumpled up the shirt. "Doesn't matter how it happened."

Her art had been stolen and sold as official *Wolf's Landing* merchandise. If she stood up and claimed the image, everyone would know her identity. Part of me didn't see the issue with that, but clearly Lydia had deep reservations. "What do you want to happen?"

"I'm not sure. Simon's gonna freak and tell me to fight. I hate that my art is being used. It's not the money—I didn't draw them for cash, you know? I did it because I love the books and the show and—" She wiped away another tear. "Fuck. I *hate* crying."

I placed my hand over hers and gave hers a little squeeze. "You've never sold any pieces, right?"

She tapped on her laptop with her other fingers and blushed. "I did once, but it was completely behind the scenes and an entirely different piece of art. This guy *begged* me to make a print of one of my drawings so he could give it as a wedding present to two big-time *Wolf's Landing* fans he knew." Her smile was faint. "I couldn't say no."

Probably not him, then. Why pay for something you could steal? "I could poke around a little at work and see if I can find out how they go about licensing stuff. Get you that info—and you can decide what you want to do about it?"

"Yeah." Lydia breathed out. "Okay. But only that, Ian. I—don't want to out myself. Not yet." She chewed her lip. "Maybe not ever." That came out as a whisper.

Anger and sorrow snaked through me. They made a killing off merchandise. If the person who'd stolen Lydia's art got a fraction of that, it was still a tidy sum. That money should be Lydia's. But I also understood her reluctance—this was Bluewater Bay. She did live here with *Wolf's Landing*, the actors, the producers, all of us.

Hell, I'd read fanfic of the show before I'd joined production, but once I'd met Carter and Levi, I couldn't read stuff that paired them together. Felt *weird* to read about them—or their characters—boning each other, then see them on set. And then they'd gone and gotten married and boy, thinking about that was weirder. "Where does personal end and professional begin?" I hadn't meant to speak out loud.

Lydia returned my squeeze. "Exactly."

A thumping sounded down the stairs, and Simon lumbered into the kitchen, all sleep and mess. He stopped short when he saw us. "Oh shit. What happened?"

Lydia repeated her story to Simon while I went and got coffee for him and refills for Lydia and me. As predicted, he freaked out.

"But you have to tell them it's stolen, Lydia! You can't let them get away with it!" Simon's voice rose and he pushed his jumble of hair around his head.

"I'm not going to stand out on a street corner and admit I draw pictures of Carter and Levi fucking! Don't shit where you live, remember!" Her eyes were wide and she'd slid off her stool.

"Guys." I set three coffee cups down on the island. "Pause for a moment."

They both stared at me. Simon rubbed the back of his neck and plopped his ass down on the stool I'd occupied. Lydia sank to sit as well. "Who takes cream?"

Lydia opted for cream, Simon for none. I fixed everyone's coffee, pushed the mugs in front of them, then pulled out another stool and sat. "Yelling's not gonna help."

Simon peered down into his coffee. "They're *stealing* from her, Ian." Hard voice. Same one I'd heard yesterday.

"I know. And it's wrong." I took a draw on my joe.

"But it's also my name and my reputation, Si," Lydia said. "I realize you want what's best, but we *live here*—and I do work in the comic-book field. I can have fan art on the side. But making money off someone else's property is right out."

"People sell their fan art *all the time* at cons!" Simon sighed and looked up. "I don't understand why it's such a big deal."

She shook her head. "I don't want to be known as the pervy chick who drew Carter and Levi dueling with their dicks."

I nearly spit coffee out my mouth. I managed to swallow, but the giggles came after. "Oh my God, really?" I couldn't stop the laughter.

Lydia turned red and then snorted and soon, all three of us were stuck in a laughing fit. When it finally subsided, I rubbed my forehead. "I get what both of you are saying. But the simple fact is that it's Lydia's art and name, and she has to do what's best for her."

Simon gazed at me for a long time, and then at Lydia. He softened. "Yeah, you're right." He seemed to struggle with what he wanted to say. There was the anger and the sadness I felt written on his face. "It's so *unfair*."

Lydia twined her fingers in his. "It is. But let me find my own way, Si. Help me, but let me steer." She reached over and grabbed my hand. "And thank you for listening."

Simon stretched his arm across and I put my other hand in his. A circle. Weird, wonderful, perfect. Now I wanted to cry.

A quirky smile formed on Simon's lips. "Thank you for talking, too."

I couldn't think of the correct words to say, so I nodded and let the Derrys hold my hands while butterflies danced in my chest and my heart beat out a steady rhythm.

Over the next week or so, I tried to find out how licensing worked and man, was that ever a tangled mess. No one on set knew. Everyone in the art department shrugged. Later on, after I'd exhausted people to ask, the art director pulled me aside. "Ian, you're not thinking of *selling* work from here, are you?"

Oh *shit*. "No!" Little prickles of cold danced across my skin. "I saw some new T-shirt designs at the shop in town and got to wondering how the heck they find the artists for those."

He relaxed and leaned against my workbench. "Gonna try your hand at graphic art?"

I laughed. He knew my two-dimensional work was . . . lacking. "I can barely draw stick figures. It's sculpture for me. I was curious, I guess. Is there some kind of in-house merchandise place, or . . .?"

"Honestly, that's a whole different side of the property. Not tied to us at all."

So, a bust. I thanked him and then showed him the work I'd been doing on the retro shoot. In the end, he was pleased, and I swallowed the lump in my throat and asked the question I didn't want to ask. "Has there been stuff vanishing from set?"

"Na. But occasionally, we get someone with the bright idea to make some bucks off old props."

"I wouldn't do that." Shit, would never have occurred to me. Stuff belonged to the studio—I was only part of the creative team. If anyone owned anything, it was Hunter Easton. Though I bet that wasn't technically true, given the arcane tomes contracts were.

He nodded. "You're probably the last one I'd suspect. You were worried about taking your badge home the first day."

God, that brought back memories. I ran a hand through my hair. "I was a little in awe of the whole place."

"Stay that way, Meyers. You're a breath of fresh air." He clapped me on the shoulder and headed out.

I asked Anna about merchandizing, but she stared at me like I'd grown an extra head. "We don't have anything to do with that."

Searching around online led to very few leads. I'd only discovered that it was pretty damn hard to find out how to submit art to Wolf's Landing. By Wednesday evening, I had nothing at all to share with the Derrys other than myself. I brought another less expensive bottle of wine over, and Simon got two large pies from Flat Earth Pizza.

Not high class, but none of us were feeling particularly snazzy, especially when Lydia pulled out a second T-shirt with her artwork on it.

"Well, fuck." I didn't know what else to say.

She tossed it down next to the pizza boxes. "I've started to get congratulation notes on Fandom Landing." She picked up her wineglass and downed half of it. "I think I'm gonna delete my account."

"No, sweetheart!" Simon rubbed her arm, his face a mess. "You love that place."

"Some backstabbing bastard from there stole my art." Her hands shook and she set down her wine. "I'm not loving it at the moment."

Deleting her account wouldn't make the situation go away or find the person who stole her work—especially if we got a lead and could dig up whoever was doing this. "Maybe . . . take a break from the site? I mean, if it's stressing you out."

The tension seemed drained from her body and she leaned against Simon. "Yeah, that's probably a rational reaction."

"I'm not exactly known for rational reactions, as you guys found out, but I've learned the nuclear option is usually the worst." I peeled open the top box. Mushroom and olive. "Oh my God, how'd you know this was my favorite?" I took two slices.

Simon had this weird expression as he watched me chow down. "I didn't."

"It's my favorite." Lydia smirked.

Apparently, we had pizza in common. "You have good taste," I said between bites.

We ate and drank in silence for a while and I kept staring at the T-shirt. Unfair. So very unfair. If people knew it was Lydia's work, she'd probably get a lot of commissions. Maybe better freelance work. Hell, with the Wolf's Landing clout, she might be able to draw for one of the major studios. "There *has* to be a way to contact the people in charge of licensing."

She shrugged, and it had all the motions of dejection. "I may let it go." Tears pricked her eyes. "Stop doing fan art."

Simon creased his brow and looked over at me, his helplessness radiating across the table.

I cleaned my fingers on a napkin. "Lyds. You gotta do what's right for you . . . but maybe wait on all that? We'll figure something out."

She nodded absently, then pushed back from the table. "I . . . think I'm gonna head upstairs. Sorry to be a downer." With that, she rose and left.

Simon rubbed his face. "I should go make sure she's okay."

Totally understood that, so I shooed him in the direction of the stairs. "I'll clean up."

Simon stood and followed after Lydia and my heart went with him. These people—I loved them both. My breath caught.

"Si?"

He stopped at the doorway.

Tell her I love her. "Tell her I care, too."

A smile that melted me from the inside. "She knows. But I'll tell her again."

I didn't expect the punch to my stomach or the dizziness that lasted as Simon headed upstairs. I sorted through the leftover pizza, putting it all into one box and stuffing it in the fridge. Dishes went into the dishwasher.

So very domestic. Normal. Loving. Nothing like I ever expected this relationship to be. If there were any silver lining to the storm cloud of Lydia's stolen artwork, it was that I'd found a place deep in their lives at the same time, though I didn't understand the pressure in my heart and head for Lydia. I didn't want her—not like I wanted Simon. I craved his touch and body and moans along with the quiet moments and the dinners and texts.

But like with Simon, I desperately wanted Lydia happy. My soul broke to see her so fucking torn up. I wanted her smile and laughter. The light in her eyes to be there again. For this all to be fixed.

I leaned into the counter and closed my eyes. We were all hurting.

Simon didn't walk lightly, so his thumps down the stairs announced his return, and I gathered my thoughts. I was trying to pull myself together when he wrapped his arms around me from behind.

"Hey." Warm breath against my ear and he kissed my neck. "Thanks for everything. You've been so understanding. You didn't sign up for this, after all."

I turned in his arms and pulled him into a kiss, needing his touch to chase away the sadness, if only for a moment. His hair was soft under my fingers. "But I *did* sign up for this. You two. Us three." That was the point of the conversation we'd had last week. "What good am I as your boyfriend and Lydia's friend, if I'm not here for you both?"

"I'm so glad you walked into my store." He hugged me tighter. "Because I don't know how to make things better. I want her to fight."

"But she doesn't want to right now."

"Yeah." The word came out airy and sad. "And I think if you weren't here, I'd be a much crappier husband." He pulled back and took my hand, drawing me out of the kitchen and into the living room.

"It's really fucked up." I sank onto the sofa. "Someone taking her drawings and passing them off as their own. Did they think she wouldn't find out?" Fandom was a tiny community. Even when the shirts were local exclusives—some merchandise was—word got passed around. People bought extra everything on their trips to Bluewater Bay and sold stuff online.

"Probably. Which is weird." Simon sat down and I curled up next to him.

"Maybe the thief isn't well connected?"

"Or they're clueless."

We settled into silence, his body warm against mine, snuggled together. I wasn't sure which of us was holding the other. Tension leaked out of Simon. Seemed the wear and tear of the past couple of days had his eyes flickering closed too.

He was exhausted. Made sense. He didn't get a break like I did since he lived and worked with Lydia—and next to Howling Moon. "Wanna watch some TV?"

He nuzzled my neck. Affection, but no heat. "Sure. I'm afraid I'm not up for anything else."

Neither was I. Still worried, still had a rock in my stomach for Lydia and this fucked-up situation. I found the remote and clicked their television on. I flipped through the schedule and found something innocuous: a documentary on the Australian Outback.

About five minutes into watching it, Simon fell asleep. I let him. Maybe when he woke, his anger and need to fix the situation right *now* would be tempered. Lydia had to find her own path and be comfortable with whatever the endgame was.

I understood that. I'd needed to know there could be an endgame with Simon. Sitting in the Derrys' living room, with Si asleep on me and the television showing beautiful countryside to the sound of lovely accents and music—well, here it was. I could have *this*.

Now we had to figure out how to give Lydia everything she wanted and needed.

CHAPTER EIGHTEEN

SIMON

I woke to Ian stroking my hair. I was lying with my head in his lap on the couch. "Oh fuck. How long have I been out?" I wasn't any good at napping—I woke up, was groggy, and couldn't sleep for the rest of the night.

"Maybe twenty minutes?" He caressed my shoulder. "Not long."

I should've sat up, but I didn't want to move from Ian. If I rose, the world would be there, lurking outside Ian's embrace. Lydia distraught. Her work stolen. Everything I didn't want to think about because I couldn't *fix* it.

It was a miracle Ian was here, on my couch, and in my life. I was so damn grateful to Lydia for dragging his ass to dinner after he'd run, and humbled that he was here now, when our life was rough and rocky. In a way, he was right—he had signed up to be in a poly relationship, which meant meeting everyone's needs. None of us had expected this crisis, but Ian had done exactly the perfect thing and balanced us all out. "Do you want to stay?"

His fingers traced over my face. "Is this a tonight question, or a long-term question?" The amusement in his voice warmed my heart.

"Tonight," I whispered.

He shifted beneath me and brushed my jaw with his thumb. Deep brown eyes gazed down. "I want to stay. Tonight. Longer." He pressed a finger against my lips. "But . . . I think you should spend the night with Lydia. She needs you."

She needed both of us. When I'd talked to her upstairs, one of her biggest fears had been that her inability to cope would drive Ian away. I didn't believe that was true at all, but his going home tonight would only fan that fear higher. "She doesn't want you to leave." I spoke against his finger.

His brows creased, not in consternation, but thought. "I suspect neither of us is up for sex."

I gave a hollow laugh. "I'm sure my dick would be into it, but not my mind."

"I'm far more interested in your mind." Ian hadn't removed his finger. "Especially for what I want to do."

I felt the hint of a shiver, the seed of desire. Yeah, I liked Ian's games and he liked mine. Now was not the time at all. "I love you."

A smile and he leaned down for a quick kiss. "Ditto." When he sat back, he pointed the remote at the TV and turned it off. "Be with Lydia tonight."

"Ian . . ."

"I'll stay. I've got a change of clothes in the guest room. We can all have breakfast together in the morning."

Oh. That might work. Goodness knows I wanted to comfort my wife, but I didn't want to do it at the expense of losing my boyfriend. And Lydia feared Ian's loss just as much. "How is it that you've taken to this so easily?"

His huff of laughter loosened a tightness in my chest. "I don't know. I'm doing what seems natural and right." That cocky smile returned. "I'm sure there's gonna be a day when you two have to deal with me falling apart."

Probably. That's how relationships worked. That's how love worked.

"True." We both rose and headed upstairs and Ian came with me to the master bedroom. Lydia was tucked under the covers, reading, her eyes still rimmed with red and a tissue nearby. I sat down at her side.

"I'm trying to distract myself." She waved at her Kindle. "You two heading to bed?"

"Kind of." I explained Ian's suggestion.

Lydia peered past me to where he stood, leaning against the doorframe. "You don't mind?"

"Not at all. It's the three of us, right? That's what we decided the other day."

She nodded.

"You need Simon right now. And I need you both well." He shrugged. "Call me selfish."

Tears welled in Lydia's eyes and she scrubbed at them. "Fuck. You're making me cry. And you're the least selfish guy I know, Ian."

"Thank you." Color on his cheeks. He pushed himself off the doorframe and strode to the bed. "I'm still convinced we'll figure this out." He brushed Lydia's hair off her forehead and pressed a quick kiss there. "You'll see."

He had the confidence I lacked. Without Lydia outing herself, there was no way to stop the thief. I held out my hand to Ian. He took it, and bent down to kiss me—a gentle one on the lips. "You two get some sleep."

Ian's smile was lovely, heartening, and warm, and we both watched him blow us a collective kiss before he slipped out of the bedroom and closed the door behind him.

When the latch clicked, Lydia breathed out. "How did he end up in our lives, Si? We totally don't deserve him."

"I have no idea. But I hope to God we can keep him with us. I can't imagine a future without him."

Same thing had happened with me and Lydia. Now it was happening with Ian—for both of us.

I woke to only Larry Purrbutt as a companion, which wasn't that unusual. Lydia said I could sleep through a ferry horn going off next to my head. She often got up before me, got dressed, and made coffee. What wasn't usual were the soft strains of conversation floating up from downstairs. Lydia's sweet voice coupled with Ian's deeper one.

Our fluffy kitty padded across the bed and flopped down for scritchies, and I indulged, enjoying the sounds of my lovers talking.

I had to be the luckiest man alive. *Had* to be. Still couldn't wrap my head around Ian, his agreeing to a relationship, and how quickly and easily he'd slipped into our lives, especially to support Lydia. If only there'd been a better, less heartbreaking reason for his understanding. But I'd take this, especially since it only highlighted the type of man Ian was, now that we were all on the same page.

I checked the clock and groaned. A few minutes before seven. *How the heck do they get up this early?* I pushed myself out of bed and headed for the bathroom. Shop opened at ten and both Lydia and I were scheduled to work, me in the morning, and her in the evening. But dollars to donuts she'd be catching up on her freelance work. The whole stolen-art situation had slowed her down something awful, which I understood, but deadlines were far less forgiving.

A half hour later, I made my way downstairs and was greeted by two smiles. My heart did one of those little flips you read about in books. Lydia was relaxed for the first time in days, her eyes no longer red and the lines of worry that had been there were nearly gone. I'd done that. But so had Ian. "Hi, guys."

"Hey there, sleepy head," she said.

Ian chuckled and sipped his coffee.

"Hey there yourself." I leaned in and claimed a kiss from her, then another from Ian that tasted of coffee and milk.

His cheeks were ruddy.

I couldn't tell if his expression was surprise or gratitude, only that he, too, was happy. "Did you sleep okay?"

"Oh, yeah," he said. "I always do here."

Lydia bumped him on the shoulder. "You know you're welcome any time."

"I—yeah?" His face lit up like a Christmas tree. *That* expression was gratitude.

One of the great things about being married for ten years is that Lydia and I had developed a way of communicating without speaking. I raised my eyebrow and tilted my head. *May I?*

Her smirk and tiny nod were the reply.

"In fact . . ." On my route to the coffee pot, I pulled a set of spare keys off a hook on the wall. "Catch." I threw them to Ian, who deftly snatched them out of the air.

Then I poured myself a cup of coffee, leaned back against the counter, and watched as he stared at the keys in his hands. So many emotions played over his face that I couldn't tell what he was thinking. His shoulders eased down when he finally met my gaze, and his eyes were a little too shiny. "Thank you. You have no idea—" His voice cracked and he shook his head.

I had some idea. So did Lydia, who leaned her head on his shoulder. "We mean it."

A faint, but joyful smile from Ian. "I know."

I took a long sip of coffee. Perfect. Almost everything was perfect. We only needed to fix the part that wasn't.

I tried not to curse in front of my employees, and especially not in front of my customers, but it was getting harder and harder, because so many of them were walking in wearing those fucking T-shirts. Enough that I abandoned my model painting halfway through Thursday evening, and took back over from Lydia as the Derry on shift.

She hadn't said anything, but her smile was forced and her voice a little too singsong. Her shoulders were so tense, you could cut diamonds with her muscles. Lydia gave my hand a squeeze, murmured her thanks, and vanished into the back.

Jesse worked with a brow furrowed into an expression I'd never seen on him before. When the shop emptied for a moment, he'd faced me, and it was like a mask had been ripped off the joking, jovial employee I'd always known. "Simon," he said. "What's going on?"

I stared at him. Jesse never used my name, in all the years he'd worked at the shop.

"This better not be about your new boy toy, because I swear—"

"You know about Ian?" It came out as a squeak.

He tossed his head. "*Everyone* knows about Ian. You guys fuck with your eyes every time you see each other."

Oh.

"Also, Lydia had it out with him inside Stomping Grounds."

Oh. And now Lydia was falling apart. *Holy shit*. The rumor mill must be grinding on *that* something awful. I pushed my hand through my hair. "It's not about Ian."

Jesse watched me in a way that I both appreciated and feared, because he stood like he would punch me, boss be damned. He might have been a twink with a penchant for putting on fabulous smoky eyes, but I had no doubt he could hold his own in a fight. There was only one course of action for me: tell the truth.

"It's not Ian." I held up my hands. "Look, we don't talk about it, but Lydia and I are poly. She's known about Ian from the start, she's fine with it, and they're good friends."

"And yet—" He gestured to the back, still eyeing me like Lydia was his sister and I was the jerk breaking her heart.

"You can't tell anyone this," I said. "Hell, Lydia will kill me for telling you."

Jesse's obvious anger softened to confusion.

"You know those new T-shirts from Howling Moon?"

Greater confusion. "Yeah? They're pretty cool."

Though we were the only two people in the store, I lowered my voice. "Some of them are stolen fan art."

Jesse's eyebrows shot up and he glanced at the door that led to the back rooms, obviously doing the math. "Are you telling me—you're telling me some of those shirts have Lydia's art?"

"Yup."

His turn to rake fingers through his hair. "I didn't know she drew Wolf's Landing stuff."

"No one does. She only posts at one place, and uses a pseudonym."

Jesse might have been a smartass, but he was also legit smart. "Is it because she lives here? Shit. You can make a huge name for yourself in fandom if you're good. And she's better than good." He glanced at the door again. "Hunter Easton encourages fan works . . ."

I nodded. Hell, Hunter married a slash writer. "She doesn't want to complicate our lives here."

"You mean, other than you two having an open marriage and you shacking up with a guy working *for* Wolf's Landing?"

I chuckled at that, but sobered fast. "It's her art, Jesse." I leaned on the counter. "I'd love for her to fight, but I can't make her."

He nodded sadly. "Yeah, I know."

Another crop of people walked in the door, and we both looked up. More customers. More T-shirts. We let them browse for a bit. Comics people hate when you jump on them as soon as they walk in.

"I'll help in whatever way I can," Jesse said.

Lydia's art was out of both our hands. But if *he* thought *Ian* had been the issue . . . "Can you help with the rumor mill?"

A laugh. "Yeah, I know a bit about managing that."
One less thing to worry about.

CHAPTER NINETEEN

IAN

Saturday was rainy as all hell, so I stayed at home during the morning and worked on some sculpting. In the back of my mind, I was thinking about Simon, the dragon I'd given him, and the relationship that had developed out of the mess I'd made, and somehow, those thoughts and feelings turned into a gryphon with wings of flame throwing itself up into the air from a rocky outcropping. I was putting the finishing touches on the wings when my cell phone blasted out the ring tone I'd set for Simon.

Shit. Too many of my fingers were covered in clay slurry. I managed to answer with my pinky and set the phone to speaker mode. "Hey, Si."

"Hi there." It came out as a weary sigh, and I held my breath. Something was most definitely not right.

"You okay?"

His grunt was answer enough. Nope. Not okay. "I'm fine, but I have to cancel tonight. I need to take Lydia's shift."

We were supposed to have a date tonight. Dinner, a movie, then he was coming over here. My heart sank, but not at the loss of the date. "Is Lydia all right?"

A heartbreaking pause, then a whisper that sounded too loud over the speaker. "Not really."

The slurry had started drying, and I picked bits off and let them fall to the table.

"What happened?"

"She was feeling better. Seeing the shirts was hard, but it wasn't killing her like it had been. Then, a new design came out."

Fuck. "Another one of hers?"

"Yeah. The last piece of art she put up before this all began—it was actually a take-off on wolf T-shirt designs from the eighties. And everyone is going fucking nuts over it, like it's the greatest thing ever."

Lydia's art *was* the greatest thing ever. "Si, *Wolf's Landing* owes her for saving our asses over the whole altar and rune mistake. *Please* let me say something?"

"God, Ian, I want you to. But I—*we*—can't go behind her back on this." There was pain in his voice.

While I wanted to rub my face with my hands, I resisted the urge. I already had enough clay on my face, in my hair, and on the drop cloth beneath my feet. "I know, I know." I couldn't break Lydia's trust any more than Simon could. "What else can I do?"

Simon blew out a breath. "Maybe *she* can be your date tonight?"

"What, dinner and a movie?"

"Pretty sure she doesn't want to go out." His voice dropped. "I'd feel better if she weren't alone tonight. She's . . . not doing well at all."

My heart fell straight to the floor. "I'll come over." Anything for Lydia. For Simon. If I could ease their pain and worry, I'd walk to the moon.

"God, Ian, I love you."

My throat tightened as my soul sang. "I love you too." *Both of you.*

We set a time for me to come over, and after Simon hung up, I gave up on sculpting and cleaned up the work area and then myself. I knew better than to badger Lydia to fight with Wolf's Landing's merchandizing partner, but I wanted to make her feel better and take her mind off the issue for *one* evening.

A plan took form in my head. It was silly and cheesy, and exactly what Lydia needed. At least, it was an evening that I wouldn't have minded when I was down. On my way out the door, I grabbed a couple of old movies. I swung by the grocery store on the way to Simon and Lydia's, then arrived at their doorstep a few minutes before Simon had asked me to arrive. My finger hovered over the doorbell, then dropped.

In my pocket were the keys they'd given me. Seemed appropriate to use them, so I did. When I walked into the kitchen, they were both there. "Hi honeys, I'm home!"

Damn if that didn't get me two smiles. Lydia's was full of tears and sadness, while Simon's was filled with hope. He crossed over the room and pulled me into a kiss that was both sweet and scorching hot. I had no idea how he managed to be lovely *and* dirty with a press of his lips and a quick swipe of his tongue. He left me breathless. Someday soon, I'd put him on his knees again, and do exactly what I wanted to do to that mouth.

But not tonight.

When we broke the kiss, Lydia was smirking a tiny bit, and there was a hell of a lot less sadness on her face. I lifted my grocery bag. "Don't worry. I have something for you, Lyds." All of us gathered around the kitchen island and I pulled out a half gallon of vanilla ice cream—the good kind, not the cheap imitation crap.

Lydia tilted her head. Simon snorted. "I never pictured you into vanilla."

"Si, ice cream is like having sex," I said. "It's all about how you do it." Next, I pulled out a bottle of Godiva chocolate liqueur and a bottle of Chambord.

Lydia exhaled. "Well, that's better."

"It's mildly kinky." I set a bag of semi-sweet chocolate chips down next to the bottles. "I mean, I could have gotten Fireball or something like that, but I wasn't sure if you were into pain play with your ice cream."

I think Simon tried to swallow his tongue. Lydia burst out laughing.

Finally, I pulled out the movies I'd grabbed from my collection— my set of cheesy eighties fantasy movies.

Simon flipped through them. "Now *this* is pain play."

Lydia punched him in the arm. "Hey now! I like those! Besides, this is *my* date night with Ian."

He held up my copy of *Ladyhawke*. "But the *music*!"

Okay. He had me there. Prog-rock didn't exactly scream medieval period, but I loved the movie anyway. "It's a product of its time."

He set the case down. "You realize we were all toddlers when these movies came out, right?"

Lydia rolled her eyes. "Don't listen to him. He gets a boner for the *Fifth Element*."

Simon tossed his hands up in the air in mock disgust, then laughed. "I'd better get to the shop." He kissed each of us goodbye, and this time, the peck didn't make me want to tie him up and fuck him—though that was still on my to-do list for the near future.

When the front door clicked closed, the smile slipped from Lydia's face. "Thanks for coming over. I know Si's worried and I'm—" Her voice cracked and she choked back the sob. I wrapped her in my arms and she pressed her face against my chest. "I'm a fucking mess," she said.

I stroked her back. "It's been a rough couple of days, that's all."

"I'm gonna lose him." Scared words spoken into the weave of my shirt.

"No, you're not. You've been married for ten years, and he loves you to pieces. You're not losing him. You're not losing me. Not anyone."

We stood there while Lydia tried not to cry and failed. "Yeah, but this is hurting him so much. I know what he wants me to do. I . . . can't, Ian."

"He realizes that. And he loves you, Lyds. You're not gonna lose him."

This would hurt for a good long time if things dragged out, but I wasn't going to say that. Not now.

She shook, then her breathing eased out. "Logically, I know that, but my heart . . ." She paused. "He's such a good man. He doesn't deserve this."

He *was* a good man, but there was more she wasn't seeing. "And you're a fantastic woman. You don't deserve this, either." A bark of a laugh escaped me. "Besides, he put up with my sorry ass. You both did. And you let me stay."

She hugged me tighter, but didn't speak for a good long time. Finally, she pulled away. "Ice cream's gonna melt."

"Mm-hmm. Would you like a bowl with the works?"

"Magic words."

I untangled myself from Lydia and made us bowls of liquored-up ice cream while she took the movies into the living room. When I walked in, the menu screen for *Ladyhawke* was already cycling.

"You're too good for us," she murmured, and took a bowl from me.

"Other way around. But thank you."

Lydia's sadness fell away for a moment. "You really don't know yourself, Ian."

I met her gaze. "Do any of us?"

A small snort. "Million-dollar question." She picked up the remote and started the movie.

Truth is, I did know myself. Maybe not perfectly, but enough to understand that what I had was far more than I deserved, especially after the blunder I'd made. But hell, if I was going to let it go. The Derrys were stuck with me, for as long as they wanted me.

I leaned back, took a spoonful of spiked ice cream, and watched a painfully young Matthew Broderick dig his way out of a prison.

Two and a half hours later, the movie was over, Lydia was curled up with her head in my lap, and we were both a little bit buzzed. She gripped my knee and let out a sigh. "I love that film."

"Me too." Despite the out-of-place soundtrack, the story and humor and romance always brought me back. The *I love you*s at the end, the way they all supported and loved— "Oh my God, they're a thruple!"

Lydia laughed and squeezed my knee. "Kinda, huh?"

I'd never seen that before. It was purely subtext, but *clearly* Philippe loved both Navarre and Isabeau—and they loved him. "Wow."

Lydia rolled over and looked up at me. "Ian, can I ask you something?"

"You just did."

She grabbed a decorative pillow and bopped me in the head. "I'm trying to have a real conversation here!"

I laughed, took the pillow away, and tossed it over by the arm of the couch. "Sorry. Slightly drunk."

"Yeah, well, whose fault is that?"

Mine. Totally. My second helping of ice cream had been in a glass and more booze than cream. "What did you want to ask?"

She fell into seriousness. "Is it okay if I'm kinda a little in love with you?"

Her words zipped through me. The back of my skull tingled and my pulse hitched up a notch. "Um. Yes?"

"Oh good." She closed her eyes and whispered, "Because I'm kinda a little in love with you."

My head spun, and I didn't think it was from the liqueurs. "I mean, I'm gay." I stared down and she opened her eyes. "But I completely understand why Simon loves you like he does. Because I probably would too, if I were straight or bi or something. Hell, I—" Words fell away.

Lydia poked my leg. "You . . .?"

Wasn't going to get away with not saying anything. "I'm kinda in love with you too." I waved at her laying on my legs. "I mean, this is *quite* a friendship."

"But boobs and pussy don't do it for you."

I shrugged and chuckled. "I've always been more of a dick and ass man."

She shrugged too, but it came out weird since she was lying down and only made me laugh. That gave her the giggles, and we snickered and snorted like two eight-year-olds with a pile of fart jokes. When we both wound down, she relaxed against my legs. "You know what I wanna watch next?"

"What?"

"*Fifth Element*. Don't tell Simon, but I fucking love that movie."

God, my cheeks would break from smiling so much. "Your secret is safe with me."

CHAPTER TWENTY

SIMON

Maybe it was because I couldn't stop worrying about Lydia, but Saturday night crept along with hardly any customers and too many minutes. I couldn't paint miniatures or models since I was the only one manning the shop, but even my normal go-to time movers like organizing back issues or bagging and boxing comics didn't help at all. I still ended up perched on a stool behind the counter trying not to seem too bored or too stressed.

Given a few looks of pity I got when the smattering of customers did check out, I'd obviously failed at one or the other. Eventually, it was close enough to closing time that I began the walk-through of the store. Mostly, it was to straighten merchandise and put issues and books that had wandered around back to where they belonged.

Of course, right when I finished tidying up the model section, not five minutes before closing, the shop door opened and closed and the murmurs of two men floated over the shelves.

Really? Why did people have to come in at the Goddamned last second to buy shit? I schooled my expression and headed out to greet them. I might hate last-minute customers, but I knew better than to let *them* know that. They were *customers*, after all.

But when I spied them, I stopped and stared. For the second time in several weeks, *Wolf's Landing* had come to visit my shop—this time in the form of Hunter Easton and Kevyan Montanari.

It was one thing to meet Hunter on the lot, *in* Wolf's Landing— quite another to have him and his co-writer and husband looking in my shop at the new comic releases.

"Why didn't I know this shop was here?" Kevyan said. "This is way closer than that place in Port Angeles."

Hunter snorted. "Because it's too damn close to Howling Moon and you never walk past there if you can help it?"

A soft chuckle. "There is that."

At least one other person in the world didn't like Howling Moon. I bit back a smile. "Hi, can I help you?"

They both turned and I had to fight to keep the professional smile on my face. Hunter was wearing one of the T-shirts sporting Lydia's designs.

Toss-up if I managed to hide my dismay. Hunter's smile didn't falter, but Kevyan's did—and Hunter clearly noticed *that*. He gestured at me. "This is Simon," he said. "The shop owner I was telling you about."

Focusing on Kevyan was easier than staring at Hunter, so I stepped forward and stuck out my hand. "Simon Derry."

His handshake was firm and short. "I'm Kevin." He glanced around the shop and there was a hint of surprise in his voice. "This is a nice place!"

Kevin. I mentally slotted that in where Kevyan had been. "Thanks! We *are* a little closer than the shops in Port Angeles. We might not carry *everything*, but if there's a title you want, we can order it."

He nodded.

"Except Wolf's Landing merchandise," Hunter said.

I flinched and saw the reaction in both men. My gaze drifted to Hunter's T-shirt. "It's a licensing issue." My words sounded rough. I swallowed.

"Sore subject?" That from Kevin.

"It's complicated." I rubbed my neck and tried to get my heart rate back under control.

A glance passed between the two of them, and I was reminded of both Lydia and Ian, and man, I wanted to be home with them even if the men standing before me were the authors of my favorite books. I shook the funk off. "I'm sure you didn't come to hear about my problems." This time, I must have managed a half-decent smile, since they both mirrored it.

Hunter cleared his throat. "I dragged Kevin with me so we could sign any books you had in stock."

"And because I didn't want to drive thirty miles to get comics." Kevin gave a small shrug, but his grin deepened. "His name's on more books than mine. Figured I could browse, too."

"Wow, um." How did signing stock work? "I've never had an author come in before, let alone two. Do you need anything?"

They both had a painfully amused look, and my grumpiness gave way to embarrassment.

"Just point us to the books. We have pens and everything." A laugh from Hunter.

I gestured for them to follow, and took them to our collection of Wolf's Landing books and graphic novels. "It's not that many."

"You have the whole series." Kevin reached for one of the books he'd co-authored. "It's more than some bookstores keep in stock."

That was true. The business person in me understood why bookstores did that, but the reader in me *hated* when the entire series wasn't available. "Nice benefit to being the owner is that I get to choose what's on the shelves."

"Believe me, we're grateful for that." No laughter from Hunter now, only appreciation.

I hovered like a mother hen for a moment, then checked my watch. "I should finish closing."

Kevin looked up. "I'm going to want to buy some comics."

After my experience with Carter Samuels, I suspected neither of these men would take me giving them comics. "That's fine. Mainly, I need to lock the front door."

I managed to slip away, lock up, and finish tidying while they autographed books. Tomorrow, I'd make a little card stating that the books were signed or something. Though, I bet the stock over at Howling Moon was too. I swallowed the lump in my throat. Before the T-shirts, I hadn't minded them as a neighbor, Marlina's possessiveness notwithstanding. But now? God, it was hard seeing Lydia's work not being recognized.

Hunter came over to the counter while Kevin browsed. "Thanks for staying open for us."

That got a chuckle out of me. "Like I'd throw you guys out of my shop."

He waved my words away. "We're people, Simon, and I have a feeling you weren't exactly happy to see us."

"It's not . . . I didn't . . ." I sighed and scrubbed my face. "Long week, that's all."

He nodded noncommittally.

My brain itched as I took in that damn T-shirt. Maybe . . . maybe he knew how merchandising worked. He owned the damn characters after all. "Hey . . . so how do they hire artists for T-shirts anyway?" I waved at my wife's design on his chest. "Or the comic books? Stuff like that."

He blew out a breath. "I'm out of the loop on the whole process." He stepped back and pulled his T-shirt out flat. "Take this, for instance. I have no idea how they got StarVixen to agree to let them use her art. I had to beg and plead and practically promise my nonexistent first child to get her to sell me a print *at cost*. And here she is on a T-shirt."

Oh *God*. I stared at Hunter. Oh *fuck*. *He'd* bought that print? The ground swam below my feet and I gripped the counter.

"Are you all right?"

Nope. Not in the least. "StarVixen didn't license the art." I barely heard my own voice over the rush of blood in my head.

Hunter stared at me.

"For the T-shirts. She didn't license it. Wasn't asked. Someone stole the art off Fandom Landing."

"What the *fuck*?" Kevin joined us at the counter, a handful of comics in his hands. "You— Please tell me you're fucking joking."

I shook my head, my throat tight and dry.

Hunter's expression turned neutral. "How are you sure the art was stolen?"

I barked a bitter laugh. "Because it's my wife's art. Wanna know why I'm a wreck tonight?" I gestured at Hunter's T-shirt.

Hunter's face lost a little color. "Your *wife* is StarVixen? Can you prove this?"

Part of me wanted to choke Hunter, but the rational side grappled for control and won. I swallowed a few breaths and nodded. Of course he'd need proof. "Yeah. I can. Her studio is in the back."

They followed me past the counter and into the back rooms, all the way to Lydia's computer. I nudged it awake, used her password to log in, and clicked through the folders until I got to her Wolf's Landing fan art. Then, one by one, I started opening files—the original Photoshop ones with all the layers and shit. After about the seventh file, Kevin spoke.

"You can stop. We believe you."

I turned. Both men were ashen. Kevin seemed worried. Hunter looked like he wanted to rip someone's head off. A spark of hope bloomed in me. Lydia might murder me, but I had a feeling Hunter could fix this.

Kevin stared at the art. "Why didn't she *say* anything? Like, when people on the forum were congratulating her and all that."

I winced. "She doesn't want anyone to know who she is. In real life."

Hunter's furious expression softened. "Because she lives here, right?"

"Yeah." I turned back to the computer and started closing files, mostly so I didn't have to *see* the emotions I'd been dealing with for over a week. Relief flooded through me. Lydia might kill me, but at least someone else knew what had happened. "I mean, she's drawn Carter and Levi—naked."

"So? I've written them fucking," Kevin said. "And I live here now."

My hand froze on the mouse.

"To be fair," Hunter said, "visual arts are a bit different than written ones when it comes to sex."

"Unless you're talking porn." Kevin's voice was just as conversational.

I finished closing out everything, logged out, and faced the two men. "I doubt there's a Wolf's Landing porno."

"There is." They spoke in unison.

Fuck me. Part of me was horrified. The other part itched to find the damn thing.

Hunter laughed, probably because I was no good at poker faces. "Hey, do you think I could talk to your wife? Art theft is pretty damn serious, and this—" He touched the T-shirt he had on and his fury returned. "This is beyond the pale."

"How soon do you want to talk to her? I'm heading home after—" I waved at the front of the store.

"Given the way you look tonight? The sooner the better, I bet."

That was about the size of it. "Let me finish locking up." I eyed his T-shirt. "Want something else to wear?" I couldn't imagine what Lydia would think if Hunter Easton walked in wearing her stolen design.

Hunter grimaced. "Please."

I gave Hunter one of the plain black T-shirts I kept handy in the back room for those occasions when I either dripped blobs of paint on myself or ended up wearing my lunch. I also rang up Kevin's comics—and as I'd suspected, trying to gift them to him didn't pass muster at *all*.

"Take my debit card like I'm a normal human being," Kevin said.

So I did—then led those normal human beings who were the heart and soul of Wolf's Landing out the back so they could follow me home.

We got to my house and I parked in the drive, while they pulled behind Ian's Mini Cooper at the curb. Despite the fading twilight, Ian's car was still brilliantly yellow.

"Nice!" Kevin said. "Yours?"

"Nah, it's my boyfriend's." The truth slipped out before my brain caught up to remind me that was *dumb* to say. My stomach tumbled. "Um. I mean . . ." I stopped on the walkway and stuffed my hands into my pockets. "Well . . ."

Hunter rolled his eyes. "You're poly?"

"Yeah." I stared at him. "I am. We are." Holy shit. Someone's first instinct was polyamory and not that I was a stinking cheating bisexual? My head spun around again.

"Good." He pointed at the door. "Go."

Kevin smirked.

God, Lydia was going to murderlate me. Couldn't keep my mouth shut about *anything* anymore. I marched up to my house, Hunter and Kevin in tow, and unlocked the door. I found Lydia resting her head in

Ian's lap in the living room and for a moment, I forgot who was at my back. "You're watching *The Fifth Element*? After all the grief I got for loving the movie?" Seriously? My lovers, conspiring together!

"It's a bad-movie-and-spiked-ice-cream night, sweetheart." Ian turned. "And this is—" His entire expression changed from snarky to horrified in an instant. "Oh shit!"

Lydia's eyes were huge as she stared beyond me. She levered herself up to sitting and Ian leapt for the remote and paused the movie.

"They need to meet Carter and Levi," Kevin murmured.

"This is my wife, Lydia. I think you've met Ian, Hunter." I took a breath and stared into Lydia's horrified gaze. "Honey, Hunter and Kevin—"

"Kevyan." Lydia spoke through the fingers covering her mouth.

"Kevin," Kevin said.

"—stopped by the store tonight to sign books."

"And I was wearing one of your T-shirts." Hunter brushed past me into the living room.

"I told him everything." I felt like absolute shit when Lydia's eyes got watery. *Way to go Simon.* "I'm sorry, but I couldn't not—and besides, he's the guy who bought your Carter and Levi print."

If I'd thought Lydia's eyes had been huge before, I'd been wrong. "*You're* Wolf Hunter?" Lydia let out a breath, grabbed one of the throw pillows and clutched it to her chest. "You shit! That's not fair! You're Hunter Easton!"

Wow. At least she hadn't lobbed the pillow *at* Hunter. "Ian, how much Chambord did you pour over my wife's ice cream?"

"A lot." Ian ran a hand through his hair. "Hi." He looked sheepish and happy and embarrassed, and I fucking loved every inch of him.

Hunter chuckled. "I met Kevin on Fandom Landing." He focused on Lydia. "Can we sit and talk? Because I think I can help you, being the rights owner of all my characters and shit."

"I can too," Kevin said, "because I bet every single worry you have about people knowing who you are, I've had first."

Lydia sat back against the cushions. "Well, fuck. This night can't get any weirder, so yeah." She waved at the couch. "Have a seat."

Ian rose. "Want some ice cream? It's vanilla, but we've got chocolate chips and liquor."

In the end, both Hunter and Kevin said yes to ice cream with chocolate chips, but hold the booze. I followed Ian into the kitchen to give Lydia, Hunter, and Kevin time to talk in private.

Ian leaned against the counter. "So that's something." He waved at the door to the living room.

"Right?" I closed in on Ian and stole a kiss that tasted of raspberry and chocolate. He turned it into something much longer and sexier. By the time he relented, I was breathless and the room was spinning. Maybe not the most apropos time to sex it up with my boyfriend, but he *was* one of the reasons Hunter and Kevin were sitting on my couch.

"I'd apologize for bringing all this Wolf's Landing chaos into your life, but I think—" Ian glanced over my shoulder at the door to the living room. "I think it's gonna work out."

I did too. Everything was going to be fine. I cupped Ian's face and kissed him again, and again until *he* was the one breathless and groaning. "We're supposed to be getting your guests ice cream." He spoke against my lips.

I smiled and nipped his neck. "We're giving *our* guests time to talk to Lydia."

Ian didn't argue. We necked until I was about ready to drag him upstairs, but then pulled away from each other and put together three bowls of ice cream, which gave us time to look less like two guys ready to fuck. When we returned to the living room, Lydia had a sober gleam in her eyes, but importantly, now radiated happiness. She seemed a little shell-shocked, but in a good way.

"So that's settled," Hunter said. "I'll talk to my lawyer and get the whole thing straightened out."

"But what if they don't agree?" Lydia breathed the words out.

Kevin snorted and took a bowl from me. "Oh, they will."

Hunter took the other from Ian. "My reputation for being a bit of a diva author is somewhat earned."

"Somewhat?" I knew the glint in Kevin's eyes. All love and snark.

Hunter's lips twitched upward. "And those on the opposite side of my lawyer think he's a psychopathic demon."

Kevin picked a chip off his ice cream and popped it into his mouth. "He's actually a really nice dude."

I was glad we bought a huge couch for the living room. Plenty of room for all. I planted myself next to Lydia, and Ian took a seat next to me.

My two loves. When I glanced up, I found Kevin smiling at me. I gave him a sheepish shrug before digging into my ice cream.

Lydia fiddled with the edge of the throw pillow she was still clutching. "About that print you bought . . . you said the people you gave it to were big fans of *Wolf's Landing*?"

Hunter licked his spoon. "It was one of my wedding presents to Carter and Levi."

"Oh *fuck*." She buried her face into the pillow and muffled words came out. "Please tell me you're joking."

"He's not. He did. But they loved it, so it's all good." Kevin elbowed Hunter. "Even if you were trying to embarrass them."

Hunter snorted, and cocked his head, suddenly very serious. "Lydia, your artwork is fantastic. StarVixen is legend in fandom circles and I get asked *all the damn time* if I know who you are. Things will change when this comes out, but I think you'll find life just as interesting and fulfilling after it does."

She lowered the pillow. "We have a rule about not shitting where you live."

"Honey, your work is so far from shit, it isn't funny." Hunter sank his spoon into his ice cream.

"But—"

"Lyds," Ian said. "Something I've learned on set is that even Anna doesn't argue with Hunter Easton when he's on a tear."

"Oh, she does. But I usually win."

"Usually." Kevin's eyes glittered with amusement. "It's fun to watch when he doesn't."

Hunter grunted. "Don't push your luck, kid."

Kevin laughed. "Too late."

I smiled down into my bowl of ice cream. Lydia was right. This night couldn't get any weirder, but that was fine. My attention strayed to the frozen image of Bruce Willis on the screen. "Hey, why don't we finish watching the movie?"

It was a plan everyone agreed to, so Ian grabbed the remote and hit Play.

By the credits, Lydia was curled up in my lap, and Ian had his head on my shoulder. My heart couldn't be more full of joy.

From the other section of the sofa, Hunter gave me a thumbs-up.

"Welcome to the Wolf's Landing family," Ian murmured.

I tousled Ian's hair, but it was Lydia who said what I thought. "Welcome to ours."

Yup. Life was weird, but absolutely perfect.

IAN

Seven months later

Moving in winter in the Pacific Northwest was a crapshoot, but nature was kind and gave us one non-rainy day to transfer all my belongings from my old place into Simon and Lydia's house. *Our* house now. Took another couple weeks to integrate my stuff into theirs and pick what we wanted to keep, what would go into storage, and what we'd sell or give away, but in the end, the house had become the three of ours. My items nestled next to Simon and Lydia's, my movies and books shelved in with theirs. I made dinners and picked up items at the store for both of them. They brought me soup in bed when I got wretchedly ill with bronchitis.

We'd become a family I'd never expected or known I could have, and I loved it. Simon was as much mine as he was Lydia's and his own, and between the two of us, we constantly reminded him that he was damn lucky to have us both.

Not that he ever forgot.

After that wacky movie night, Lydia and I ended up instituting regular date nights for us—a way to bond and have a relationship separate from Simon—and I found myself inexplicably head over heels for her too. Still had no desire to fall into bed with her, but I loved her, down to feeling giddy to my toes when she smiled at me. The internet told me this was actually a thing—that romance and sexual attraction weren't the same. And yeah, that was me: in a romantic relationship with both my partners, but only interested in banging one of them.

I did that in spades, and so did Lydia. Simon was insatiable and delighted and well and truly fucked. A week after I moved in, over dinner, he blurted out, "I don't want anyone else."

Warmth from my head to my toes. Good. Yes. We hadn't talked about the openness of our relationship, but I'd already decided I'd found perfection. "That's fine with me." I'd made curried chicken for dinner. I pushed some rice into the sauce. "I got more than I bargained for with the two of you. I don't think I could handle another person."

Lydia patted my arm and grinned. "You poor man." She studied her wine glass. "I love you both. You're both my everything."

"But . . ." Nothing but adoration in Simon's voice.

"I'm still figuring things out," she said.

"We have time." Maybe it was because I'd worried so much about being the third wheel in the beginning, but I kind of understood the hesitation to change up what had worked for her. I *was* a huge difference in their lives.

"All the time in the world." Simon reached over and took Lydia's hand. "Let us know if or when that changes."

"Always."

So that was that. We all had each other. Simon and I were both fine with our little trio—and fine with Lydia potentially wanting someone else besides, as long as we all knew what was going on. I waited for the pang of jealousy, but none came. None had ever with these two.

I was happy. Incredibly so.

We were also all incredibly *busy*. When the news broke about the art theft, not only did Lydia eventually end up with a tidy pile of money—payment for her stolen work—she ended up with the recognition she so rightly deserved. Because of that—and her newfound friendship with Hunter and Kevin—she was invited to be the artist for a new Wolf's Landing graphic novel they were writing.

It was Kevin who'd finally uncovered the identity of the thief. Just as we'd thought, it was one of the users on the Fandom Landing site—a woman who'd ended up meeting a Wolf's Landing merchandizing guy at a bar during WolfCon the previous year, gotten into him, and lied about being an artist to keep the dude interested in *her*. When he wanted to see her art, she followed up by sending him

Lydia's work and of course he'd gone nuts over it. The whole situation was stupid, yeah, but lust made you do weird shit.

Unsurprisingly, End o' Earth had become a happening place to be—as crowded as Howling Moon—especially when Carter and Levi swung by for their comics.

With Lydia's schedule changing and the extra customers, Simon had scrambled to hire and train new employees to fill in the gaps. Jesse had taken over as assistant manager and ran the shop with glitter and pink and a no-nonsense attitude that had everything working smoothly. Dexy had as many hours as she wanted. Even I worked a few shifts on weekends.

In return, sometimes Simon came with me to the set and helped out when we needed an extra hand in props. That was all *before* Lydia had gotten the invite to be a guest artist at WolfCon. Now? God, we were in a hurricane of activity.

So, I'd no idea how Simon had managed to do what he'd done without me knowing, but there it was, on the kitchen island when I walked in, a month to the day after we'd unloaded my life into theirs.

The dragon. The one I'd given him to paint.

What had been so dark and horrible all those months ago had been transformed into something so beautiful it made my skin ache. My work, yes, but Simon's too. He'd taken anger and sorrow and hope and crafted it all into love on top of love.

Our dragon was now a brilliantly painted masterpiece, complete with intricate lines of gold between the scales. It launched itself into the sky on iridescent wings that shimmered in the light and seemed to move as I did. Scales rippled. Eyes gleamed. Every inch was incredible.

Every bit of the detail I'd sculpted was there—and more. So much more.

I was so damn grateful no one else was home, because I dropped the grocery bag, cracking half the eggs I'd bought, and I'd broke down and cried like a baby. Tears down my face and everything. I was still misty-eyed when Simon had come home.

He circled me in his arms, pulling me back against his very solid body. "You like it?"

"Of course I do." I leaned into his heat.

"Lydia painted the base." Warm words spoken into my hair.

Even better. "It's perfection," I said. "Utterly."

He kissed the side of my neck. "It's *us*."

I closed my eyes and in that moment, I was the one soaring into the air. "It sure is."

EXPLORE MORE OF BLUEWATER BAY

A BLUEWATER BAY STORY

For more, visit:
riptidepublishing.com/titles/universe/bluewater-bay

Dear Reader,

Thank you for reading Anna Zabo's *Outside the Lines*!

We know your time is precious and you have many, many entertainment options, so it means a lot that you've chosen to spend your time reading. We really hope you enjoyed it.

We'd be honored if you'd consider posting a review—good or bad—on sites like **Amazon, Barnes & Noble, Kobo, Goodreads, Twitter, Facebook, Tumblr,** and your blog or website. We'd also be honored if you told your friends and family about this book. Word of mouth is a book's lifeblood!

For more information on upcoming releases, author interviews, blog tours, contests, giveaways, and more, please sign up for our weekly, spam-free newsletter and visit us around the web:

Newsletter: tinyurl.com/RiptideSignup
Twitter: twitter.com/RiptideBooks
Facebook: facebook.com/RiptidePublishing
Goodreads: tinyurl.com/RiptideOnGoodreads
Tumblr: riptidepublishing.tumblr.com

Thank you so much for Reading the Rainbow!

RiptidePublishing.com

One of the things I truly believe is that everyone deserves a happy ever after. Sometimes those HEAs may be a little different than others. This is a book for those for whom the concept of family doesn't just mean one other partner. Thank you to the poly people in my life.

I also have to thank L.A. Witt for her unwavering support while writing this, and for letting me borrow some of her characters so I could play in the sandbox she helped build. I'm also very grateful for the editing skills of Caz Galloway and Sarah Lyons.

And much thanks to my agent, Jennifer Udden.

Close Quarter

The Takeover series
Takeover
Just Business
Due Diligence
Daily Grind

CTRL me (in the *Rules to Live By* anthology)

Anna Zabo writes contemporary and paranormal romance for all colors of the rainbow and lives in Pittsburgh, Pennsylvania, which isn't nearly as boring as most people think.

Anna has an MFA in Writing Popular Fiction from Seton Hill University, where they fell in with a roving band of romance writers and never looked back. They also have a BA in Creative Writing from Carnegie Mellon University.

You can find Anna online at annazabo.com, on Facebook at facebook.com/annazabo, or on twitter as @amergina.

Enjoy more stories like
Outside the Lines
at RiptidePublishing.com!

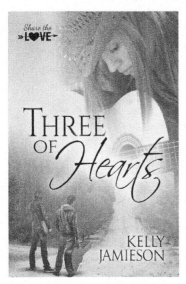

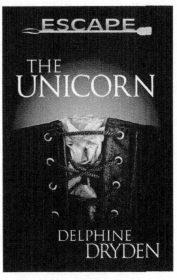

| Three of Hearts | The Unicorn |
| ISBN: 978-1-62649-255-4 | ISBN: 978-1-62649-372-8 |

Earn Bonus Bucks!
Earn 1 Bonus Buck for each dollar you spend. Find out how at
RiptidePublishing.com/news/bonus-bucks.

Win Free Ebooks for a Year!
Pre-order coming soon titles directly through our site and you'll
receive one entry into a drawing for a chance to win free books for
a year! Get the details at RiptidePublishing.com/contests.

CPSIA information can be obtained
at www.ICGtesting.com
Printed in the USA
LVOW03s2305281217
561165LV00001B/153/P